D1565220

MISTRESS MIAO

A Novel

Yun Rou

For my writing teachers, Joe Frank and Gordon Lish.

Nine bows, Joe, for showing me what is possible and why it is important. I only wish you were here to see the fruits of your sage counsel.

Nine more, Gordon, for showing me what not to do and who not to become. Your voice is ever in my ear.

Mistress Miao

By Yun Rou

ISBN-13: 978-988-8552-75-7

Author photo credit: Angela Alvarez

FICTION / Magical Realism

EB137

Published by Earnshaw Books Ltd. (Hong Kong)

God does not play games of chance.
Chance plays games of God.

1

I WAS RUNNING along the beach in Santa Barbara when she came out of the marine layer in front of me, high-stepping like a plover, black hair shiny with the mist, green eyes glowing, cheekbones like machetes. I stopped and she stopped and we looked at each other as if we were each apparitions where only the elements of sand and air and water should be. I stammered something and she smiled, then right away guessed, incorrectly, that I was a hedge fund manager or a programmer. I suggested she might be Korean, an insult in kind, it turned out, because Chinese people prefer to be recognized as such. She offered me another chance at an opening line and I told her how when I was a kid, I used to save balloon scraps in a cedar cigar box I deemed a coffin after the balloons popped, and then hold funerals for them. She said I was strange, but in a good way, and agreed to coffee and olive rolls at a downtown bakery where the railroad tracks and the freeway run close.

I watched her thread a spoon through her toes the way magicians do with coins. I asked her if her green eyes were contact lenses or real and she told me they were real, a genetic anomaly, something passed down to certain women in her line. I told her that I was a photographer with the Old Testament name, Solomon, and I told her that the world made the most sense to me when I saw it through a camera lens. She knew about Ansel Adams and Mary Ellen Mark and Paul Strand and Dorothea Lange. She told me she went by Lulu, but her birth name was something else. She spoke glowingly of the struggle of the Han people — Chinese who looked like her — against nomadic people like the Mongols and the Jurchens who founded the Jin dynasty in a world full of traitorous nobles, scheming eunuchs and opportunistic generals. Everyone switched sides, she told me. Nobody was who they appeared to be. There was no firm ground in which to stake a flag of principle. She told me she loved history and came from a Qingdao family at least 900 years old. I told her I knew about the beer from her home town of Qingdao, but that was all I knew. She said that was okay because we would never, ever talk about her past again. We spent the day together and returned to the beach at sunset.

If a courtship implies effort and design, we didn't have one; rather, everything just flowed. She had a roommate and no privacy, so she started staying over at my place, a rented townhouse not far from the Earl Warren Showgrounds. First, she left a toothbrush, then her flute, which she played softly at all hours, then she had a drawer, and then she moved in. In the days and weeks and months that followed, I became progressively more intoxicated by how completely spontaneous and unencumbered by expectation and convention she was. My own limited exposure to my generation of Asian-Americans told me they were very strong scholastically, they had dragon moms, they were brand conscious, they didn't care much about the old traditions, history, the old ways; they looked forward. They wanted to be America with a nod to their ethnicity but not much more. I brought this up once with Lulu.

"You're completely a stereotype white guy when you talk like this. Racist!"

"How could I be a racist and want to be with you? I'm confessing I'm a rube. I haven't spent much time with Asian people. Where else would I get my ideas? I can only base my conclusions on my experience and on what I've been told. Everyone is a victim of how they're raised. It's what we do with what we're given and told that makes or breaks us. I'm trying to learn."

"We're not victims," she told me fiercely. "History has taught me to reject the whole idea of being a victim. It's all in how you see it. We can't ever control anything but ourselves. That's a core tenet of Taoism."

I didn't know what Taoism was and I asked her. She shrugged, not really eager to talk about it. I pressed her and she admitted it was the religious tradition within which she was raised.

"It's the yin/yang symbol on every bumper sticker. It's the going-with-the-flow that California surf culture is based on. It's the rebellion against tyranny and freedom from regimentation we see in sci-fi movies. It's about loving nature, cherishing harmony, never using force against force, going with the flow, keeping your eye on the big picture. It started with Neolithic shamans, medicine men who healed the sick and spent thousands of hours watching grass grow and rivers flow. No Internet back then, Solomon. No streaming music of videos. No TV. It's an ancient thing."

"But why do you care about all that?"

"Because those people really knew how to live," she snapped at me. "We're so lost now. We all care way too much about what other people think of us, what other people do. And when I go looking for deeper knowledge about anything, I find it in those family traditions."

To say I'd never met anyone like her would be an understatement. She would intimidate most men, or at best be misunderstood. Beauty is great, but it only gets a person so far. You have to be agreeable if you want to be in a relationship. You have to compromise. You have to care. Lulu was beautiful but not easy, stingy with her caring, and unlikely to give an inch. She was a force of nature unaffected by obstacles or society or culture.

"Settling down?" she scoffed. "What are you talking about? You're so old-fashioned.'

"We both are, don't you think? In our own ways? I mean you've got your ancient religion and interest in history, right? Anyway, I'm just talking about committing to a relationship."

"I'm committed to you, in case you can't tell," she said. "Isn't that enough?"

It was enough because what she meant by commitment was a wild intensity I'd never experienced before in any kind of relationship. She might have been a prickly person but if she decided you were the person for her, the result was pure magic. Of course, it took me a while to understand what she saw in me. Where she was impulsive, I was methodical; where she was mercurial, I was rock-steady; where she bit through the hard candy and cracked it into powder the minute it hit her teeth, I sucked and savored to make the sweetness and flavor last. I once made the mistake of asking her what she saw in me.

"A confident man doesn't ask that question."

"A curious man does."

"And here I thought you were such a smart guy. I've already explained this to you. It's a religious thing."

My first thought was that she was referring to our adventures in bed. She got that, and rolled her eyes at me. "I mean Taoism," she said. "You're the yin to my yang."

"Wait," I said. "I read about this. Isn't the man usually yang and the woman yin?"

She waved her hand dismissively. "More stereotypes. In the yin/yang symbol, there are two fish in a circle, right? The white one with a black eye and the black one with a white eye? Well what everybody gets wrong, and what you should understand, not only as my man but as a photographer, is that that symbol is a video not a still. Those fish aren't static opposites frozen in time and space; they're swimming. They change places constantly, and each has a bit of the other in it. Together, they make an integrated system — a whole."

"You're saying we complete each other," I said.

"You're so mushy."

"But you are, aren't you?"

She shoved me hard against the wall. I thought that was her way of being yang and I was going to get lucky, but all she did was pick my pocket, take out some cash from my wallet, and tell me she was going to the store.

***

Lulu was a sexual omnivore. Sometimes she brought new friends to bed, mostly women. Sharing that bed with her was an adventure — not so much because of the sex itself, which, admittedly, was creative and wild and sometimes even a bit scary, but because of the nightmares. One night she split my lip with a backfist when I shook her awake.

"Please tell me what's going on," I said, holding a washcloth to my face.

"I can't talk about it."

"When you start hitting me, you really have to."

"I see terrible things, okay?"

I turned on the gooseneck bed lamp. Lulu's face was all angles and contrasts in the shadows. There were tear tracks on her cheeks. The clock said it was 2:45 AM.

"What kind of terrible things?"

When she wouldn't answer, I asked if they were memories of her secret past. I asked if anything bad was happening at school, if she was afraid of someone or something. I even asked her if she had a stalker.

"We all carry someone around with us," she said.

"I don't. I'm not sure I really know anyone who does... Besides you, I guess."

She shrugged.

"Do you hear voices?"

"I don't need a shrink, if that's what you're implying," she said, heading for the bathroom.

I followed her and took a seat on the closed lid of the toilet. I pulled my feet up like a gargoyle as she took a shower, squaring my fingers and pretending to photograph her through the steamy shower door. I thought then that if I never had another view of a woman, any woman, it would be okay. That's how beautiful she was. That's how happy she made me. That's how perfect everything about her was, everything about *us* was, nightmares be damned.

"Let's get married," I said.

She shut off the water and stood there dripping and staring at me, her hands clenching and unclenching.

"I've been waiting to tell you. I heard today that I've been accepted into the photography program at UCLA."

She clapped her hands. "Awesome," she said. "I know how much you want that."

"But I don't want it if it means being without you. I want you to go with me."

"We don't have to get married. I can just go.

"Well, I signed up for Mandarin classes, too."

"Good. You need all the help you can get."

"And I talked to the Dean of the Asian Studies program. You could apply. Drown yourself in history there. I mean, not just love it, learn it. Live it every day. Become a professor, if you want. Maybe that would help with the nightmares. Help you confront whatever's bugging you. Being busy like that, I mean. And having a focus."

Moving very deliberately, she stepped out of the stall and wrapped herself around me, dripping wet.

"So, will you go with me? Will you be my wife?"

"You're such a silly boy," she whispered.

"What's your answer? Will you make me the happiest man in the world?"

I took her tears for a yes and covered her lips with mine.

We had been together a year.

***

Do young people in love generally incorporate astronomical events into the life they build together? I doubt it. Lulu and I certainly didn't. Our world together was so intimate and our respective commitment to our work so deep — Lulu to her studies of Chinese folklore and I to photography and my UCLA Master of Fine Arts degree — that news of the total solar eclipse simply floated past us. Later, I would ask myself if we would have delayed our departure to join the millions of people watching the Christmas-day event live or online. The honest answer was no. Lulu's nightmares had eased since we tied the knot, and even celestial events could not derail the forward-racing bubble-of-secrets-on-wheels that was our marriage.

I'd seen an eclipse once before, when I was a six-year-old boy. My Grandpa Henry used a piece of emulsion and a pinhole camera made from a grocery box to show it to me safely. I saw the source of all life disappear as if extinguishing the world, then gradually reappear, first as a thin white line on the cardboard, eventually as a full and blazing orb strong enough to scorch paper. It didn't occur to me then that if the sun could disappear, nothing in life could be taken for granted. I had not yet learned that aboriginal people live in awe of such celestial events, and that the Chinese in particular consider eclipses to be auspicious signs.

The freeway south to my parents' home in Palos Verdes was at a standstill. I'd picked up holiday-sale roof tiles for my father and Lulu had done the grocery shopping for my mother. We had a lot to carry, so we took two different cars, my old Ford pickup truck and her little Honda SUV. She had our three house cats with her. Lulu had this strange love/hate relationship with felines. She was always cursing them and kicking them when they came close, but also insisted on having them around, something she refused to explain. After sitting motionless for an hour, Lulu launched a traffic app. It dropped us into a maze of surface streets. At a red light, I caught her gazing back at me through her side mirror. She blew me a kiss and smiled. When we took off again, she did so with a squeal of tires and a fist pump out the window. For a moment, I mistook her enthusiasm at having solved the traffic problem for enthusiasm at the prospect of visiting my family.

My fall semester had centered on film, an obsolete medium but fascinating to me for the way it demanded absolute discipline in composition, no do-overs, no second chances like the ones the digital world. The coursework was a trip back in time, first to Ansel Adams' zones of gray and perfectly balanced composition and then, right before the semester break, to Henri Cartier-Bresson and his emphasis on releasing the shutter at the decisive moment. I was romantically fascinated with seeing the world through the lens. Everyone else was addicted to a smart phone; I was addicted to my camera, and also, more and more, to Mandarin, which Lulu insisted on using whenever we were at home and especially in bed.

Following Lulu along the edge of the *barrio* that was East LA, I captured street scene after street scene at every stop light and slowdown: a mother nursing her baby on the curb, a knife fight in standoff mode, a naked woman pushing a cart full of clothes, a young couple grinding hips against the hood of a lowered muscle car. Every shot seemed to require that I open the lens aperture to let in more light. I picked up the phone and called Lulu.

"Lulu's grocery delivery," she answered cheerily.

"Check out the sky. I don't see any clouds but it looks like the sun is setting at 10:00 in the morning."

I watched her look upward through her windshield. "How could they miss a storm like this?" she asked. "LA weather forecasters are the worst."

"Maybe it's first contact and some giant alien ship is blotting out the sun."

"Forget the weather. The best Christmas present of your life is coming your way."

A mile down the road, I called her again.

"I think we should find our way back to the freeway. This neighborhood's really dicey."

"Don't worry. We'll be out of it soon. The app says the freeway's still a parking lot."

As we slowed to a stop at the next intersection, the idea of an eclipse wispily nudged its way into my head. Most of the streetlights around us were shattered but one flickered on feebly. The untimely darkness reminded me of the time my older brother, Bryce, locked me in a basement closet because I ate his ice cream cone. All those years later, the terror of being alone in the dark in a tight space came rushing back. I turned on my headlights. Lulu's came on automatically.

With no warning at all, a wiry Hispanic man carrying a semiautomatic rifle burst out of a convenience store on the near right corner. Paper currency spilled out of his backpack as he ran in front of Lulu's car. Lulu laid on the car horn. The thief turned. His eyebrows rose like a theater curtain. He pulled back his lips to bare his teeth and erected a middle finger. Lulu rolled down her window and responded in kind.

As I knew they would, subsequent tests showed Lulu's blood to be clean of any untoward influences. I smoked a joint once in a while but Lulu never joined me. She claimed she was allergic to marijuana, that it made her heart race. The thief, however, tested positive for methamphetamines. Perhaps that was why he raised his shotgun and unloaded it right into Lulu's windshield.

A cloud of glass glittered in the strange light. Lulu slumped forward, her foot dropped heavily on the pedal, and a burp of smoke issued from her Honda's tailpipe. The thief leapt sideways but not fast enough. I heard two thumps as he fell beneath Lulu's SUV, which continued to accelerate before smashing into a lamp post at the far end of the street.

My tongue turned to cotton. I couldn't move, could barely breathe. The door to the store opened and a group of people eased out. They followed the trail of bills across the street. A man prodded the inert body of the thief with his foot. A teenager tried to remove his knapsack. An overweight woman drifted towards Lulu's wreck. I saw two people working their phones.

Forcing myself to get out of my car was the hardest thing I'd ever done in my life. Every step was like pulling a piano using a wire cable looped around my neck. I noticed a purple Charlie Chaplin bowler hat, Lulu's favorite, lying in the street. When I reached the Honda, I didn't see Lulu right away; her body occupied a blind spot. Not the kind my optics professor had explained was the result of a normal lack of photoreceptors at a particular spot on the retina, but rather the kind the brain creates when confronted with information it simply cannot process.

I ran my fingers over the edge of Lulu's door, inches from her, and found the metal cool. The road grew lighter and lighter as the sun and the moon moved beyond their brief assignation and returned to their proper spots in the heavens. The world grew warmer. People gathered around me. Numbly, I watched Tiger One and Tiger Two being pulled from the car. They were dead in their pet carriers, their heads hanging limply to the side. I saw nothing of Tiger Three and never would again.

I did see something shaped like a human head lying on the dashboard. I examined it curiously. A piece of it seemed to be missing, and one eyeball hung down its cheek. Someone began to scream Lulu's name in a voice I didn't recognize. Someone else put his hand over my mouth and the screaming stopped. Gently but firmly, I was muscled away and down the road.

In the distance, I heard sirens and I saw lights.

2

GRANDMOTHER SQUATS at the base of a crusty birch tree, snaps off the bright red pod from a choice ginseng plant, and buries the seeds before extracting the root. She's old but she has power in her body that makes men look at her, power in her hands that makes her work go quickly, power in her spear that makes enemies fear her, power in her eyes that helps her see everything. When I grow up, I want to understand nature so I can control it the way she does. She's humming and smiling and looking at me. She says I'm even wilder and stranger than *she* was when she was ten years old. There is so much love in her look; I feel bad for having smeared the charcoal from the teapot fire all over my tunic.

"Make me some tea, Miao," she says. "Watch for bubbles the size of crab eyes so you'll know when the water's ready."

"I don't have to watch. I can tell the water's ready just by listening."

She stops digging for a moment. "Of course, you can," she smiles.

"I don't think a doctor should be out here digging around in the cold ground."

Grandmother leaves her work to crouch beside me, her knees reaching almost to her shoulders. "A doctor's fingers can feel the

12 pulses and find healing herbs, too."

"You promised me a spear lesson today."

Grandmother takes a sip of her bitter tea. "You have to learn the sword first, remember?"

Suddenly, I have to move. That's the way it is for me. I can't sit still for long. The forest canopy beckons me, each branch a crooked and enticing finger. "Swords let people get too close," I call back as I climb.

I'm not even halfway up this big oak when the sky goes pale. It feels strange and happens fast, without any of dusk's fiery round clouds.

"Come down now, Miao! The eclipse is here early."

"Already? I thought you said we had another hour."

"Precisely predicting such things is difficult. Now, please climb down."

Squirrels above mock me with their chatter, but warily. They know my little stick lacks an iron tip but is chiseled sharp nonetheless. They've lost friends to me, those squirrels, and I've been hoping a strange sun will serve more of them up to me, and maybe a pangolin too. That happy prospect is squashed by a sudden wave of tiger musk. This very morning, Father argued with Grandmother about staying home because a big male killed a water buffalo on the edge of town and two deer here in the forest as well. Grandmother insisted we go out anyway, telling Father it was worth the risk because medicinal herbs collected under a hiding sun have especially strong curative powers.

"Miao," she calls calmly. "I've changed my mind. Don't come down just yet. Climb higher. When it gets dark, just hold the tree tightly and wait. The light will return."

She lowers her teacup and takes up her spear. The green oak shaft stores her energy and shouldn't be touched by anyone but her, yet I have licked it with my tongue and tasted her sweat on it and understand how it reassures her. A single leaf flutters past me and I watch it drift downward. I barely catch its whisper when it touches ground. That's how quiet the forest has become. That's how still are all the twittering birds. Grandmother feeds the fire and it roars before the tiger does.

When the cat finally appears, his step is so light, he doesn't even crack a twig. His eyes glow in the firelight and I can feel his stare between my ears. Grandmother puts the fire between them and works the handle of her spear down into the dirt so his attack will not knock it from her hands.

"Come on," she urges the striped and stinking giant. "Don't keep a lady waiting."

Instead of jumping over the fire to reach her, the beast retreats into the darkness. I hold my breath and hold it some more. I know he's still here but I don't know where. Faint yellow stars appear behind my eyes, and my legs and my grip on the branch feel weak. Moving faster than a shooting star, the tiger is suddenly behind Grandmother. She whirls. Towering over her, he swats away her spear with one giant paw and sinks his long fangs deep into her belly.

When she carried me around as an infant, that belly felt as hard as a wall, unyielding, tight with muscles from twisting and from crouching, from bending and from giving birth. Now the wall is down and Grandmother's innards spill out in a steaming purple swarm. I want to look away when the tiger begins to chew, but I cannot. Grandmother screams and I scream with her and the tiger glances up at me, his jowls red, his teeth stained, his whiskers awry. I leap from my perch, bent on destruction. Taking lessons from flying squirrels, I twist and turn to avoid branches on my way down and land atop him, my legs astride his shoulders. The hard heat of him shocks me. His coat abrades my thighs and makes them bleed. I expect him to flick me off his back as a horse would twitch a fly, but he is buried so deeply in Grandmother, he does little more than arch his back.

My stick is made from the same wax wood as Grandmother's spear. Like hers, it is hardened by sweat. Unlike hers, it is also soaked with the blood of squirrels and monkeys and birds. Hunting everything from mice to monkeys and once even an antelope, Grandmother has shown me that no matter how big the prey, the target is always small. I know I cannot reach the tiger's heart but I think I can reach its brain. I stretch upward to the blurred sun. I feel the tendons in the back of my arms stretch, feel my shoulders open, feel my ribs spread.

When my elbows pass the top of my head, I point my stick downward and thrust it as hard as I can into the base of the tiger's neck. It goes in as easily as a needle passes cloth and keeps on going through the skin and the fat and the muscle and the gristle, not stopping until it passes all the way to his tongue and until there is no more shaft in my hands.

Now the tiger answers me. His head pulls back, his neck muscles turn to cords, his eyes roll back to meet mine. He hisses like a snake. He bucks and shakes. I grab his ears for handles and hold on, pinching my knees like a Mongolian pony rider. His rear legs spasm. His eyes lose focus. His breathing stops and he collapses. I jump off and kick his black lips and punch at his bloody nose. I strain and shove but Grandmother is trapped beneath him and I cannot set her free.

She beckons with one free hand. I kneel to her.

"Miao," she says, her eyes wide.

"I'm here."

"This is not the end; the cycle is endless."

"Grandmother!"

Her breath rattles. I have killed enough monkeys to know what this means.

"Lord Hun lives in us," she whispers. "He will want you to serve him again and again, life after life. I haven't had time to properly train you, but don't worry, green-eyed girl. Others will."

And then she is gone and I am up and headed for Yidu Town, tears streaming down my face. I hear the voices of demons, fox sprites. I hear the Gods of the Four Directions argue about me as I run.

Trip her. Kill her. Eat her for killing the tiger.

Why not reward her instead? His paws are bigger than her head. She had no chance and yet she triumphed.

The old woman should have done more. There is weakness in the family line. It taints their blood.

Are you mad? The blood is strong. The woman tried her best. The light played tricks.

She waited so long in the tree.

The sun makes choices and the child made hers. She leapt onto the tiger's back. I'll claim the line if you won't.

She is not ours to claim. Another already has her.

Another? Who?

You know very well who.

I can reach her foot just now. I can bring her to ground.

Do so at your peril. If you annoy him, he will turn your world upside down.

Then let him keep her then. Who would want to deal with so much confusion and pain in a minion? Stay clear of her.

I dash through the town gate and leave the voices behind. I avoid puddles and dodge the pig dung. Chickens flee, trapped between my footfalls and cooks with cleavers. I pass the central market but there are no flowers today, no fresh vegetables, no embroidered fabrics. The Jurchens have been raiding so there are only knives, arrows, bows, straight swords, curved swords, daggers, axes, clay jugs, water pots, dried fruit, bales of rice, and salted meat.

"I'll never touch animal flesh again!" I scream, but on the inside.

3

THE PARAMEDICS used the Jaws of Life to extract Lulu from her crumpled car. At the hospital, they swaddled her in what would have been a pristine white landscape of care, save for oozing spots of brown and yellow and red. I spent the first night searching for her in dreamland and the next day bumping into objects, denying the feel of the ground beneath my feet, utterly unwilling to give substance to my new reality. After her first week in a coma, I began sleepwalking. A psychiatrist I consulted, really just to have someone to talk to, explained that people rarely actually sleepwalk purposefully. Rather, we just spontaneously wander as a symptom of sleep deprivation. It turns out we can no more stay awake forever than we can live without dying. Sleep cleans the brain. Without it, choking toxins accrue and we die bit by bit, evoking strange visions along the way, some of which are linked to the world of blood and flesh, others only wispy and imagined.

I watched Lulu retreat from me one day at a time. I couldn't see the lips I longed to kiss for the medical mask holding her face together, nor recognize, for the forest of splints and casts, wires and screws, the sweet body in which I had so often taken refuge. Sometimes, when it was all too much for me, I would take out my camera. Carefully avoiding Lulu, I would aim it at objects around the room: a transom over her bed, a pan of bloody gauze, pale urine in her catheter line, a fitness magazine one of the nurses had left by the window, a bottle of juice I'd brought in from a nearby market. Reducing the scale of reality to manageable bits helped keep me sane. In the face of abject horror the mundane became my salvation.

"I'm sorry for not protecting you from this nightmare," I whispered in her ear on the morning of her twenty-first day away. "I'd change places with you in a heartbeat. Wherever you are, I'll be right here waiting whenever you get back. It doesn't matter how long it takes."

It did matter, of course. Before the eclipse, life had been long weeks of study punctuated by weekends of making love and watching movies together, our limbs entwined. In those days, I measured moments by how long her smile took to bloom after I ventured a joke. By the end of the first month of Lulu's coma, I felt as if I was perpetually dangling a thousand feet above a frigid lake. My heart beat wildly and the doctors diagnosed a benign stress-induced cardiac arrhythmia, implying it would pass when my wife did.

I read stories to Lulu all day long, and even scoured magazines so as to concoct a travelogue for her about far-away places we would visit together when she was better; exciting destinations she would take by storm, wowing the locals with her beauty and brains. Because of her appetites, I rated the attractiveness of Lulu's nurses for her, identifying ones I knew she would fancy, particularly the one with close-cropped blonde hair whose nametag identified her as Coraline. When those same nurses caught me sleepwalking, they shook their heads. I heard them talk about the weight I was losing and how they thought I was suffering more than Lulu was, an assertion that drove me crazy. They would sometimes fall silent the moment I walked into the room, as if they were keeping some secret from me.

My physician father flung nothing but grave terms in my direction. I supposed it made him feel like he had some control of things if he could name them. My mother sent flowers. My sister, a red-headed single mom named Ginger, visited often and spent her time shooting me mournful looks. My brother, Bryce, now a sports agent in New York, called daily to check on me. Everyone acted as if Lulu was already dead but I rejected their opinions, stubbornly insisting I was no widower yet and would never be one.

***

At the end of the first month, my father called in a San Francisco specialist for a consultation. Determined not to hear his verdict, I hit the stairs just as he exited the elevator. I left the hospital by a back door, ran to my old truck, and drove aimlessly, ending up at a mall in Beverly Hills. I wandered around until a security guard felt the need to escort me out of a woman's shoe emporium, claiming I was a fetishist staring mutely at women's feet and ignoring all offers of help from the sales staff.

I was bewildered. I didn't remember staring at anyone and I didn't hear anyone speaking to me. As I passed a kiosk selling cellphone cases, a girl approached. "May I speak with you a moment?" she asked in accented English.

I've seen puzzles designed by brain researchers to confirm perceptual pathways and processes, to turn a dolphin into a vase in the blink of an eye, or a woman to a wolf, a commando knife to a race car, a landscape to a locust. So it was with this girl. In the first instant, she was my Lulu; in the next, she was not. They were the same, but she was soft where Lulu was hard, peaceful and still where Lulu vibrated wildness. I gaped.

"You're Solomon Miller, yes? Named for a wise, biblical King?"

I managed a nod.

She took my elbow gently and guided me to a plastic bench.

"I'm Lulu's twin sister. My name is Dongmei. You can call me Dora."

"Her shooter belonged to a Latino street gang," I said.

"I know."

"He was in jail until the day before. He got $300 out of that speedy-mart till."

"I know that, too."

"He shot her because she honked at him. She has a temper."

"That's for sure."

"He gave her the finger and she gave it back. Then he pulled the trigger."

She closed her eyes. A family walked by, two teenage kids and their parents. The mother wore too much makeup and too much jewelry and too much perfume. Next to her, Dora looked as simple as a flower, and yet, somehow askew. I looked at her more closely and noticed tiny differences between her features and Lulu's: her eyes were bigger, for one thing, and her nose perhaps a smidgen wider. Her hair gathered in a peak in the center of her forehead. Lulu's did too, but not quite so clearly.

"She should have just let it go," I said.

"She never could do that."

"And you're exactly like her?"

She shook her head. "We're twins on the outside but inside we're totally different."

I took a full and normal breath. The ringing in my ears eased up a bit. I wasn't happy to be awake, but I wasn't sad about it either.

"Twins," I repeated.

"She never mentioned me, did she?"

I shook my head.

"I live in China but went online to rent an apartment here. I arrived last night and came to the hospital just as you were leaving. I recognized you from your photo and followed you."

We ended up at one of the mall restaurants, a cake chain popular for giant portions. When the waiter came, Dora ordered a giant slab of chocolate cake. She told me the family had received word of the shooting but was vague about how. She told me they had sent her as their emissary, that she was younger than my wife by eight minutes, that both she and Lulu had studied English in school, and that she liked to do multimedia works with bits of things she found around Chinese cities attached to canvases. By bits she meant small things she could buy, pieces of colorful action figures from cultural museums, stamps, and images she took with her camera. I figured out she was the one who had taught Lulu about great American photographers. At one point, I asked her if I could sniff her. I know it was a strange request, about as strange as finding out your comatose wife has a twin sister. She offered me the inside of her elbow and I buried my nose in it while she watched me carefully, her cake fork poised in mid-air. She smelled different than Lulu did, but not so different.

Of course, in those days, Lulu smelled mostly of disinfectant.

***

Dora's place was in Brentwood. We took a cab there. The place came with a sound system and I connected it to my phone and played Otis Taylor, which was the first time she'd heard blues music. I was glad to have something somewhat normal to do, just sit around and listen to music.

"Tell me how my sister was with you," she said.

"We were inseparable," I said, my voice cracking.

"Did she get angry easily? Or sad?"

"The only time she got emotional was when she had a nightmare. The rest of the time she was super controlled."

"What kind of nightmare?"

"She never told me. They got better after we were married."

"And what did she do with her time?" Dora asked, leaning forward.

"You obviously didn't speak with her at all."

"No."

"But you knew all about her accident."

"Please just tell me about her," Dora urged.

"She studied Chinese history at UCLA," I sighed. "She was interested in the time of the Mongols, talked about this woman who she said was one of the first female rulers in China, wanted to maybe do a Ph.D. about her."

"Do you remember the woman's name?"

"I am to Mandarin as a butcher is to Brahms."

"Yang Miao Zhen?"

"Yes, I think that's it. How did you know?"

"She's a distant ancestor. Lulu was always fascinated by her. Tell me, did my sister ever do magic for you?"

I feel my eyes filling with tears. "Everything about her is magic for me…"

"I mean the little things," Dora interrupted. "Clocks running backwards, animals with human faces appearing in corners of your house. Tree branches bending out of her path before she reached them. Strange music where there was no instrument, no orchestra, no electronic player."

"I don't…."

"Tea cups hovering in the air. Clothes moving around with no one inside them."

"You need to stop," I said. "I don't know what you're talking about."

"Try to remember," she urged me. "You must have noticed something unusual."

I made a stab at thinking about it, but I couldn't tease the strange from the wonderful in my brief life with Lulu. That was the thing I loved most about her, the way there was nothing normal about her, at least to me. She was so beautiful and exotic that even watching her do dishes or sit in front of a movie was somehow special.

"I wouldn't have noticed anything like that," I said quietly. "Love is more powerful than whatever force you're talking about. It erases all disbelief."

Dora looked at me for a long time, then put her arm around me. "Do you want to have sex?" she asked at last. "You could pretend I'm Lulu."

Lulu had once explained to me that what had held Chinese culture together for thousands of years was the teachings of Confucius, who set up roles for people, defined relationships, developed rituals for people to follow, and gave explicit directions on how they should behave. She told me that when Mao took power in China, he uprooted all the culture just the way the first Chinese emperor had done to the lands and traditions of the kingdoms he united under his rule. They both burned books and the intellectuals who wrote them. They left modern China to figure out a lot of stuff all over again. I figured this awkwardness with Dora was an example of that.

"You know that's inappropriate, right?" I said.

She turned red. "I'm sorry. I shouldn't have said that. I just have no idea what to do or say in this situation. It's so horrible."

What I didn't tell her was that I was so lonely and in such pain that if she had phrased her proposition differently, if she'd offered to make love instead of have sex, I might have agreed. As it was, we fell asleep at opposite ends of the couch, only our toes touching.

When morning light chiseled through her venetian blinds and woke us, Dora told me she'd found me in the kitchen at 3:00 AM, in the midst of a walking dream, yelling in a terrible way. She asked me if I remembered the dream. I said I didn't, but I did. I had been on a sailboat anchored off a postcard-perfect beach in the Marquesas Islands, the air redolent of marine diesel and coconut tanning oil, the setting sun centered directly over Lulu, on the foredeck, in a purple swimsuit. I'd tried to talk to her but she'd put her finger over her lips and shook her head. I'd tried again, more loudly this time, insisting she answer, but she'd refused.

"I need to get back to the hospital," I said.

"I understand," she replied. "I'll be here if you feel like some company later."

4

According to Grandmother, a giant named Pangu created Earth and sky after he awakened from his slumber inside an enormous egg. The effort exhausted him so completely that when he stood up, he died. His body gave rise to mountains and waterways, animals and plants, and a nearly omnipotent being named Hua Hsu, who birthed twins, Fuxi and Nüwa, with human faces and the bodies of snakes. These twins crafted the first humans from clay and set them to live in a giant tree that linked heaven and Earth. These human ancestors were as agile as monkeys and as fierce as leopards. Only when Fuxi coaxed them down to eat what grows in the ground did they become docile and tame and able to get along. Then they populated the Middle Kingdom.

In the five years since I killed the tiger, the people of Yidu have come to see me as one of the tree people reborn. They can tell I am most comfortable in the forest, and they hear tales that I hold a spear even when eating and sleeping. It's obvious I care more for the ways of nature than the ways of men, and most of all for refining my spear techniques. My brother, An Er, leader of the Red Jacket rebels, wants me to fight for him as one of his top lieutenants. I want nothing to do with such politics, and my mother supports me in this.

"You don't realize how beautiful your sister is," she scolds him. "All she will do is drive your men to distraction."

"And *you* don't realize how much skill she has with her weapon. She's worth twenty of my men even on her worst day. Such skill is wasted sitting by a cooking fire or helping you sweep the floor. If she's here when the Jurchens come through, they'll make a whore of her. At least with me and my men she will have a fighting chance."

"I'll die before I become some man's whore," I say. "I'll choose whom to be with and when, and that's that. Anyway, nobody will catch me because nobody climbs trees the way I do."

My brother laughs. "You'll have to come down sometime. And you're going to want men just as much as they want you. You're a girl with desires. Any fool can see that."

"Get out of this house if you're going to speak to your sister that way," says my mother.

In an effort to change the direction of the conversation, Father brings up the subject of a warrior named Li Quan.

"Have you considered having him join you?" he asks my brother.

"If I do, he'll take over my men," An Er answers. He seems a bit annoyed by the question and shows it by throwing rice at me. I take aim at one of the grains with my spear, hitting it in midair.

"No waving that thing in the house!" my mother cries.

I think of Grandmother. I think of the tiger. I think of the days to come. Despite the fact that my parents have forbidden me to do so, and despite a dust storm swirling in from the Gobi Desert, I cannot sit still for family bickering; instead, I head off to practice in the forest. I choose to go east, the only realistic option when Jurchen spies trickle in from the west, Genghis Khan's scouts dart in from the north on ponies, and the treacherous southern Song send weekly raiding parties our way.

It is dark when I arrive at my secret grove, but the full moon, glowing brown because of the dust particles in the air, delights me with its mood. I have six favorite birch trees here, closely-spaced as grains of sand in the Taklamakan Desert. I use their trunks as targets and also bring along targets made of mulberry paper, which I suspend from the branches. Mulberry is heavy enough not to dance too much in the wind and not to fall apart in a light rain. Such fine and special goods abounded along the trade roads before the nomadic Jurchen and the Mongols started killing merchants. Now, they are rare and prized, and Father spoils me with the paper because he knows how much I love my practice and because he knows the townspeople treat me warily, secretly believing no normal child should be able to kill a tiger. Sometimes, I think they would have preferred I had just died.

Over and over, tens of thousands of times now, I repeat the techniques Grandmother taught me and ones I have learned from watching An Er's men. Every day I collapse when my muscles finally fail, and every day that failure takes just a little longer to occur. My arms and legs have become as strong and flexible as bow strings, and the muscles in my belly and my rear and my loins have grown hard as stones. My palms are pure callouses. Knobs of bone have sprung up along the base of my fingers where they contact the wax wood shaft of my spear, which was once my grandmother's.

I love to seek out and uncover the rhythms and cycles of nature when I move, to anticipate when and in which direction the wind will gust and my papers will swing. I position targets to represent the six sections of the human body: upper left, upper right, middle left, middle right, lower left, and lower right. Where once I used tea-fire soot for camouflage, tonight I blend with the forest as the storm deposits layer after layer of Gobi topsoil upon my robe. I dance through the dust, a devil-child enshrouded, practicing clockwise and counterclockwise circular deflections, envisioning neither soldiers nor rapists, drunken lechers nor confident seducers, but rather big, striped cats.

All alone, I fight them all. Not just a reincarnation of the single Amur Siberian that ravaged Grandmother but a swarm of like monsters, all eleven feet long and heavy as five men, all alert, eyes fixed on me, claws protruding, fangs bared, muscles tensed, murder in mind, and after murder, feeding. I practice with my eyes closed, having memorized the location of my targets. My imagination is as powerful as my techniques. I not only see the tigers, I smell their rancid tongues as they pant and inhale their musk—for they are always males—feel the rough presence of their fur as they brush by me, read the hunger in their eyes as they pounce.

Tonight, and for the first time, I discover how to relax and link hand to hip, to connect the forward movement of my spear point to the upward push of the ground into my feet. Blowing the dust from my targets, I see my puncture holes are cleaner than they have ever been, with no bits of fiber visible. This means I am striking faster and more cleanly. It means I have reached a new level of power and skill.

A wolf howls in the distance and then another one. Wolves are often around. I respect them but do not fear them. Perhaps they fear me.

I stuff the paper targets into my tunic and smile.

5

WHEN THE hospital hired a new head of neurology, I made an appointment to see him in hopes he would have a new approach to Lulu's long coma. We sat at opposite ends of a conference table commodious enough to have served King Arthur and his knights. Dr. Granate told me he had treated many celebrities, had published numerous articles in famous medical journals, and had written the gold standard book on managing head injuries.

"People don't wake up from coma the way they do from a night's sleep," he told me. "They rise from its depths slowly, nearly always with residual deficits, and those depths have no link to this world. The nurses will tell you otherwise. They'll tell you to be careful what you say in front of your wife because she's somehow aware of what's going on. Don't listen to those superstitious people. They think they see ghosts of dead patients in the ladies' room and spectral physicians floating around the ambulance bay at night. Their ignorant theories are born of long shifts, exhausted minds, and a lack of education."

Listening to him, it occurred to me he was the one who was ignorant and lacking in education. He was new in the job. I wondered how long he'd been in his last job and how long he would last in this one.

His assistant brought a plate of crudités for his lunch, a

plastic platter from a local deli. There were carrot sticks, broccoli flowers, zucchini strips, and tomatoes on one side, and seven strawberries and two strips of honeydew melon on the other. Granate held up a piece of carrot.

"This is your wife," he said without preamble. "It's time you got used to it. The woman you loved is gone. Even if by some miracle she were to emerge today from her vegetative state, she wouldn't remember anything about you."

I know I should have been outraged by his lack of sensitivity but all I could do was ask him how he knew that. He told me he'd seen everything in the world when it came to coma. He also told me that the gangbanger's bullet was still in her brain. I hadn't realized that. I wondered if that's what the nurses had been whispering about. Suddenly, the bullet was an entity in my life, and an enemy, too.

"It's too close to the brainstem for us to risk removing it," Granate said.

"Call it Hector," I said. "That was the shooter's name."

"The cerebrospinal fluid creeps as subtly as a long tide. Over time, it pushes the bullet through the brain. The toxic lead causes ongoing tissue damage."

Looking down, I found the carpet was surprisingly dirty, as if armies of men with muddy boots had advanced to the bookshelves and then retreated, over and over again. It didn't seem to me to be a carpet that belonged in LA, where everything was always sunny and clean and bright. It was a carpet from hell.

"Hector has to go," I said. "Really. If you take him out, she can heal. And I believe everything the nurses say."

It was a small and possibly even childish pushback. Granate sighed, "Even if removing the bullet didn't kill her, the procedure would certainly terminate the pregnancy."

My mouth went dry again, just like the day it happened, my

tongue swollen into cotton once more.

"What did you just say?"

"It's too early for the twins to survive. Even if they did survive, they've already been damaged by the medications that we've had no choice but to pump into Lulu's bloodstream."

"Twins?"

He stared at me a long moment. "I'm sorry," he said at last. "I assumed you'd been told."

Finally, I understood the secret, the nurses' whispers, Lulu's knowing smile on the morning it all turned to shit. My usual grasp on the facts of my life felt rubbery and loose.

"They were supposed to be my Christmas gift," I said when I felt it was safe for me to try and speak. "The best one ever."

Granate nodded sympathetically. "This kind of thing can be so terribly sad."

There was nothing I could do but flee to Lulu's room.

My sister, Ginger was there, staring at a romance novel through thick reading glasses. Her five-year-old, Nash, was playing with the pedals, levers, and knobs beneath Lulu's elevated bed. I closed the door behind me and climbed into bed with Lulu and pressed tightly against her, the seizure restraints hard against my skin. Her hand was balled spastically against her chin. I pried it off and wound it around my neck so she could pull me to her the way she used to when we made love. Even in the absence of tenderness, I relished the skin of her cheek against my day-old beard. My fingertips fluttered over her closed eyelids. I placed my hand on her belly and pressed down gently. I wanted to feel the babies.

"So now you know," Ginger said, watching me. "The whole family found out the first day."

I wanted to be mad about this conspiracy of silence, but I just couldn't manage it.

"We kept it from you because we didn't know what would happen," Ginger went on. "You were suffering enough."

I looked up at the bright, round, fluorescent hospital light. "See that lamp?"

"I see it."

"That thing's become the sun and moon to me these days."

"There's nothing you can do for her, Solomon. Not for the babies, either."

Ginger was named for a TV castaway diva because she had red hair and a mole on her cheek. Her hair color was a genetic impossibility in my family unless my mother had strayed, a fact the entire family ignored. She brushed the mole with her finger, a nervous habit. "I can't imagine how this must be for you. Can't imagine how it must be for her."

"Maybe the matrix is true," I said. "Maybe everything really is a simulacrum on some alien computer. Maybe one of them will push a button and I'll have Lulu back. I can't focus on anything. Can't study, can't read, can't even follow a TV show."

"The twins can't live, Solomon. You have to let them all go and move on."

"My shrink wants to give me meds," I said. "He wants me to be numb, to just walk through this without feeling anything. But you know what? I don't think Lulu's numb. I think she's living some kind of life somewhere. Dreaming of ancient China, maybe, or maybe reliving whatever memories give her nightmares. Either way, I know she feels everything and I want to also."

Nurse Coraline came in and fussed over Lulu, talking to her in soft tones as if she were a child not a woman. "Let's just get you covered up and comfy," she said. "These hospital rooms are so cold."

Before the shooting, I'd seemed slothful next to Lulu, with all her crazy energy. Now that she couldn't move, I couldn't stay still. When Ginger began crying, I left the room and left the hospital and stepped out into the night. If Los Angeles ever felt like a cage to any gangbanger, love slave, or lonely old man, it felt an even tighter, dingier, dirtier cage to me. Bursting with souls, there seemed no space for air. Meandering toward my truck in the hospital parking lot, I answered my ringing phone.

"So now you know about the twins," my father announced. "As harsh as it may sound, letting nature take its course is probably the best thing."

"Orientals have different values," my mother's voice chimed in. "Your marriage wasn't going to end well. If you'd asked us beforehand, we would have told you. And with twins, well, you can imagine the burden of a divorce."

I pulled the phone from my ear and stared at it a long moment before continuing the conversation.

"We know this is difficult," my father said. "But things happen for a reason."

"Let me be sure I understand what you're saying," I said. "You think I'm better off because someone shot my wife and endangered my unborn children?"

"Even if she wakes up, she will never again be the woman you married. And those fetuses aren't children yet," said my mother. "It's important to remember that."

"Even if they were, who really knows whose they are?" my father added. "I mean with the liberation of college girls and all."

I hung up and drove aimlessly away from the hospital, ending up in front of Canter's Deli on Fairfax Avenue. It was Lulu's favorite place. "The smoked fish makes me think of a stir-fried Jinan dish, although ours was a little sweet," she'd said. "And these *kreplach* remind me of dumplings I had with Father once, on a trip to Beijing."

"Even Jewish people only pretend to like this food," I

remembered telling her.

"I don't think that's true, and anyway, I do like it. Chinese food in America isn't Chinese food at all and Italian food here isn't Italian either. This food is much more authentic. That's what I find interesting."

I went in and ordered a knish. It tasted like chipped wood. I ordered vegetable soup but found it too salty. I paid the check, left the food uneaten on the table, and went outside. I sat down on the sidewalk and pressed my back against the restaurant wall. I noticed the bits of quartz blended into the concrete as a hard hedge against the heels of the millions of steps of restaurant-goers. The hostess came out and shooed me away for loitering. I rang Dora on the cell phone number she'd given me.

"Lulu's pregnant with twins," I said on the phone.

She made a noise.

"Obviously runs in the family," I went on. "Everyone knew except me. I'm sick of being in the dark about everything."

I heard Dora sigh. "Being in the dark can be a good thing. Your darkness spares you things the light would reveal."

"Spares me?" I repeated. "What the hell is that supposed to mean?"

No answer came over the line.

6

THE ROOF NEEDS patching. My mother doesn't want Father to do it because his back is sore, so she sends me to fetch my brother. I know he'll be at the Red Jacket camp beyond town. The autumn grass is still green and the horizon is still blue and the dusk fills my lungs with optimism and energy, so I run all the way there. The wind shifts as I close in, brining the scent of salt and kelp from the coast, driving the men from their posts in pursuit of dreams and desires.

Sure enough, my brother's tent is empty save for a baby-faced young man reclining on his pillows.

"Where is An Er?" I demand, lowering my spear to the ground.

"Who's asking?"

"His sister."

"I thought so. I've heard plenty about you. They're off whoring, the lot of them."

"Our mother is ill and she's asking for him."

"Well, he won't be doctoring her tonight. Come in out of the cold."

I point at the pot of sorghum wine on the floor beside him. "You're drunk."

"Not too drunk to know a lie. You're mother's not ill. She has the tongue of a snake. No dampness or wind could get past it."

"Show some respect!"

Liu pats the pillow beside him. "Come sit by me and I'll show you plenty. You're letting winter in."

I edge in, the tent flap still open behind me. "Tell me which whorehouse my brother favors. I'll go get him."

Liu's gaze devours me from neck to knees. He grins.

I reach behind me for the flap of the tent. "Never mind. I'll find him."

The next instant, Liu's hand is around my neck. He pulls me to the bedclothes. I could resist but I'm interested to see what feelings arise. I notice the contrast between us. He gasps; I sip air. My muscles are relaxed; his twitch like squirrel whiskers. His eyes are half-closed; mine are wide open. Baijiu seeps from his skin. I've never tasted it, so I run my tongue across the skin on the back of his arm. He grunts.

"You're as strange as they say. How old are you now?"

"16."

He shoves both his hands inside my tunic and squeezes my breasts. To my mother's consternation they have only just arrived — late, she says — and are thus nearly as new to me as they are to him. I find his touch agreeable and wait for more. He straddles me. I am more comfortable on top so I squirm to switch positions. Beneath me now, he bucks like a nervous pony and reaches between my legs.

"No," I say.

He ignores me, tearing at my billowy pants. I know how sex works. I've seen it in goats and dogs and horses. I feel a flicker of the urgency Liu seems to feel, but his gritty skin and the stink of his breath tamps it down. Pig milk cures addiction to baijiu. Perhaps Liu should try some. The more he paws at me, the more I realize something is missing. Perhaps it is tenderness and love, those things people say are absent in wartime, when we build walls around ourselves for fear of being pierced and penetrated. I try to stand but he won't allow it. He presses his fingers into me with one hand while liberating his little white worm with the other. I reach down for it with two hands. He smiles at first but when I twist, he howls. If there is one thing I know how to do, it is to twist a shaft.

"Bitch!" he screams.

He tries to bat away my hands, but they are strong and trained and not so easy to loosen. He kicks me and I let go.

Duck, Miao. Run like a snake. He has a knife.

It's as if Grandmother is standing right next to me and whispering in my ear. Later, I will hear of Liu's temper. If I'd known of it then, I would not have turned my back to him in my bid to escape the tent, would not have missed him reaching for his dagger. I might even have been able to dodge it. The blade catches me in the buttocks, on the right side. It would have hit my heart or lungs if I hadn't unhesitatingly followed Grandmother's advice. With one quick movement, I yank it out and throw it back. It's just a spear with a short handle, so my aim is true.

Liu receives it squarely in his eye.

***

I touch my wound and sniff my finger for poison. I find none. I thank Grandmother for watching over me and pause for a moment in hopes of a reply. None comes. I reenter the tent. Liu's is motionless, his face a frozen mask of surprise. I retrieve my spear. I could ask my father to protect me but I don't want trouble to follow me home. Instead, I fix my eye on the Pole Star and run towards the north woods, a perilous province populated by large carnivores and Jurchen outlaws and spies. It is a place for traitors and crooks on the lam. It is a place for the likes of me, once a killer of monkeys and squirrels, then a killer of tigers, and now murderer of a man.

I veer off the main horse route and pick my way through low scrub. Though its flowers are shutting down for the night, I identify yarrow root by its fragrance and pack my wound with its leaves. I sit and rest on the ground. Saplings dance lightly in the kind of breeze Grandmother told me serves predators the aroma of prey, yet I sense no threat. I find a strip of *chaga* bark fungus, break it off and chew it, savoring its smoky flavor. I work my wounded leg to test it and find the flow of blood has lessened.

I gaze up at the sky through the loosely entwined branches at the canopy of elm and birch. My heart slows, each contraction coming more assuredly. I worry about being punished for killing Liu. I didn't have to throw the dagger back, after all. I could have just run. The problem with running is that others can run too. The dagger throw ended the problem and I'm not sorry for it. My mother once told me that in the old days a magistrate was called when a crime was committed. Now, when even steppe ponies conspire over the change in dynasty and owls decide night matters with their talons and beaks, there is no rule of law. Even if there were, the word of a girl counts for nothing against the testimony of a soldier.

I hear a buzzing in the distance, faint, delicate, and low in pitch. Strange, as the season for insects has passed. Taking it for the secret warbling of a war party and resolved to find any enemy before he finds me, I track the noise to a clearing. In the near darkness, I see an enormous cocoon woven around a man-size sapling. Oversize green-and-orange wasps circle it, their wings long and slender, their stingers sharp as Liu's dagger. Up close, their sound is deafening. They pay no attention as I approach the hive and find its silver mesh cool to the touch and more like silk than wasp paper. Whatever lies within it swells against the pressure of my fingers. Beyond the cocoon, birds crowd a great oak. Closer, I see they are ravens but with red feathers, not black. Closer still, I see each perching on three legs.

Grandmother told me of such creatures. She called them *sanzuwu*, sun crows, and said they feed on immortality grass and take turns lighting up the heavens in their transit across the sky. She said one day they will color the sky in a giant cloud and burn clean the surface of the world. Right now, they just watch me as I dig my fingers into the cocoon and pull off layer after layer of its delicate flesh. Why am I doing this? I cannot say. Everyone around me seems to think so hard about everything; I just do what I sense needs to be done.

Once, I saw a mantis dead in a market stall, a southern insect stiffened to a crisp by a northern clime. The vendor offered it as an exotic dish to shopping chefs. I wonder if I will find a giant one like it inside all this wrapping, as magical as the red ravens. The darkness deepens and I hear desperate cries erupt to the south along with the distant thud of battering rams and the far-off clanging of swords. I should be worried about my family, as it sounds like a Jurchen raid, but I trust my brother has pulled himself away from his women by now and will fend off any and all invaders.

The layers of the cocoon pile up like shorn wool until, at last, I break free a man clad in a rough hemp robe and wearing the kind of domed woolen hat I've seen mountain folk wear. He stands taller than I do and his matted beard sheds dust and mold. The *sanzuwu* surround him in one perfectly choreographed hop to the ground. He fixes his gaze upon me and a pinprick of citrus-colored light arises behind his eyes. He smiles and extracts something dark and sweet-smelling from his robe. I don't object when he shoves some of it into my wound, thumbing out the yarrow at the same time. He grins. His teeth are bright as stars. He raises his hands above his head, gives a single clap, and sets the birds to singing. To their melody, he begins to dance.

I've been cold and worried for hours, but when he offers his hands and I take them, I feel warm and free of cares. His touch is softer than mulberry paper and his fingertips bear no nails. The birds coo. The birch trees rustle. The moon glows. I laugh. I tell him I'll kill again if I have to, to protect myself and those I love. He nods as if he has known this, and me, for eons. We swirl as we dance, spiraling high and low. Despite my clothes, I feel stripped bare. Despite the madness of it all, I find he and I are one; even more, we two are part of everything else, so three, and then back to one again.

I have never felt happier.

7

IT TOOK FOUR hours to get in to see Granate. When I finally gained an audience, I asked him if he believed in God. He told me he thought the universe was intelligently designed, so I asked him whether he though so highly of himself that he would keep even that intelligent designer waiting for four hours. He told me emergencies happen but offered no apology.

"I don't believe my wife is gone," I said.

"Believe what you like but I'm telling you she is devoid of consciousness," he replied, going through the mail on his desk, not even looking at me. I wondered how he could be so sure of the things he said. My own short life had taught me that the more dogmatic people were, the less likely they were to know what they were talking about.

"From what I've read nobody even knows what consciousness is," I said. "Some scientists think it's just a function of complexity; others say it pervades every bit of matter in the universe. By either definition, it sounds like Lulu still has it."

Granate loosed a histrionic sigh. "What I can tell you with certainty is that neither your wife nor the fetuses have any future."

"Who can be certain of the future? You could get hit by a bus this afternoon. I could eat tainted sushi and die."

He said I was welcome to get another opinion, but even if I did, he was transferring Lulu to a long-term facility outside the hospital. His only answer to further questions was to pretend I had evaporated like a puddle on the chair across from him. Once again, I beat a retreat to Lulu's room. When I got there, Coraline with short-cropped hair thrust a pen and clipboard into my hands.

"What's this for?"

"Withdrawal of support."

"You mean medicine?'

"Food, water, medication, everything that's keeping her alive. I'm so sorry."

She dimmed the room lights on the way out. I washed my face and hands in the sink then surfed the television channels, seeing details of a stop-and-frisk police action gone wrong, breaking news about an eleven-car pileup on the San Diego Freeway, and political candidates hurling invectives at each other. Everything felt irrelevant and remote. I fell asleep, staunchly ignoring the paper I was supposed to sign, and only woke up when Dora shook my shoulder.

"I hope it's all right that I've come. You never really invited me."

"She's your sister," I said. "You don't need my invitation."

"How's she doing?"

"They want me to sign this form so they can send her someplace to die."

She took the clipboard from my hand, read the form, and handed it back to me without comment. "What about the children?" she said.

"I guess they want to withdraw support from them, too."

Dora chewed her lip. "You're sure they are not viable?"

"How can you ask me that? The only thing I'm sure of is that

43

we don't appreciate what we have until it's gone."

"You loved my sister. You will always have that."

Suddenly, Lulu's monitor began to beep and flash. She convulsed, her toes making moguls against the sheets at the bottom of the bed, her back arching violently. A rumbling noise came through her breathing tube and her lips drew back. Her fists tightened until her nails drew blood from the base of her palms. A nurse I didn't recognize rushed in, took one look, and ran out again.

"Somebody do something," I yelled.

A young doctor burst through the door, glanced at the monitor, and injected something into Lulu's IV line.

"What's happening?" I cried.

"Coma's a strange trip," he answered, calmly tossing the syringe in the red waste bucket. "For all we know, she's remembering a rock concert."

When the thrashing stopped and she was stable again, the doctor left. The episode had exposed Lulu's armpit, and with it, the purple tattoo I'd had needled into my own arm to please her.

混沌

I asked Dora what she knew about it, telling her Lulu had been mum on the subject. She shrugged.

"There's also this," I said, fishing Lulu's jade pendant out of my pocket. "She wore it all the time. Literally never took it off. I guess it's a tiger or some other kind of symbol. You know how she feels about cats. This is her blood on it. From the shooting. From the crash. I couldn't bring myself to wash it."

Dora stared at the thing for a long time, then pulled a chair next to Lulu's bed, rested her forehead on Lulu's belly, and cried. I wanted to comfort her but I couldn't. Instead, I just clutched the pendant in my hand. After a while, she sat up.

"China's a different world," she told me. "As far as a Westerner goes, it might as well be the planet Jupiter. I'm not just talking about the customs and the culture and the politics, I'm talking about what happens to the collective mind after thousands of years of living under imperial rule."

"Lulu told me it's the symbol for some crazy old Taoist god. Someone else told me Triad members use it. A Chinese secret society of criminals. Lulu told me a bit about Taoism. She didn't mention any gods."

"At the very beginning, Taoists were just shamans. They worshipped trees and rivers and such. I suppose you could say they treated natural phenomena as gods. Then there was this philosophical period where it was all just about the nature of things, the way things worked, Tao itself, which I suppose you can just think of as things moving forward. Tao's no entity and it's not god, either. Some people say it's just the ongoing, ever-changing, evolving process of everything that happens in the universe.

Buddhism brought the promise of an afterlife to Chinese people. The idea of accruing good karma during daily life so as to end up in a Heavenly place was attractive to a poor, suffering population. Taoism had to adopt similar ideas to compete, so it made up gods to pray to and even included Buddha and the Virgin Mary in Taoist temples."

"Lulu didn't tell me any of this. Actually, she doesn't really like to talk about it. I sense it is super important to her, though."

Dora massaged her temples and took a big breath. "Oh, it's important to her all right. You have no idea. But nothing is as simple as people make it out to be. There's so very much about China you don't understand. China still has Buddhism and it still has Taoism, even though they're hidden more now and absorbed by culture. In the old days, emperors adopted Buddhism or

Taoism. Things are different now. These days, religion and government don't mix. But people hold onto their beliefs. Some of us believe that holding on is the most important thing there is, sometimes even as a way of speaking truth to power and dealing with injustice. Some of what you call Triads were just advocates for the peasants brought over by American railroad companies as cheap labor. Chinese people trust each other more then they trust foreigners when those foreigners are their overlords, so Triad members served to settle disputes between Chinese laborers, too. Five thousand years of defiance takes a toll but also molds people, simmers in their souls, lives in their houses, bubbles up in quiet, secret meetings, hides in tiny signals and written codes and scrolls stuffed down into urns."

"In tattoos."

"You mean in symbols? Then yes. But you can also find defiance in classic books that say one thing and mean another. You can see it expressed in architecture that leads people in circles. You can find it in medicine that yields both cures and poisons. Defiance can also be seen in a thousand little acts that lead to a revolution that kills millions."

"We had a revolution," I said. "Ours was over religious freedom. Taxes. The yoke of monarchy."

"Nothing in your revolution can prepare you for China. America is a childishly new experiment; China is a seasoned, mature culture."

"A mature, seasoned culture with old secret societies still operating in the modern world."

"The West has such things, too. Regional, organizational, familial. It's not such a radical thing. People are tribal, Solomon. You're Jewish. Surely you understand that."

"I don't have anything to do with all that, but I take your point. But wait, are you telling me I married into the mob?

"We don't call it that. The best definition, I think, would be cult. And yes, we worship the god of chaos. His name is Hun. Believe it or not, you know him from what you call won ton soup."

I blinked in confusion. "Wait. What?"

"Think about the dumplings in the soup," she said. "They don't have any prescribed shape like they might in an Italian pasta dish. They're not spirals or strings or bowties but just lumps of dough with meat in the middle."

"I guess," I said slowly.

"Their signature is their vague, amorphous shape, and that's because they're named after the God of Chaos. We call him Lord Hun. My family worships him and his work in the world, creating opportunities — though rarely where you expect them — reshuffling things when they are stiff or stuck, providing a propulsive force to untangle problems and situations but always in an indirect way that makes both his form and his actions subtle and hard to detect without paying a lot of attention."

"What does it mean to follow him?"

"We have some rituals that just express our devotion to him, but also we have practices that heighten our ability to see his hand at work."

"Like Taoist meditation searching for the immortal Tao or Buddhists cultivating the ways of Buddha in their own lives."

She nodded.

"Strange kind of god," I said. "But a cool idea."

"Oh, Hun is strange all right," Dora gave me a small smile. "And yes, he can be kind of cool, too. And cruel. But he also can be kind, especially in the way he gives us things."

"What kind of things?"

She looked right at me.

"Second chances," she said. "They're his specialty."

I, in turn, looked at Lulu.

47

8

THE DANCING exhausts me and I collapse to the ground in the middle of the clearing. When I awaken, the dusty man is holding a gourd to my lips. The rind is hard and the edge is fleshy but the water inside is cold and pure. I drink sloppily, like a soldier, then check my wound with my finger. I find no crusty scab, no fibrous bump, no gap in the flesh, no tenderness under pressure. Wondering if perhaps I dreamed the attack, I twist around to inspect myself. There, in the dim light of dawn, I find a tiny pink line in my flesh.

"The last trace will fade by sundown," my dance partner tells me.

I'm startled by his voice and realize I haven't heard it before. Looking at him now, I can scarcely connect the man before me to the one I danced with last night. His skin is smooth and his gleaming hair is pulled back behind his head. There is no trace of dirt on his skin, no trace of the forest on his tunic. His formerly dun-colored eyes are piercing and black. I ask who he is and he tells me his name is Mu. I blink, confused. The only Mu I know is the hunchbacked old shaman who lives on a platform in a tree on the edge of town. I've heard he holds forth for anyone who will listen about the pervasive presence of the ancestors, about heavenly signs, war, rebellion, floods, snows, omens in the form of snow-white deer, fish swimming against the flow of the river, and about worried glances from heavenly sages. I know Father is among a small group of people who take his utterances to heart. Anyway, old Mu grunts in granular tones whereas this young man — and yes, in the morning light, he is clearly young — has a voice like a temple bell. Might I still be dreaming?

"Life is a dream within a dream within a dream," says Mu, as if reading my mind. "But here and now you're awake and yes, I am the Mu you thought you knew, and yes, I always know the thoughts of my dance partner, even though you're the first one I've had in some centuries."

The spell of Mu's wasps has so beguiled and confused me that I see birch trees and oaks as the legs of giants, immodestly covered by the holdover leaves of autumn. Too, I notice for the first time a high mountain behind us that was invisible during my night flight through the dark forest.

"Did you say centuries?"

Mu nods. "I've been watching you since you were born. I know about the terrible tiger and all the tigers since, and I know about your practice east of town. I know about the mulberry paper your father steals for you."

"He doesn't steal it; he buys it at the market."

"So he would have you believe. He tells me everything, you see. He has since he was a little boy. I knew you were coming. Not just to me here in the forest, but coming into this world again at this time and in this place, first to kill a soldier, then to find me sleeping with my wasps."

"I didn't kill anyone."

Mu laughs. "You can't lie to me. I know of your explorations, of your growing appetites, and of your uncertainty around how to control them. I will help you open yourself to Hun and thereby you will grow."

I nod slowly. "First, tell me of this Hun."

"He lives in us."

"Grandmother mentioned him when she died."

Mu nods. "She would have. And she would have told you more if she could. Hun is Emperor of the Center. He is the god of creation and she was his devoted servant."

"Where does he live?"

"In coincidence, though of course there is no such thing, and in the wispy, invisible tendrils that hold our world together. He manifests betwixt and between the familiar cycles in your life, such as the change of seasons and the appearance of your monthly bleed. He is there when things disintegrate, and also when a poor plan succeeds against all odds and expectations. When an excellent technique fails or a good pact falls apart, those, too, are his doing. Hun supports every winning underdog and sends snow in summer and a year's worth of rain in a week. Every great gain is his design, as is every time luck leaves you like a fickle lover. All that is Hun, the weaver of the very fabric upon which the drama of human life is written. The women in your grandmother's line serve him, as do I."

"I don't serve anyone," I say.

"Ah, but you do."

"I say I do not."

Again, Mu laughs. "Hun is generous and kind in ways you cannot presently imagine. Everything about him flies in the face of the normal and expected. It is an honor to belong to him."

"If he's the god of accidents, he sent the tiger to eat Grandmother."

Mu nods. "Yes, he did. But only after providing her a lifetime of gifts."

"Gifts? Her husband died young and left her alone, my mother hated her, and then she got eaten by a tiger."

"Longevity is not the only way Hun shows favor. Can you not tell that Yang Nuo moved with alacrity through the spirit realm, and she does so still? Have you forgotten her great talent with her spear, which she shared with you? Do you not remember how easily she found highly-prized ginseng roots even in the dead of winter, even under a foot of snow, and dug them out with her hard fingers to keep your family alive during the lean times? She could sniff the great birch mushrooms from half a *li* away and sell them to doctors for potions and cures, too. Our chaotic master rewarded her very well, Miao."

"And what has he given you?"

"We'll talk about that later. Right now, you must follow me to the lake."

"Fine," I say. "I need a bath."

9

THERE WAS something about the angle of Dora's head as it rested on Lulu's sheets that stirred the photographer in me. I suppose at some point all lensmen yearn for the emotion that absolutely compels the shutter finger, an urge that arises in the belly like a craving for apple pie or ice cream or steak, the desire to consume the image, eat it, preserve it, own it. I set up the image as if doing a commercial shoot, positioning a bottle of shampoo by a vase of flowers, say, or a tube of toothpaste emerging from beach sand like a Spanish doubloon uncovered by a storm.

I used a wide-angle lens to intentionally mess with perspective and introduce distortion. I draped a clump of electrical leads over Dora's head like a tiara. Deep in some communion with Lulu, she waved me away but I persisted and eventually she gave in. I shifted the view to include the pole holding Lulu's IV bag and a wash of light from the window. I laid a kidney-shaped bedpan on the gleaming sheet next to Dora's elbow as a prop, careful not to catch my own reflection in the shiny metal. When everything was just so, I gently pressed the shutter button.

That was when I saw Lulu's right arm move, saw her triceps war with her apparently uncooperative biceps to deliberately extend her left arm from where it had rested, spastic, below her chin, until her fist lay on the bed. Her fingers, so long locked and curled, straightened and stretched one by one. Then I saw her thumb and first two fingers come together at the tips and her wrist began to swing from side to side.

I hit the call button dangling from the bed frame. Coraline appeared. I pointed at Lulu's hand. I could hear my own breathing. Dora chewed her lip. Coraline frowned. Lulu became increasingly agitated in her movement until she was shaking her hand so violently the bed moved with her.

"I think I know what she wants," Coraline declared. She grabbed the pen and pad of paper from beside the room phone, levered the pen into Lulu's grip and slid the paper under it. Despite the rhythmic whoosh of the respirator and the various and sundry beeps and clicks of the equipment keeping Lulu alive, the room was quiet enough for us to actually hear the scratch of pen on paper.

Lulu's writing was understandably wobbly, her atrophied muscles employed in a task she could not see. Even so, the handwriting was so entirely alien I couldn't help but wonder whether the woman I had married really was done and gone as Dr. Granate had said. After several minutes of excruciating effort, she put the pen down. I picked up the paper to read it.

Get my wasps China now

"Wasps?" I said. "Is that the word she wrote?"

"I don't see any other way to read it," said Coraline, inspecting the pad. "I've never seen a patient do anything like this."

"How did you know she wanted to write?"

"I've gotten to know her," Coraline smiled.

A moment later, Lulu's left arm repeated the battle her right one had just fought, her brow evidencing the concentration required. At length, the hand was down, the fingers unfurled, the movement of the wrist beginning. Coraline transferred the pad and pen, ripping off the message to provide a new sheet.

Dora pointed at Lulu's fingers, no longer curled tight. "You had her nails done?"

"It felt good to do something so I painted them myself," I said. "I did her toes, too, under the compression socks. I used Butter London's La Moss Lacquer. It's her favorite. She says it's vampy."

Lulu stopped writing. The three of us looked at the pad. This time she wrote in Chinese.

I'm sorry Daddy

The penmanship was so different, it appeared written by a different person not merely a different hand.

"What is she sorry about?" I asked Dora.

Dora looked suddenly defensive. "How would I know?"

"You're her sister."

"Nobody ever knew what she was thinking."

"Do you know why she would ask about wasps?"

Dora hesitated. "I'm not sure."

"Well, she obviously wants me to go to China. If I go, will you and your family help me?"

"This is complicated," said Dora.

"Hey, do you even *want* her to recover?" I demanded.

I was sorry the instant I said that, but before I could apologize, Dora left the room. Coraline gave me a hug. Not a pat-on-the-back kind of hug but a real one.

"I've never seen a coma that didn't wreck worlds," she said.

10

WALKING BEHIND Mu, I am impressed by the length of his stride. It seems his legs grow stronger at every step. As we near the lake, I detect a hint of watercress in the air and the aroma of catfish, too. When we finally arrive at the water, I see a panoply of peaks reflected on the surface, along with the last vestiges of the stubborn morning moon. The edges of the lake are jagged, as if the fingernails of a giant hand have gouged it out of the mountain range. I had no idea I climbed so high in my flight from An Er's camp. I touch the surface and lick my finger, savoring the freshness and the cold. I start to strip but Mu restrains me.

"Wait," he says. "I want to show you something first."

He crouches to select a stone from a patch of mud. He takes his time with the process, turning each one in his hand, running his fingers over it, cleaning it before discarding it, and trying another.

"What are you doing?"

"The glorious, long-tailed, rainbow-colored phoenix gave rise to the Shang. My people."

"I've seen red crows with three legs," I say.

He waves his hands dismissively. "Minions of Hun. Friends of Mu. The phoenix is the mistress of resurrection and rebirth."

I try to understand what he's saying. I think about the cocoon and the wasps. "I really need a bath," I say.

He finally finds a stone he likes, flat and smooth and oval, dark with glinting veins of white running irregularly through it. "This is you," he says, hefting it. "Watch and learn."

With a deft flick of his wrist, he sends it skimming across the surface of the lake. After sparkling and spinning in the morning sun, it makes landfall on the far shore. He jogs off to retrieve it and I follow through the reeds where the last frogs of the year leap up and away when I step too close. He picks up the stone and shows it to me.

"You see how the lake has kissed the bottom but not the top?"

"You mean it's dry on one side?"

"You go through all your lives like this stone, Miao. You skip, you touch, and you move on. Life after life, you never get fully engaged or involved. You never get trapped, either, but you do get wet because in the end, no matter what we do, the underside of life is always full of blood and water and snot and piss. Up top, though, ah, there things are different. Up top is where you're special. It's where you are warmed by the rays of the sun. It's where you connect with Heaven. That top side gives you perspective and understanding. That's where you can fly through time and space. That's your gift from Hun, a bit of joy and exhilaration in all that chaos and filth. Your grandmother recognized this about you and so do I."

I begin to take off my clothes. "I really don't know what you're talking about."

I feel his eyes on me as I remove my last bit of clothing and lower my toes into the mud. The water is just off ice. I wonder how the thin-skinned frogs can stand it. I turn my face to the sun and breathe deeply, feeling the pounding of my heart and the squeeze of my empty stomach. I'm about to mention how hungry I am when a stick floats past. I can't resist grabbing it and peeling the twigs off until it's smooth, paying more attention to crafting it into a miniature spear than I pay to the dull, apple-sized ache at the site of my now invisible wound. I launch it at Mu and when it hits his hard belly, he shakes his head, amazed I can throw it with such force.

I duck under the water and open my eyes in frigid blurry world. My thoughts go to Hun and then to whether there might be tigers by the lake. I think about Grandmother's voice in my head. I worry about who might find Liu's body. I think about the wasps and the cocoon and about how Mu can possibly be so old. I consider the prospect of coupling with him. I wonder if it's true that my father steals the mulberry paper for me.

Mu watches me break the surface, raise my arms, and put my hands around to the back of my hair to squeeze the lake from my hair. "A perfect phoenix," he says.

Then he's naked and in the lake with me. I don't go to him, nor do I back away. I simply wait. I have spent a great deal of time developing patience, hard work because it does not come naturally to me.

"I've seen you polishing your parents' ceremonial *ding*," says Mu. "The way you take your time with it, the way you work your brush into every crack and crevice, the way you raise it to the window to see it shine."

"If something is worth doing, it's worth doing well," I say. "Besides, the regional governor gave my family that *ding*."

Mu nods, approaching me slowly. "Being a governor meant something back then, but now, in the chaos, your skill with your spear is more important than family connections. I've hidden behind the birches to watch you. Your performances are always remarkable."

"I'm glad you think so but I don't like people who spy."

He shrugs. "As this is your first time making love, you should know that no normal man can do what I can do, and certainly not in ice water, which will shrivel a man's root the way plants shrink to bulbs in winter. Look here now."

With this, he points at that which has broken the surface of the water and is standing as straight and tall as a baby birch.

"I'm curious," I say.

"About everything," he confirms. "I know."

"About the wasps."

"You must not get hurt in the dead of winter," he says. "In the dead of winter, they cannot help you."

"It is cold now."

"But not the *dead* of winter."

"And if I do get hurt then? If you do?"

"We die," says Mu.

His arms are thick and strong around me and his hands gentle as he cradles my face, his thumbs tracing a path from the outer edges of my eyes to the edges of my mouth. He kisses me in a way that Liu did not, moving from my lips to the white span of the tops of my shoulders. I notice his hair is still tainted by a few flecks of hive so I gently push him underwater to rinse them out. He pulls me down after him. I giggle as he nibbles my sensitive places. His breath penetrates the spot that once tied me to Mother, using the conduit as a way to connect his energy to mine.

I can't believe he can hold his breath for so long.

I have explored every inch of my own body. I have listened to its rhythms while timing the thrusts of my spear, learned to find quiet places in which I can synchronize all my muscles without distraction and to the end of a perfectly placed thrust. I have learned about my breathing and the heat I make in the cold and aloft in trees in summer. Never before, in all that time, have I felt the small sun that now glows between my legs. My brow beads with perspiration despite the frigid water in which Mu remains submerged, too busy to come up to breathe.

When at last he does come up, he bursts out of the lake like a crocodile after a bird, gulping air with an enormous gasp. Then, without warning, he impales me. I want what he's giving. I grab his haunches hungrily. He disengages and withdraws.

"Hun teaches us about cycles, dear Miao," he says, noting my disappointed expression. "Not all cold and not all hot; not all forward and not all back; not all fast and not all slow. We build greater things with subtlety than we do with brute force. Anticipation brings focus. Focus sharpens feeling."

He begins again. Soon, his movements become spirals, stimulating me at the front and at the back, to the left and to the right. He seems able to control the temperature of his stalk, one moment it burns me, the next it is cool as stone.

"*Ming men*," he says, placing his palms at the small of my back. "Life's gate. The place you store your life force, our *qi*, between your lives; the place you draw upon to stay coherent and follow the thread Hun has laid out for you when you have no body; the place you draw upon to steer your life when you do...."

"...and the place the wasps go in winter," I finish.

"Yes!" he grins.

"Good," I say, wrapping my arms around him. "Now be quiet."

As my hands range far and wide, I burn memories I know I will someday draw upon when I am with other men, measuring what I feel then against the unquenchable passion I feel now.

"Too much thinking," he tells me, breaking the requested silence at last. "There are things to learn with a different part of the mind. Stop analyzing. Let go."

As if to underscore his point, he begins a gyre of the flesh, drawing the lake into a pale, patterned pool around us. Steam rises. My head grows light and my mouth grows dry. I feel his tongue behind my front teeth, completing the circuit he began when he kissed my navel. I feel energy run crazily up my spine, down my chest and belly, then all the way to the center of the earth. My climaxes crash through me without mercy. At the peak of them, when I am so lost, I cannot even remember who or what I am, I dig my feet into the cold black mud of the lake, toss back my head, and howl.

When at last I open my eyes, the first thing I see are the three-legged sun crows, the *sanzuwu*, watching me in a silent circle. They give a single flap of their wings. It's like applause.

11

My parents' Palos Verdes neighborhood was a paean to optimism, abundance, and the American Way. Most of the year, the sun was so bright, people drove the surrounding boulevards with their sunshades dropped, even at high noon. Their house itself was a big square thing with half a dozen desert tortoises living in the courtyard carved out of its middle. My brother, Bryce had brought the endangered animals in from the national monument at Joshua Tree, unfazed by the laws protecting them from precisely such a fate. They survived in my parents' yard on *Opuntia* cactus, tomatoes, and lettuce the Mexican gardener left for them every week when he came with his leaf blower and his rake.

Bryce and I sat on a bench and watched the little reptiles circle us warily, eager for a drink from my mom's gurgling fountain. My mother had wanted a courtyard and fountain even before my father's medical practice took off, even when they were living in Burbank in a house a quarter the size, even when she was at Claremont College. She'd have you believe this courtyard was all she needed to be happy, all she had ever needed, even when she was just a little girl. The strange thing was, she never ventured into it. The sight of it through the kitchen window, she said, was enough to reassure her that all was right with her life.

I thanked my big brother for flying across the country to be with me.

"When your shit is all over the fan, I have nothing more important to do," he said, tipping back a bottle of beer. "By the way, do you ever think about time travel, like if you could go back and stop Lulu from honking at her shooter?"

"No," I said. "My heart can't handle thoughts like that right now."

He nodded. "So, I've heard some crazy stories. And Lulu writing messages on paper when her brain is dead? There's so much shit we don't understand. Forces. Energies. A whole shadow world."

One of the tortoises took a bite of my sneaker. I jerked away and Bryce looked at me accusingly. "He didn't mean anything by it. That blue on your sneaker, it's like a wildflower to him. Ginger says you've got some smokin' hot nurse? Short blonde hair and long legs? Sounds like she'd look great in a bikini, playing volleyball on Venice Beach."

"Coraline. She was tough in the beginning, giving me papers and all. She's nicer now. Must be difficult working in a place like that."

"Yeah, well Ginger likes her. When's our sister going to come out of the closet, anyway?"

"The day she does is the day Dad dies."

"Maybe you should ask out that nurse."

"Jesus, Bryce. Lulu's in a coma."

My father has a face like a knife and a cutting tongue to match, no doubt the reason he chose dermatology, a medical specialty in which doctor-patient interactions are short and generally predictable. When he opened the front door, the air around us fell away.

"Hot day for winter," he called, and then, when he got a little closer. "You know, it's damn strange you never met Lulu's family, that they didn't come to the wedding, that they have never invited you to China, and that this sister suddenly materializes from nowhere."

"Every family's different," I shrugged.

My mom opened the bay window. She's my father's opposite. Everything about her is as soft and round as a pecan roll, a shape she's proud of not only because she loves pastries but because she believes women with round faces don't show their age.

"The hummingbirds are back," she called to me. "There's a nest under the eave by the garage and another one in the planter by the pool in that Asian tree that's too tall for the pot now."

"I hear Lulu wrote gibberish words on a piece of paper," my father ventured.

"Not gibberish," I replied. "She asked for her father. I talked to Dr. Granate about it. He said he wasn't sure what it meant."

"I spoke to him, too," my father said. "He's not sure any of that happened. Wasn't in the room. Says he reviewed her scans. Says they don't support that kind of brain function."

"He doesn't think it *happened*?" I answered incredulously. "We have the evidence. Two pieces of paper."

"Coma does strange things to people. You don't have to be a neurologist to know that. Wishful thinking born of desperation, for example. Making something out of unintelligible scribbling."

"Are you saying I'm making it up? It was legible. The nurse was right there. Dora, too. We all saw it and read it."

My father shrugged. "Granate says if it *did* happen, it was likely random movement."

"Random movement doesn't write words! And it sure as hell doesn't know my name or compose sentences."

"Reliving a memory, then. I remind you, there haven't been any further signs of improvement. None at all."

I felt a wave of anger rise in me.

"Why does no one want my wife to get better?" I shouted. "What's wrong with you people?"

Before my father could shout back, a car pulled up at the curb and Ginger and Nash got out. My mother appeared. "Let's go inside," she said, clapping her hands. "You all simply must see my latest watercolor."

***

My mother's art studio was an airy space with heavy blackout curtains pulled aside to let in light from the courtyard. Brightly-colored tapestries rendering parrots—my mother especially loves tropical birds—and trees hung from the walls, souvenirs of my parents' regular sojourns to Mexico. Shelves that had once held books and camera gear now bristled with orchids and bromeliads, sketch pads and paints.

The studio had been my room and was the only quarters to have been turned to fresh duty; Ginger's bedroom was as it had been the day she moved out. Bryce's too. The rationale was that Bryce lived far away and needed a place to stay when he came to visit, while Ginger's situation was unstable and might require her to return home at any moment. I, by contrast, was not expected to return; I was married.

I can't say I minded. I very much admired my mother's artistic talent and thought it perfectly appropriate she have her own studio. In fact, I often told her I hoped one day to become as good a photographer as she was an artist. There was a tall easel in the middle of the room, the exact spot where a sloe-eyed high school girl named Carmen had unzipped the trousers of a shy boy named Solomon and left him a virgin no more. On that easel sat my mom's latest work, a landscape with mountains in the background, tipped in snow. Waterfalls cascaded through little pools into a lake at the bottom, and around the lake a beautifully-rendered tiger put tongue to water. Along a rocky ledge, a group of nine farmers—an older couple, four adults, and three children—looked on.

"Wow," said Ginger. "I've never seen you do anything like this before."

"A whole new level, Mom," said Bryce. "Really."

"It's classical Chinese style," said my mother. "I've been studying it since Solomon met Lulu. You see how tiny the people are in comparison to everything else? It's to show how we are just one small part of nature, and not the most important part, either."

"Nine people just like all of us plus the babies in Lulu's tummy," said Nash.

"Those aren't babies yet, Nash," said my father. "They're just pre-babies. Proto-babies, better."

"Dora seems to think the only way I can help Lulu is to go to China," I interrupted.

My mother frowned. "Your wife is here. Why in the world would you leave? And isn't she waking up? I mean, wouldn't you help her best by being there when she opens her eyes?"

"She needs something to heal the rest of the way," I explained. "Something I have to bring back for her."

My father rolled his eyes. "I truly hope you're not talking about mumbo-jumbo herbs. You have to be careful with that stuff. Full of lead and other industrial contaminants. They don't work, anyway. Stick with real medicine."

Briefly, I considered telling them that Dora had quizzed me about Lulu's supernatural abilities, had implied there was much about my wife I didn't know, information that was only in China and that I felt I needed to know. I even considered mentioning the wasps. I nearly gave voice to the conviction, born of hundreds of hours of agonizing inquiry, that the only way I could reach Lulu was to pry into her past. The thought startled me; I had not had it before.

"It's better to do something than nothing," I said. "Better to try than just give up."

"You've never been long in the patience department," my father opined.

"If it will make you feel better, you should go," my mother suggested, quite to my amazement. "You'll need money. You're a student and traveling across the world is expensive. Come with me, sweetheart, and I'll write you a check. Just promise me you won't be gone too long."

I might not have known Lulu's mother, but at that moment I was very grateful to know my own.

12

I N T H E Y E A R S that follow, remnants of the Northern Song Dynasty gather together in our growing town of Yidu. They are trying to survive the ongoing scourge of the Jurchens, the random campaigns of the nervous Southern Song to the south, and the occasional scouting forays of the Mongols. My brother's Red Jacket militia helps stabilize things, but even so, we all feel squashed together in a cooking pot with a fire burning below us. Often, I wonder how long this small pot will be able to contain all the secrets of a girl who murdered a soldier.

It was exactly as I think these thoughts one morning when I realize someone is following me. He appears early in the morning in the courtyard of the Buddhist temple, falling in step behind me as I set out to meet Mu. I feel his presence as I bow to the monks streaming into their meditation hall. He's trying to stay far enough back so I won't know I'm being followed and I let him think I don't. I go the stone archway at the north end of the temple, I pass the row of sago palms brought in seed form as a gift for the local abbot by an itinerant monk from the far-off island empire of Nippon. When we are no longer visible to the temple hall, I turn around suddenly to surprise him.

Ha! He is Ye Gui, teenage son of the local sword merchant and the last person I expect to see. Last year, claiming they were needed to save our province, my brother confiscated many of his father's swords before our own father him to give them back. It was a humiliating event for all, and sparked a conflict that continues to smolder. I figure this is the reason the boy is following me. That and the general effect my maturing body has on every male in the village, the way they lust after me, trail me, skulk around hoping for a chance to sweet talk me.

"Did you really think I wouldn't notice you behind me? A tree could hear your nervous footfalls," I demand.

"I only want to talk," he says.

"What else could you possibly want?"

"I was watching for rebels on sentry duty at the soldier camp that night."

"What night is that?" I ask, bluffing.

"Ha. I saw everything. I saw what happened."

"You didn't see anything."

"Oh, but I did. I know you went to get your brother and he wasn't there but Liu invited you in. I watched you by torchlight, your shadows against the tent."

"You son of a turtle."

He seems to enjoy the insult, as he goes on to gleefully recount everything that happened, including his appreciation of my light and gliding steps. He tells me he snuck up close and peeked through the tent flap, says he was to be able to smell us doing what we did. He confesses the sight of me made his temples sweat, made his armpits drip despite the chilly air, made his breathing short and tight. He tells me he heard Liu curse me, even saw him go for his blade. He tells me he had to duck out of sight or I would have run right into him after I yanked the dagger from my flesh and threw it back at Liu's eye. He tells me he wanted to follow me as I ran away, limping, but he was afraid. He tells me he had to wait for fifteen clouds to pass overhead before he found the courage to go check on Liu. He tells me he has kept my secret, thinking about me every day.

"Now our families are arguing again and your brother owes my father, so finally, a taste of Miao will be my reward and nobody will say a thing," he says, smacking his lips.

I surprise myself by thinking of Mu. It is only Mu I want between my legs, only Mu to teach me the skills of love and the command of wasps. I have seen him a number of times. It is my right to do so. My destiny. I was not made to be with a boy like Gui.

"No," I say, pushing my spear point into the base of his neck.

"Oh yes," Gui smiles. "You're going to lie with me in the hay loft behind my father's house. We're going to go there right now."

"Ridiculous."

"Not to Liu's family."

"Tell me why I shouldn't just stab right through this scrawny throat of yours."

"Two murders, twice the likelihood someone will tie them together," he says, pushing my blade away carefully. "We have judges. We have magistrates. Your father is an important man, but mine is richer."

"You saw Liu abuse me. You saw him throw the dagger first."

"I saw you go to him willingly. I saw you enjoy it and then I saw you kill him. If I put out the word, soldiers will tie you to a tree and let the tigers come. Or maybe they'll shove a sword between your legs and let you bleed out in the town square in front of everyone. When you beg them to chop off your head, they'll tie your arms and legs to horses and tear you apart. Even your brother won't be able to save you."

I feel something boiling up in me. Rage at being judged by people who don't understand me, who can't do the things I can do, who don't know the world the way I do. Rage at the way women must kowtow and grovel at the power of men.

"Do we have a deal?" Little Gui persists, suggestively moving his hips. "The hay bed is waiting."

"Let's do it right here among the sacred trees," I say quietly.

"Here?" he sputters, looking around. Clearly, this is not what he has been expecting.

"Monks are at morning prayer. Merchants are already at work. It's safe. Nobody will see us."

"But the hay bed will be more comfortable..."

"Are you man enough to take me now or not?" I demand, somehow knowing this will not be the last time I ask this question.

He blushes. I take his hand and lead him behind the thickest stand of palms. "Clothes," I say, pointing.

He strips slowly. "You too," he says.

"You have to win me," I say, when his pants are off and his tunic loose and his sandals lie at an angle to each other in the dirt, one upside down.

"I'm winning you by keeping your secret."

"What says you won't come back for more?"

He grins. "If you're lucky, I will."

I slap him hard on the face. He slaps me back. I punch him under the chin. He goes to his knees and a tooth with a long bloody root appears on the ground. His manhood was a banner pole but now it droops. He snatches at his tooth and holds it up, dripping blood.

"Crazy bitch," he yells, smearing the bloody tooth against my cheek, then spinning me around and using his weight to force me onto all fours.

I wriggle but can't dislodge him. he yanks down my billowy pants. Hands splayed out in front of me, knees in the dirt, Hun avails me. I am suddenly aware of being part of a much larger world, one that extends up to Heaven and down to the center of the Earth. My hearing sharpens and I hear the blood rushing through Gui's veins, the crazy heartbeats of nearby mice, the palm trees breathing, the downward pressure of gathering clouds. I see things in the dirt, too, the patterns of fallen leaves and the caravan trails of ants.

And I see the snake.

It's a small pit viper. Its body is gray, its markings are pale, and white lines run from its nose to its chin. It has been camouflaged in a patch of leaves, warming in a sunny spot, taking in the last of the autumn warmth. I understand it has spent its whole life beneath these trees, growing fat and happy, protected by the Buddhists' reverence for life, feasting on the parade of mice moving from the cover of the forest to the monks' mess hall. Directly beneath my chest, it flicks out its dark tongue, lazily. As Gui fusses and groans. I shift and free a hand and grab the viper behind its head. It shows a cottony mouth and long fangs dripping venom. I shove it back between my legs, plunging those fangs into Gui's manhood just as he prepares to thrust.

I expect Gui to scream but he falls silent in shock. I turn over and wrap my legs around his neck. Weakly, he attempts to writhe free but I will not let go, will not be torn apart by horses for the sake of his lust, nor left for tiger food. I will not see Father's heart broken, my brother's position weakened, Mother disappointed, my family dishonored. I squeeze harder. Gui's face reddens. I see the snake's glands pulse as they deliver venom. Gui's dirty nails dig into my thighs, drawing blood. I swat him hard on the head. He gasps but cannot fill his lungs. Even when his eyes roll up and he twitches spasmodically, I will not relent.

When he is dead and I have caught my breath, I arrange him in a forward crouch, head slumped forward, snake still dangling between his legs. I use a palm branch to clean the ground of evidence of our struggle. Whoever finds him will construe that

Gui went behind the bushes to relieve himself and had the misfortune to be fatally bitten. I smooth his hair. I adjust my tunic.

It is time to go to Mu.

13

THE PLANE taking me to Beijing was called a Dreamliner. It was certainly a dream to me, as my father's aerophobia had always kept our family firmly on the ground. We crossed the country to Florida in an RV once, and another time went all the way up to Vancouver along the Coast Highway with Ginger vomiting every ten minutes in the cramped onboard toilet at every hairpin turn. After that, the only trips we made were straight down south to Baja California, sometimes all the way to Cabo San Lucas, which Dad viewed as a desert-meets-ocean paradise. I didn't see Baja the way he did. There was too much poverty and too much sloppy boozing, especially around surfing hot spots — I had championship ambitions with a short board back then — and at the bottom of the peninsula.

If those trips to Mexico failed to prepare me for a Chinese wife who belonged to a dubious secret society, they did help me realize I saw shapes and colors differently than other people did — a gift, assumedly courtesy of my mother. I saw *people* differently, too, especially the few descendants of the long-gone *Pai Pai* and *Waicuri* tribes about whom I learned by talking to a hotel pool cleaner one year and a hotel maid the next.

I found the sadness of the handful of surviving indigenous peoples of Baja to be very much worth photographing. I was taken by the contrast between their dark skin and their white teeth, by their slight frames, and by their air of suffering and acceptance, which I sought to document. I learned much about the power of light and shadow from them too, in the desert, at daybreak and at sunset. When I finally grew old enough to disappear from our camper for hours without question on our yearly trips, I followed my indigenous friends to their homes. Their villages were long gone, so their houses were just shanties on the edges of towns — tin-roof shacks with dirt floors and, for the most part, no electricity, television, or Internet access.

I listened to their stories of the power of the land, of the spirit incarnations of the creatures of the coastal desert. In return for my interest in animism, shamanism, and the spirit world of their ancestors — the existence of a magical world fully as real as our own yet invisible to non-believers — they graced my lens without reservation. Even the *curanderos*, the medicine men, so careful and shy they attached importance to the merest glance from an eagle, let me photograph them. The people of Baja taught me not only to use my eyes but to trust them. I shall always be grateful to them for that.

The images I assembled during those teen years moved my mother very much. She wanted me to submit them to a museum or at very least share them as a project at school. I told her they represented a personal pact between me and my friends in Baja and that I would not use them for commercial purposes. Even after I stopped going there and decided to pursue photography as a career, I honored that relationship. It was not until I applied to UCLA that I showed them to anyone, and then only upon Lulu's urging, and for no other reason than to gain admission to the photography program. They did the trick.

Sitting in the first row of the Dreamliner's main cabin, I tried to envision what my first meeting with Lulu's family would look like. Dora had declined to travel with me, arguing that one of us needed to stay with Lulu. She promised someone would meet me at the airport and emailed me photos of the family so I'd have an easier time identifying them. Despite all that, I sensed she was uncomfortable with my decision, perhaps because of Lulu's evidently fraught relationship with her parents, perhaps because of the family being involved in a criminal enterprise. When it came right down to it, I had absolutely no idea what to expect in terms of a reception, no idea whether or if I would be in any way welcome.

I tried to sleep but was plagued with visions of Lulu as a one-eyed, bandaged, emaciated creature wearing diapers and enduring needles and tubes. The phrase "please, Baby, stay alive" became my mantra. I repeated it while walking back and forth from the restroom, and while touching my toes and doing backbends as the plane passed Hawaii and reached the midway point over the seemingly endless Pacific Ocean. I repeated the mantra, too, as I gazed out the airplane window at the distant, twinkling stars, knowing from my camera work that when the eye relaxes to the horizon, the heart relaxes, too.

Sometime after midnight, birds suddenly appeared outside the airplane window. At first, I assumed they were Demoiselle cranes, a species my mother once told me were the supreme athletes of the avian world, able to fly over the top of the Himalayas, flapping away for days without respite on their yearly migration between China and Africa. Big as birds go, they are the smallest of the cranes and wont to fall prey to eagles. Someday, I would like to see one, but that night I was looking at far smaller creatures, obviously crows, though blood red with black beaks and dark eyes. They flew close enough to the window for me to see that tucked against their bodies, trailing behind them as they flew, they had an extra leg. Genetic mutants,

I figured. Very strange.

"Look!" I cried, spontaneously and to no one in particular. "Birds outside the plane!"

The flight attendant who'd been serving me meals and snacks immediately slid into the empty seat beside me and unabashedly shoved me out of the way to get a view out the window.

"They test jet engines for bird handling these days," she said. "What comes out looks like a bloody blender drink so you really don't have to worry, but anyway, where are these birds? I see only darkness."

I leaned forward to restore my view. They were right there, closer than ever, their eyes gleaming in the wash of the wing lights, their wings flapping furiously, their strange legs dangling, claws tight against the wind. "Are you kidding me?" I said. "It's a whole flock. Hundreds. Here. Just sit here for a second. I think the problem is the cabin reflection."

She was big and ash-blonde and it took her a little work to squeeze past me and press her face to the window between cupped hands. I know she saw the the birds because suddenly her airline-issue blouse grew damp at the armpits and I could smell a mixture of perspiration, orange blossom perfume, and laundry detergent. Suddenly there was a strong jolt and it felt like the airplane had dropped 5,000 feet, which maybe it had. The passengers around me screamed and the seatbelt sign chimed. The cabin lights came up and the flight attendant went back to work. The birds were gone but the sky was suddenly alive with columns of ominous-looking clouds, each flashing and glowing with electrical discharges. The plane shook like a wet dog, then suddenly banked sharply.

We lost more altitude. Sodas and juices and wine bottles flew as a service cart went over on two wheels and slid down the aisle. A beautiful wave of blue sparks spread across the wing.

The interior lights blinked off. Overhead storage bins popped open and small bags fell out. A violin in a hard case hit a nun on the head. A bag of baby diapers hovered, split open, and scattered. The passenger across the aisle from me gripped his tray table so tightly, he ripped it from its armatures. My stomach rose to the back of my throat then settled down again. I heard people retching.

And then it was over. The storms vanished, the flight leveled off, the engines wound down, and the wings stopped flapping. The pilot finally took to the intercom, apologized for the ride, announced that the storms had come out of nowhere, and asked us to help the flight attendants by cleaning up the areas around our seats.

"There was some loose talk of birds outside the airplane," he chuckled. "We're way too high for our feathered friends to keep us company, folks, and going far too fast. My advice to whomever saw them is to give that sleeping pill a dry run at home instead of testing your reaction to it during an international fight."

I hadn't taken any pills. I'd never heard of a red crow with three legs. I was entirely certain of what I saw. I kept my eyes on the night sky even as it turned faintly orange, then bright and clear with the light of a Chinese dawn.

It would be some time before I saw the crows again.

14

I AWAKEN the next morning to find An Er rhythmically kicking the bottom of my foot. He bears a sheen of perspiration and his legs are shaking slightly, both signs he has been leaping and jumping around with his sword. He points at my Grandmother's mother-of-pearl comb lying atop a bundle of clothing on the floor.

"Going somewhere?"

I wipe the sleep from my eyes. The skin on my knees stings when I point my toes and stretch my legs. I recall the humiliation of Gui forcing me down. I run my tongue over my teeth.

"To practice my spear, of course."

"With Grandmother's comb?"

"It brings me comfort."

Though I have become a practiced liar in a very short time, my brother appears not to be fooled. He tells me another of his men is dead and I feign surprise. He asks if I saw anything and I tell him I didn't. He says my mother claims she sent me to the camp and I tell him I didn't go, that I went to the woods instead. He mentions a dagger. I don't react. He describes a venomous snake. I shudder with revulsion.

"You're such a beauty," he says, reaching out to touch my hair and gently caress my cheek. "Just because I'm your brother doesn't mean I can't see it. The men love your impossible green eyes. They love that you're tall and that your mouth is wide and your lips are full. They love your curves, just right, not too big, not too small, everything in perfect proportion. They love your little feet and your slender fingers and your long legs. Small wonder all this is going on. Come, I have something I want to show you."

I tell him I have to clean my mouth and go do so, needing some time to think. If he's asking about snakes, Gui's body has been discovered. I imagine it lying in the dirt as I have seen monkey and squirrel carcasses in the forest, besieged by flies, bedazzling in utter rank and ruin. I do my toilet and meet An Er outside the house. He interlaces his fingers intimately with mine, something he hasn't done since I was a toddler. His expression speaks of a sense of loss. Mostly, I think, it's about me growing up and away. An Er cares about justice and fights hard for it. He thinks too well of himself, is a bit grandiose, but inside he's soft on family and resistant to change, even though the times we live in are so rough. I ask him where we're going but he doesn't answer.

We head south past the temple grounds and the border fields and the fruit orchards and past the river, too, to the edge of Southern Song territory. Borders are fluid these days, but I'm nonetheless wary of bandits out here, where caravans pass and women are scarce. We climb a rise and come to a copse of evergreens. An Er picks up a pine needle, and uses it on his teeth. He seems so peaceful, almost as if he has simply taken this hike to find a safe place for us to talk. This worries me. My brother shifts quickly between yin and yang, and is always quietest right before he becomes furiously dangerous. I love him but he scares me.

"What do you think is down there?" he asks.

"I don't know."

"Oh, but I think you do."

He leads me down into the valley. Straight ahead, the sky is still purple and the morning mist still lingers on the ground. Some geese call. Through the mist, I can just make out flashes of red. Drawing in a breath, I smell a cooking fire. Rabbit, maybe, and duck and ginger root. I hear clanking sounds in the distance. Irregular cackles punctuate a sea of thrumming voices.

The sun burns away the mist and the air is clearer. The voices get louder, the aromas more distinct. A hedgehog crosses our path, spines bristling. The shadow of an eagle caresses the ground. We come to a dirt road and step onto it, following the sounds and the aroma of cooking fires until the red I saw from the hill resolves into a dozen tents teaming with people.

"A festival?" I ask expectantly.

An Er smiles at last. "And with some very special people here, too."

I clap my hands in delight. I've always loved festivals. The last one I attended was with Grandmother, the year the tiger killed her. I relished the food and music and acrobats and, most of all, the choreographed dances. Those memories have grown wispy over the years but suddenly they are bright and clear again. Spear tucked behind my arm, I dash down the muddy path like a little girl, my feet kicking up the fetid froth trapped in the wheel tracks of hand barrows and ox carts, and in the hoof prints of horses, buffalo, donkeys and camels.

My brother follows me, fingering coins in a little pouch tied to the rope around his waist, underneath his cloak. When we reach the tents, he buys me an apple laced with molasses. The brisk walk and my nervousness have made me ravenous and I devour it in six bites, moving on to corn and roasted chestnuts and peppered yam. An Er chooses river fish staked through and roasted, eyes shrunken and cloudy. He spits out the bones and grinds them under his foot as we watch the traveling troupes performing: a beggar juggling stones the size of winter melons, men from the Han-controlled lands to the south showing other, more martial skills. An Er explains to me that such displays are illegal down in this territory because the emperor's chief official, the one they call the Crooked Chancellor, is worried about uprisings. The festival has to stay hidden because even officials as lowly as my own father worry that hungry strangers from outlying provinces will take food from local mouths. There are women performing too, not to show their fighting prowess but to attract men with their sense of rhythm and style and color, and, of course, their toned muscles and flexible spines. An Er says the festival is an opportunity for men to find mistresses and wives.

"When you say find, you mean buy," I say.

My brother tells me that's the way of things and I should get used to it. He tells me sooner or later someone will want me, too, so long as I'm not branded a killer. I don't reply. Seeing he can't bait me, An Er beckons a small group of women and they come to our table. One of them, a dark-skinned girl wearing bangles from elbows to wrists, tells me I'm pretty.

"I'm not pretty," I say. "I'm beautiful.

The girl laughs and pulls over a friend to have a look at me. The friend has blue eyes. She cups my chin and turns it from side to side. She tells me if I really want to be beautiful, I have to learn how to dress. She unwraps a long red scarf from her hair and drapes it over my shoulders. Her long, golden locks fall free and I feel my mouth go dry with both envy and desire.

Thick-shouldered men wearing silver pendants hung on leather thongs — a flower, an arrowhead, a character from their language — begin hitting barrel-drum skins with batons. The girls rise again to dance on the raised wooden platform. An Er claps his hands loudly when I join them, glad I am their dancing equal, hopeful some rich man will marry me and spirit me beyond the reach of retribution of the Liu or Gui families.

All goes well until a long-nosed girl from the Western provinces produces a pair of butterfly knives and suggestively applies their cutting edges to the fabric covering her breasts. The spirit of competition takes me and I grab my spear and wring the shaft in my hands, setting the tip to bouncing. I mime smashing the top of a tiger's head and gutting his belly. I mime climbing the tree and dropping with spread arms to save Grandmother. My moves are both combative and seductive, and the drummers, topless but sweating despite the cold, follow my tempo. My audience grows. Within a few minutes, I am the center of attention. My brother looks at my moves like the military commander he is. I can tell he's thinking he could use me as a seductive spy, an asset in his campaign against the generals of the Southern Song.

A gust of wind stokes the coals and a thick cloud of onion-and-pepper-roasted pork smoke drifts over the platform, obscuring everything but the tip of my raised spear. Some of the girls cough and stop moving. The people in the audience cover their mouths and noses with fabric but continue watching me as, oblivious to the air, I dance the way of Hun.

A sharp, clanking sound arises, random and discordant. A pair of tree-trunk legs appear in the smoke, ankles angular as ram horns, calves disappearing into the bottom edges of thick, dirty pantaloons, feet with pear-sized toes.

"It's Two-Sword Wong," I hear someone say.

The wind shifts and the smoke rises and I find myself facing a giant armed with a pair of broadswords. I attack him without hesitation and the crowd roars. He responds fluidly, blocking my thrusts, pivoting to belie his bulk, avoiding my strikes, steadily forcing me to retreat. An Er jumps up on the stage to defend me but I put my hand on his arm and tell him I'm alright. He backs off reluctantly but stays close.

"I'm just dancing," I say.

"You can't fool me," Wong replies. "I know you're a killer."

He moves in again, his swords scissoring the air, sweat on his brow, his joints creaking, his breath loud and rasping. Whenever I press my own attack, he uses one blade to parry and the other to close the distance between us. I issue a furious bout of whacking and thrusting but all he does is laugh and pivot away so my spear point finds nothing but air. When at last I stumble, he tickles my throat with his blade, places his boot on my belly, straddles me, and gloats. I place the sharp point of my spear against *huiyin*, the perineal *qi* point, the spot which, if I pierce it, will permanently wrinkle his root.

"Toss your swords to my brother," I say.

"Tricky," he answers, considering his options.

"Every battle's a deception."

He throws one sword to An Er. I sense it's his turn for subterfuge. Why not throw both at once? As I'm thinking, he yanks my spear from my grasp and puts the remaining sword against my throat again, this time drawing blood.

"You have talent but you have no experience. Do you have a teacher?"

I think about Mu, and how he could teach me some spell to be rid of this clunker, some potion or power to seduce and reduce him, some wisdom to accept the way things are in contrast to the way I would have them. It occurs to me that it also wouldn't be bad to learn to fight from someone other than a trickster or a tiger.

"I do now," I say.

The crowd erupts like a thunderstorm.

15

Off the plane and on the way to immigration, baggage claim, and customs at Beijing Capital Airport, I was jet-lagged, bleary-eyed, and stumbling. In the broad, dimly-lit hallway, I passed through a line of temperature sensors designed to protect China from incoming pathogens. It was late at night and there was only one official present, a woman in uniform looking bored and playing with her smartphone. When an alarm suddenly sounded, she leapt into our path. Away from the cover of her desk, she was tall enough to play professional ball.

She entered the crowd with a high-tech handheld thermometer. She was so intent in her inspection she might have been using a Geiger counter to find uranium. At last, she identified the culprit, an infant in the arms of a diminutive woman holding a Pakistani passport in her hand. When she tried to explain, in English, that the baby was sick, the mother became hysterical, pivoting, ducking, and dodging to keep the baby out of reach.

Obviously perplexed by this reaction, the officer grabbed the woman. A few more officers appeared. They patiently explained that the baby needed medical attention and could not be admitted into the People's Republic of China without a doctor's sign-off. Her only answer was to scream.

I was not a seasoned traveler. I had not known to call the airline in advance and order a vegetarian meal for the long flight from LA. After ten hours with nothing to eat and deeply disquieted by the red crows, I had relented and devoured a carnivore's dinner—a drab bit of plasticky pork in a plastic dish on a plastic tray under a plastic wrapper. Later, sitting alone in a detention room, I would have time to wonder if what Lulu told me is true, that eating animals makes us more aggressive. If so, it would explain why I felt bold enough to intervene when the officers surrounding the woman began to corral her in the direction of their brightly-lit office.

My intention was merely to reassure her, to perhaps briefly keep her company so she wasn't alone with officials who obviously terrified her. In trying to reach her, however, I stumbled when another passenger's carry-on bag tipped over, catching my foot in the telescoping handle. Hand outstretched, I fell directly into the tall officer, who went backward, arms wheeling, with me more or less on top of her.

I'd never been squeamish, had even dissected a live frog and watched its beating heart, but the sight of the glistening white bones protruding from her wrist weakened my knees. Speakers overhead erupted in sirens and a couple of the other officers took me to the ground, mashing my face against the floor. A golf-cart ambulance wheeled up silently marked with a red-and-white cross and two medics jumped off. One immediately went to the injured officer, the other attended the sick baby. The remaining officers now encircled me. I did what anyone in the situation might do—I took out my phone and started a video.

"I was just trying to help," I said. "It was an accident. I'm so sorry."

I heard a couple of my fellow travelers rising to my defense but the officers weren't impressed. One of them took away my phone, stopped the recording. I tried to snatch the phone back and found myself in handcuffs.

"Tell them you're American," I heard someone say.

I did but to no avail. I sat on the floor, hands locked behind me. The injured officer was taken away. I called out an apology, but she gave no sign of having heard me. As the other passengers moved off and away, the officers examined my passport and my phone, too.

That was when they found the pictures of Lulu.

That was when they found the pictures of her family.

When they dragged me off, I did not go easily. The tops of my loafers polished the floor.

***

The heavy silence in the airport holding cell made me think of how my wife loved quiet, how she made a point of moving quietly, taking dishes out of the cupboard without a sound, breathing gently, even moaning in low tones when we made love. I wondered whether her coma was quiet or whether the world inside her head was loudly bedeviled by the ogres of yearning and the fiends of frustration, monsters of her secret past. I know she would have been offended by the raspy breathing of the short-haired, middle-aged woman who at long last appeared at my cell, and by the loud drag she took from a cigarette she lit using a plastic lighter decorated with black dragons. I know Lulu would have winced when the woman loudly scraped the feet of her metal chair on the floor, turning it until she faced me directly, her knees tight under her skirt, her white silk blouse open at the neck to reveal a thin gold chain.

"Mr. Solomon Miller. Welcome to the People's Republic of China. Am I pronouncing your name correctly?"

"I'm sure you know your English is excellent."

"Thank you for saying so. It is a difficult language. My name is Ping. I am a Colonel in the Ministry of Public Security."

"I want my clothes back. This is all a mistake."

She gesturing at a ceiling cam high up in the corner of the room. "Let's not have any more such mistakes. We are being carefully watched. If you try to break my bones, believe me when I tell you things will become far worse for you than they already are."

"I was exhausted. Jetlagged. I tripped on a bag handle," I said, aware that I smelled of nervous sweat even in the fresh prison garb.

She sighed. "And broke an immigration officer's wrist."

"I'm deeply sorry. Like I said, it was an accident."

"Thousands of travelers go through our checkpoint every day, often after trips longer than yours, and yet do not attack airport staff."

"I didn't attack anyone! I saw a woman in distress and was just trying to help. I'm sorry about what happened to the officer. I meant no harm."

"Yet after the attack you resisted arrest."

"I just said it wasn't an attack. And nobody told me where they were taking me or why. They never said I was under arrest, either."

"Did you think you were being invited to a dance?"

I closed my eyes in frustration. "How is the sick child?"

"She is being evaluated in the hospital. She has a respiratory infection. It may be the flu. That is the purpose of the health screening you violently interrupted. To help people receive medical attention."

"And your officer?"

"Her injury is serious. Surgery has been required. Her wrist may never be the same. Tell me, Mr. Miller, what was your intended address in China?"

"I believe I'm going to Qingdao," I said. "Family was to have met me. I'm sure they're worried. Look, I would like to speak to someone at the American embassy."

Colonel Ping engaged in an examination of every molecule of her cigarette, the white wrapping paper, the interior of tobacco leaf, the addictive additives, the chemicals and fillers. Given her apparently genuine curiosity, anyone would be forgiven for believing it was the first time she'd seen fire.

"I'm sure you do," she said after a time. "But you won't be speaking to any Americans until I have the names and addresses of everyone you know in China, as well as any and all information you have about the serial killer, Yang Lihua."

"The serial killer!"

She gave me the first smile I'd seen since landing in China. Her small teeth were white and even. The smile was awful.

Criminals often think they are smarter than they really are," she said, blowing smoke. "They all fail in the end, members of your family included."

"Really, Colonel, I have no idea what you're talking about."

"The mark on your arm tells a different story. At this point, Mr. Miller, you need to know that unless you cooperate with me, you will never again see your physician father, your artist mother, your homosexual sister, or your alcoholic brother."

"My brother's no alcoholic," I said, trying to hide my surprise at her synopsis.

She inclined her head graciously. "If you say so."

"And I've never heard of someone called Yang Lihua."

"And yet you have pictures of her on your phone," she said, holding it up, an image of Lulu on the screen. "Romantic pictures, Mr. Miller. Quite touching. If there hadn't been so very many of them, perhaps the officer wouldn't have recognized her and called me. But there *were* so many, and pictures of the rest of her family, too."

I was slow on the uptake. I admit I was. Lulu was Lulu to me, not someone named Yang Lihua. I protested Ping's violation of my phone, she responded by ridiculing the American preoccupation with individual rights. I told her all I'd done was try and help a crying woman and her sick child. She contemplated her cigarette again, moving it close to her wrist and holding it there until the skin reddened.

"You've also married a serial killer."

"I've done no such thing."

"You hate that term, don't you? Her whole family hates it. Makes you think of sadists and perverts, sociopaths and psychos who take pleasure in killing."

"I don't know anyone like that."

"Of course you don't. Tell me, do you really believe you're in a Hollywood movie right now? Do you think you're about to be rescued by commandoes jumping from a low-flying jet plane?"

When I didn't answer, she began to nod slowly, and to talk to herself as much as to me.

"Because you are from sunny southern California, I am going to be sure and send you somewhere north, a cold place where the bread and the ground are hard as ice, and the handle of the shovel you will use every day shreds your soft skin. That's where your whole family should be, a place where no flowers grow, where screams of righteous indignation are lost to a frigid and merciless wind, somewhere the concrete and the iron bars and the endless desert neither hear you nor care for you."

"You have to stop this," I implored. "I don't know any serial killers. I'm innocent."

She rose from her chair and pushed it neatly into place beneath the table. "What you are, Solomon Miller, is in very deep trouble."

When she left the room, I stared defiantly up at the camera, but after just a few minutes, I broke down and wept in frustration.

16

NESTLED IN THE crooked branches of his favorite oak tree, Mu inhales a thin column of fragrant smoke from a ceremonial cauldron the size of a squirrel's bathtub. His fingers play across its decorative bronze phoenixes. His legs dangle so loosely, the wind plays them like clouds.

"Wake up," I call to him. "I've come to say goodbye."

He unwraps his cloak and points at his erect member. "Sit here before you go."

I climb up onto the tree, pull aside my purple pantaloons, and settle onto him with a languorous wiggle. "I leave tomorrow. You won't see me for a while."

"Your brother only took you to the festival because he wants to see who Li Quan recruits from that ragged bunch."

"I didn't see anyone doing any recruiting."

"Have you met Li?"

"I have no idea what he looks like but I'm sure my brother would have said something."

"Don't count on it. The two of them are rivals in ways you don't know. Anyway, if Li's not there, he's recruiting somewhere else. He's nothing like your brother, who will take even highway bandits. Li wants real soldiers. Men with discipline and character."

"I don't care about this Li Quan. I just want to learn to fight men as well as I fight tigers."

"Breathe the smoke," he says.

I do, and my sensations sharpen, making me more aware of his flesh inside me, his tongue and the fire between us. As he moves I feel energy go straight back from *qi hai*, the energy point just below my navel to *mingmen*, the energy gate Mu says orients connects me to Lord Hun.

"Can you feel him?" he whispers in my ear.

"I feel you."

"Not me. Him."

Since Lord Hun influences the way the world progresses and unfolds and is a god in the Taoist pantheon, I live in hope I can somehow see him. Feeling his presence is not enough, I tell Mu. I want a vision of the great lord to appear before me, a grand emperor, perhaps, in black robes holding a scroll in one hand and a sword in the other. Mu reprimands me for this. Despite the engravings and carvings people make of him, Mu reminds me that Hun has no permanent form but is fully as as irregular and chaotic in his manifestations as the world for which he is responsible. He will come to me, Mu says, but won't show himself directly. I have to look for clues to him, vague signposts and ciphers.

I groan in frustration. How can anything, even a god, be formless? Everything has a shape. How can I conjure a vision of something that doesn't exist? I turn my head so more of the smoke goes up my nose. I notice it's bluer now. Thicker. I feel the pressure as it fills my head. I gag and shut my eyes and Mu tells me to open them again. I do, and retch as bats flit about the ragged borders of my vision. He tells me he knows what I'm seeing, those shapes at the edge, that they're neither ancestors, ghosts, nor motes in my eye but the dark multitudes in service to Hun. He wants me to study them closely, memorize them as I would important allies, find the rhythms and the patterns in their movements, look to them and know they look to me, too. If I can suss out the threads connecting them to each other and to me, I should also be able to see Hun's dark fingers guiding them like puppets.

"Hun has been behind every seemingly inexplicable coincidence and event, every unexplained noise in the night," Mu continues, still moving in and out of me. "He is behind every bowl tumbling off a shelf without a rat's snout pushing it, every pot or barrel rolling across the road with no merchant's foot behind it, every piece of fruit falling before you with no tree or farmer's bucket in view. Chance, fate, and fortune are all our lord's doing.

"Hun has his agents, his spies, and, of course, his librarians. His agents are the animals of the wood, the birds on the wing, the fish in the sea, anything that can see and understand the Great Unfolding, even if only from a narrow point of view. Their collective intelligence, the experience of the fox running from the wolf, the bird hatching from the egg, the taste of the soil to empire-building ants, the thickness of water to the tail of the fish, all this and more is recorded by the trees, who also work for Hun.

"Trees, you see, do not stand alone as they appear to do, but rather are connected in ways we cannot see, not by the fragrance of their flowers or the way pollen is scattered from one to the other by butterflies, but by the intricate entwining of their roots underground. Along subterranean songlines of fungus, trees share their individual fear of fire and axe and their collective love of the sun. When they are not turning the light of day into sweetness in their leaves, they are recording stories of all the creatures who share lessons with them during the hours, weeks, or years they find succor in branches or shade."

I accept this description with gratitude and wonder then redouble my search for Hun. I look for him in the dark world I know is right at my shoulder, behind my knee, in the space beneath my ear, all those secret and occult hiding places in which I know he dwells. Silence billows. Suddenly, though I have done nothing at all, Hun appears. I know him by the way my skin reacts to his presence. He touches my forehead with a flaming finger. He is not a vision; he is a feeling. He is a voice whispering like water over smooth stones in a river.

The fire between your legs will never burn out.

Full of yearning, I quicken my pace atop Mu. Despite his magic, the old man flags, tired despite his youthful disguise. I scream at him not to stop, the smoke still flowing into my nose. He tries to keep going but his thrusts grow shallower just as my need grows stronger. I put my hands around his throat and squeeze. I know how he desires me, how he longs to meld his flesh with mine, but now he can't breathe and he tears at my arms and finally frees himself, gulping air in great wheezing gasps. It is only when his heart finally slows that he notices I have trapped his root.

"Release me," he says.

I tell him that he has seen my true nature and he admits it is true. I tell him that he therefore knows he cannot be free of me without using a knife on himself. He responds by twisting my head away from the smoke. I twist it back and sense his surprise at how strong I've become. He asks me what I want.

"Tell me the secret of the wasps," I say.

"I intend to. There's no need to act this way," he protests.

"But you wouldn't tell me everything. You never do. You always hold something back because you like to stay in control. I've seen that about you."

"My father learned the wasps from his father, who learned it from his father and on down the generations all the way back to the phoenixes," Mu croaks. "Our way is to celebrate nature, to worship its wisdom, to accept its unfolding. The wasps know us for what we are. They sense our humble attitude, the way we regard ourselves as insignificant beings in the face of the great Tao. They wrap us when we call them, and embrace us in their welcoming hive. Their soft, gray, paper draws the evils of aging from our skins and vibrates the pain of memories loose from our bones."

"I understand all that. What I need to know now is how to summon them," I say.

"You smell like fire when you're angry," he tells me. "What do you need them for? You're young. Just a girl. Healthy. No pain. What do you want with the wasps?"

I tense up and twist. He gasps. "Don't toy with me," I warn. "I'm not too young to know things happen to the body. Just today I had a man's sword at my throat."

Mu drops his hips, tries to pull away, fails, sighs, and raises his hands in surrender. "You have to be able to summon the right ingredient," he says. "This is not always so easy. More than one wandering shaman of my Phoenix Clan has succumbed to wounds and age for lack of this one key thing. Our wasps know the secret requirement. If you present them with it, they will unfailingly appear to do what is needed. If not, you can cajole and plead and beg and die and they will not offer so much as a buzz."

"Everything of value in this world has a secret. Tell me what it is the wasps need."

"When the time comes, you will know," Mu answers. "Until then, even if you send me to Hun, you will not have the answer."

17

LULU KEPT a glass statue the size of a breadbox on the bathroom windowsill of our LA apartment. It was a striking sculpture, particularly when lit by morning light. It might have been a standing dog without any ears or eyes, a blunt tip rather than a defined nose, feet but no claws, a clump behind it rather than a tail. It was amorphous, blurred, striking, even eerie. I asked her about it and she got mad and told me it was none of my business. I wasn't in a great mood that day and didn't accept that. I told her the apartment, including the bathroom, belonged to both of us and I wasn't objecting to the statue I was just curious about it. She told me to fuck off, so I took a picture of it with my phone and posted it online. One person told me it was a melted candle. Someone else said it looked like a guardian angel for the legions of the underground, the hellion Cerberus with its three heads squashed together. Someone else said he thought it was some kind of guardian totem.

Lulu got mad again later and so did I. "You think I don't know you talk to that thing at night?" I shouted at her. "I swear, I think it talks back! If it didn't sound so crazy, I'd tell you I've seen it talk back to you, seen what passes for its lips moving, though I can't hear what it says."

She put up her hands at that. "Fine," she said.

"So am I crazy?"

"You're not."

"So you do talk to it."

"It's my guardian. It's a Taoist god called Hun. A family superstition."

"If it's only a superstition, how come I see it talking back."

"You've been smoking weed lately," she said dismissively.

"Yeah, well I think it talked to me, too."

She was startled by that. "What did it say?" she asked suspiciously.

"I can't be sure. My Mandarin is not up to it. And honestly, I think it has some kind of accent. It doesn't sound like you. It doesn't sound like the language I'm learning in school."

"Take a guess," she said. "I mean, like what you *think* it might have said."

"I got the sense it was transmitting a warning. But I think it was meant for you, not me. I think it was trying to tell me that something was going to happen."

I hadn't thought about the episode again until I found myself chained by the ankles to a van departing the airport. Whether I was high that night or not, whether that thing spoke to me or not—and after seeing those crows I found myself wondering whether I hadn't been missing evidence of magic in my life with Lulu—I sure wished I had a guardian of my own right then. If not that, then it would at least have been nice for the driver to treat me like any kind of dog at all and toss me a pork *bao* from the box he had on his lap. The savory aroma percolated in the small space and drove me crazy with hunger. Since landing in Beijing, I'd eaten nothing but a cold bowl of thin rice gruel, offered to me without a word of comfort. It seemed the cops were in collusion with the airlines to break my vegetarian vows.

Vows were the least of it, of course. Survival in some frozen wasteland was likely a bigger priority. Every mile I rode alone in the back of an unmarked van left me more suspicious of Colonel Ping. Since being put in my cell I'd been given no inkling of charges, process, or rights, and I had the growing and deeply unsettling feeling that Ping was acting out of something other than official capacity.

I wondered what was happening on the world outside my van. Had Dora's parents called her to report me a no-show? Had Dora tried to reach me? Were my own parents worried about me? I had received two texts from Ginger upon landing, so she was sure to find the ensuing silence strange. Had my brother tried to call? How long would everyone who knew I was traveling ascribe my silence to a missed flight, jet-lagged sleep, or a single-minded dedication to my mission before they started worrying and making inquiries?

I'd been drowning in an ocean of despair since Christmas Day, repeatedly breaking the surface like a cormorant for a breath of what substituted for air — the love of my family, Dora's brief attention, the sight of a group of happy-go-lucky surfers on the way to the beach — and then sliding back underwater again. That Beijing morning found me at my most desperate. The sun, no more than a glow behind a gray sky, revealed ever-narrower and more remote roads. Stripped of my coat and with no heat in the back of the van, I shivered harder than ever before in my life. The cold grooves in the floor cut lines in my flesh whether I sat up or lay down.

What I could see of the highway traffic through the van's barred back window and narrow side view slits was heavy with cars and trucks and motorbikes. Tiny particles in the air made dirt-brown halos around streetlights and headlights. Most drivers stared straight ahead as the van passed by. It may not have had markings, but the windows screamed cops.

Beijing's endless urban sprawl gave way slowly to suburbs dotted with the odd high-rise complex, then at last to boondocks dotted with wooden-plank shanties covered by tin roofs and surrounded by piles of garbage and patches of gray snow. Through the bars and dirty windows, I saw people bustling along, warm in faux North Face jackets, scarves and hats. Some stopped to chat and shared tea in hot thermoses, the steam fogging their glasses. We came to a market by the side of the road. I'd seen videos of markets in India built right over train tracks, vendors pulling back their wares to within inches of the passing cars when the twice-daily train came through, then resuming their occupation of railroad real estate as soon as the train passed. Those images were a panoply of color, monks in saffron robes, red tents, black, yellow, and brown spices in bins, deep indigo fabric on rolls. There was nothing quite that colorful here on the outskirts of Beijing, although there were hanging strings of dried red peppers and a table of yellow rayon kung fu uniforms wrapped in clear plastic.

Suddenly, an elongated, three-wheel delivery bike tipped over right in front of us, sending its cargo, hundreds of Mandarin oranges, skittering across the roadway. The driver could have driven right over them, he was a policeman after all, but he came to a halt. Office workers on motorbikes sounded their horns. A few elderly men and women, the vendors, shouted at us. When my driver didn't move, they began slapping the sides of the van with open palms and the street erupted into a riot of gestures and shouts. The driver got out. His gun and his police uniform didn't seem to impress anyone. The next moment, he was invisible, surrounded by the angry crowd.

The van rocked. I smelled burning paint and heard metal shriek. The door fell open and a thin man wearing a knapsack and a hoodie climbed aboard. He used a bolt cutter on the chain holding me to the floor.

"Follow me," he said.

"Okay," I answered in Mandarin, glad for my university Chinese and for Lulu's help in achieving reasonable fluency.

The driver glanced up as we moved away from the van. His face showed nothing and he didn't say a word; in fact, he seemed busy buying produce. My rescuer's hair smelled like smoke. He cut me free, then shoved bolt cutters, cuffs, torch, and crowbar under a pile of trash. He led me down an alley between a row of houses. When we were safe from view, he pulled a navy-blue hoodie like his own from the bag and pushed it at me. It fit perfectly. Next came my carry-on knapsack containing my wallet, passport, tablet, wristwatch, American dollars, and a thin wad of Chinese renminbi I'd exchanged at Los Angeles airport.

"My phone?"

"Working on it."

"Ping still has it?"

"She found all your photos quite incriminating. We have freed you from her but expect her to follow. We must gain distance from her."

"When you say we, you mean my wife's family?"

"My name is Vincent. We need to get you to Qingdao, but no more airplanes, buses, or trains. The only anonymous way is by car. I don't want anyone to see the transfer so I've parked a few blocks away."

He led me toward a waiting scooter. He stuck his arms into something between a windshield and a cloak and climbed aboard. I got on behind him and we went puttering off. The wind stung my face. I put my lips next to his ear. "Colonel Ping asked me about your family. Asked me about my wife."

Victor didn't answer. When I leaned around in the wind for a look at his face, he seemed lost in thought. There was nothing further from him until we arrived at a waiting, white Buick. He ditched the scooter and directed me to the back seat.

"Harder for the cameras to see you back there. Keep your hood up and tight around your face."

"You knew exactly where I would be and when," I said. "And you weren't surprised about Ping. What did you guys do, hack the police computer system and bribe the driver? The whole market thing was a diversion?"

He offered a thin smile as we drove off.

"You didn't happen to retrieve my toothbrush, did you?"

"No toothbrush, crazy American. We'll get you one in Qingdao. Now be patient like a bird waiting for worms. It's a long drive. I put a new card in your phone, so you can use it if you like."

I wanted to ask him why everything about my life had suddenly become secret and occult, why nobody connected to Lulu seemed able to just say what they meant without a whole hidden level of meaning and dramatic rigmarole. Instead, I closed my eyes and slept.

18

Two-Sword Wong stands motionless at the back of the festival grounds in a spot folks use as a latrine. The gourd-size muscles of his shoulders hold his arms up as if he's hugging a tree, which he isn't. The stench around us is terrible, but you wouldn't know it from the way he is smiling. I want to shake him, to tell him it's time we get started with the training he promised. I want to tell him that my brother has already figured out I'm a murderess and others will too: constables, men who don't like me because they can't have me, women who are jealous of my looks, bored folks who have nothing better to do than spread rumors. He needs to know that someone in town will soon come for me. Of course I say none of this.

"I know you think meditation is useless," Wong intones. "But we are following in the path of the early Taoists. They were hermits, scholars, revelers, making love for days, drinking, and dancing...."

"I'm not bedding you," I interrupt.

".... then meditating for months in a cave or standing in the forest like trees," he continues, his eyes still closed, "breathing in clouds and exhaling streams, rectifying their bodies, stilling their minds, directing *qi* to their organs, moving their weapons as slowly as grass grows, and concentrating to feel every breath of wind on their spears, every bug passing by their staffs and blades."

"I'm no hermit and I'm no scholar, so why do I care?"

"Because the best of them were warriors beyond your wildest imagination. They were sensitive enough to feel the breath of a moth on their skin. They had minds quiet enough to hear field mice break wind half a *li* away and eyes sharp enough to know when mountain passes were melting just by staring at the silt in riverbeds fed from up high."

"You think I could be that good?"

"If you follow my training. Now don't talk and don't move. Just stand as I am standing. If you so much as twitch, we stand an extra hour. You won't care much for that. It's going to be a long, cold night, so quiet that darting mind of yours."

"Hard to think of anything but the stench of this place," I mutter.

"Shit is always available for our consideration," Wong chuckles. "That or lack of shit, which frankly, at my age, can be more uncomfortable. The point is not what you smell, the point is to find Tao in the low places as well as the high. Now, let me ask you something. Have you ever seen bamboo? The tall grass from down south?"

"I have."

"Have you noticed the rings across the stalks? Think of yourself as a stalk of bamboo with those same rings crossing your body. Each of your rings is a reminder for you to break a habit and let go of something."

"What are you on about?"

"You hold tension in your body. Tension slows you down. It diminishes your ability to attend to the present. Your mind should be a clear blue sky but instead it is full of storm clouds obscuring your view of reality. You worry about what people think of you, for instance, and you relive painful events from your childhood. Fixated upon certain outcome or ideas, you lose freedom of movement, including the ability to change direction quickly so as to retrieve balance or strategic advantage. As you stand quietly with me, review these rings. Start at the top of your head and move your mind, ring by ring, to the bottom. In this way, you will find freedom."

"My balance is better than yours. Than any other fat man's, too."

"If that were true, it wouldn't have been my blade at your throat."

"And my spear at your balls?"

"Balance is in the mind as well as the body. Had you been clearer and calmer you would have seen through my ruse."

I want to keep arguing but I knows it's pointless. He parries every objection I have in the same infuriating way he parries my spear thrusts, always coming up with something unexpected, something I wish he wouldn't say, something to make me uncomfortable. He returns to his meditation and I look him up and down. I don't want him and I don't want him to want me. He has the belly of a pig and the musty stink of a weasel, an animal I knows is sly and stealthy and as likely to steal and replace a girl's soul as to stalk a mouse. I've been watching my own soul carefully for any sign of an invasion. Now that I'm aware of Hun, I know anything can happen, anyone can pretend to be anyone else. It turns out there is no man I've yet met, even Father, who isn't hiding something, even if it's just that he steals paper or fears his sharp-tongued wife.

Yes, Wong must be a soul thief or a demon for me to loathe him so hard. What was I thinking when I asked to learn from him? As the ooze bubbles between his spade-like toes, he tells me he could be anywhere, that he's journeyed far from here in his mind. A flower falls from the tree above him, a peony even though the tree is bare, and it's not the season, and peonies grow on bushes not trees. Another flower flutters down, and then one after that. Soon, there is a rainbow of petals sticking even to the bulbous veins of his legs. I remember the way the wasps covered Mu, but this is different. Wong's with some other god, I can tell that now. There is no vibration, no buzzing, no healing, no rebirth. I watch one of the boils on his face erupt, sending pus and blood down his cheek. I can't imagine how miming a shaft of bamboo could cause *that*. A little mountain above his lip grows red and angry and it, too, explodes. Quite the paradox really, that a pig like him has the power of mind over skin. I know he's putting on a show for me, juxtaposing talent and filth to underscore the harmonious dance of opposing forces that he says is the way of Nature.

Opposites at work. Inhaling and exhaling. There's shit and then there isn't. The foul coexists with the fragrant. Yin and yang.

It's Hun explaining my lesson, paying Wong no mind.

I breathe. I drift. Time passes. The wind picks up from absolutely still to a chilly, gusty assault. It starts to rain and the temperature drops. I'm cold and I've had enough of standing next to shit. I open my eyes and go for my spear, which leans against a tree covered by an oiled cloth. Wong hears me move.

"What are you doing, wench?" he whispers.

I don't bother to answer him, since it's clear he knows. I come at him at full speed and his swords appear from under his cloak. He parries and I attack again, and we move back and forth and I sense his anger fade. He begins to laugh. We work the angles, stepping forward and back, high and low, our weapons clattering and banging against each other. I find that if I keep Hun's notion of yin and yang in mind and see us both as part of a single reciprocating system, I can anticipate Wong's attacks easily in a single, fluid unfolding.

We move like water.

Yes.

"Ha!" says Wong. "So much for learning nothing by standing between shit and flowers."

We go on like this well into the night. Finally, I grow tired and the fat man grows hungry.

19

WATCHING THE WORLD rush past, pressed against the car window, my hat pulled down and my collar up obscuring all traces of my white face, dirty blonde hair, and round eyes, I felt as if my efforts to make myself invisible were having more than merely their intended effect. Being alone in such a totally alien place left me feeling rootless and insubstantial. Absent the reference points that defined me, including friends, family, and my marriage, I found myself also without a framework for ideas about spirits, saints or an afterlife. I didn't know how to feel about Lulu's alleged criminal past, nor the outlaw present of the family I was about to meet. I didn't know what to choose as my moral touchstone. Should it be karma? Reincarnation? Holy edicts? Biblical laws? My mother, devoted more to watercolor painting than any particular religion, had a Jewish grandmother on her father's side and an Asian-Indian, devout Hindu, on her mother's. Despite coming from a German Lutheran clan, my father disdained organized religion even more than air travel. Nothing in this heterogeneous family mix seemed to have stuck with my brother, my sister, or me. At most, we were atheists; at least we were agnostics. More accurately, we didn't think much about the religious consequences of our actions. Certainly *I* had not, at least until Lulu was shot.

I did think about the Baja *curanderos* though, particularly the way they accessed a rich tableau of spirits through rituals and healing smoke. I thought about the impossible birds I'd seen aloft, too, and of Granate's comments regarding the superstitions of nurses. I considered Lulu's nightmares and what Dora seemed to know about them. I closed my eyes against the passing scenery and imagined the alternate universe they all seemed to know. I furrowed my brow in concentration and tried to punch straight through to my ailing wife and tell her I was here in China to do whatever she needed. I waited for her to let me know I'd reached her. The resulting silence was deafening.

When we finally reached Qingdao, I found the air better than what I had encountered in Beijing and enjoyed the ocean views appearing between red-roofed buildings. We pulled up in front of a nondescript building of modular concrete, a tower, and a long low section for what I took to be conference rooms. A Holiday Inn. After a Chinese holding cell, an American-branded hotel seemed incredibly welcoming.

"It'll be dark soon," said Victor. "Get some rest. Someone will be by for you."

I got out of the car and he drove off. I went into the hotel and found check-in a breeze. I was obviously expected. My room was on the top floor of the tower with a view of the ocean. My suitcase was on the bed. Opening it, it was clear someone had been respectively through my things, repacking and refolding when done. My cell phone lay on top of the clothes. I turned it on and found it sported a new memory card and therefore bore no messages at all from anyone, including nothing from my family and nothing from Dora. I sent her a text, told her where I was, but got no reply. I showered, ate some crackers from the minibar, and waited fruitlessly for word from Lulu's family. I fluffed the pillows, lay down on the bed, and surfed channels on the TV. The sports stations made me think of my brother. One Chinese serial, an historical epic featuring sword-toting Chinese men wearing fake beards and traditional robes, was briefly interesting for its demure and beautiful actresses but I couldn't follow the story. I watched an English-language news channel for a while, then drifted off.

In the earliest hours of morning, the whine and click of a key card in my hotel room door lock woke me. I leapt out of bed and ducked into the clothes closet just as someone slipped sideways into the room and the door closed quietly. Looking for the shadow of a gun in the faint wash of light from the green numerals of the digital clock on the credenza, I saw the silhouette of a woman. When she opened the drapes, the multicolored glow of the city illuminated Dora's face. She approached my bed and touched the coverlet gingerly. Mistaking bunched up pillows for my body, she whispered my name once, twice, a third time more loudly.

I suppose I should have come out at that point, but there had been so much flat-out strangeness since I arrived in China, I was hesitant reveal myself. Instead, I stayed hidden as she checked the room and bathroom, then gracefully lowered herself to the carpet in front of the TV and started sobbing quietly. At that point, I emerged. She leapt up and hit me on the chest.

"Were you spying on me?"

"Since I left home on this crazy mission, I've been arrested, threatened with exile to a frigid prison, told my wife is a serial killer, and busted out of a prison van. Then you sneak into my room without so much as a knock. So, yes, I'm a bit cautious."

Dora sat down on the edge of the bed and stared at me. "Everything's shifting right now," she said.

"What does that even mean?"

"You know the part of the beach that is alternately wet and

dry, the long, wide line where the water comes in and goes out again? Right now, we're all in a place where even a super computer can't calculate the pull of the moon and the effect of storms and tell us when the tide will turn."

"Just tell me my wife's no serial killer."

"That's a terrible term. Who used?"

"Your friend, Colonel Ping, of course."

"Well, she shouldn't have."

"Then why did she?"

"There's a history there."

"I'm not asking about history, I'm asking whether my wife is a killer."

"She doesn't accept any rules. Culture, family, friends, conventions, authority, none of those matter to Lihua."

"You're describing a sociopath," I said. "She wasn't that way with me at all. Edgy sometimes. Even rough. But not a sociopath. And you haven't answered my question."

"There were misunderstandings," she said. "People died. After that, she went to America, met you, took a new name, focused on her studies. Who knows how long she could have sustained her new persona if things had turned out differently?"

Some realizations no matter their perfidy or glory, scuttle along one's mental baseboards until their movement reveals them. That was the way I came to understand I had always known Lulu was profoundly disturbed, and that Dora knew I was going to find out the truth.

"Your family was waiting for me at the Beijing airport and when they found out that crazy rogue colonel got to me they broke me out, right? She is some kind of vigilante cop, yes?"

"Yes and yes."

Someone pounded on the door and called my name. Dora put a finger to her lips. The pounding continued. Then someone operated the lock. Dora pushed me aside, and when the first of Colonel Ping's men came through the door, she kicked him in the head and knocked him out cold. Other men came through, but it was bottleneck and Dora was a kicking machine, axe kicks to the top of the head, snap kicks to the groin, heel kicks to the knees. Men went down. People shouted. Dora grabbed my hand, I grabbed my knapsack, and we dashed down the hall past the elevators to the hotel stairwell. That door was bigger and heavier. Fireproof. I held it shut while Dora pulled the fire hose off the wall, opened the valve and loosed a stream. This time when men came through the door, they met a river goddess who left them slipping and sliding under a rainbow mixture of spray and fluorescent light. Through that miasma strode Colonel Ping, impossibly, dry and composed, her eyes burning with a flame the hose could not extinguish.

20

Fᴀᴛ Mᴀsᴛᴇʀ Wᴏɴɢ just loves to eat. He tells me that the only other place to find food as good as what's at the festival is in the Song capital of Lin'an down south, but of course it is so much more expensive there, as tea houses charge a fortune for the same wild game and rare herbs that festival-goers hunt and gather themselves. The way he shovels down his food, he might as well be digging a ditch, but he is keen on the energetic dimension of food and tells me I can calm my agitated mind with sour soup, relieve a painful knee with beef tendon, move sluggish bowels with melon, and free a frozen shoulder with salted fish. He recommends I carry dried hot peppers in a satchel all winter long in the event of an invasion of my nose, chest, or throat.

I tell him I don't get sick. In response, he reaches out for my chin and runs his thumb over a bump there, pointing out that even though I'm young and strong and accustomed to training outdoors, I still get pimples and am not as perfectly healthy as I think I am. There's too much yang and not enough yin in you, he says, which I take as him making an excuse for finding me such a difficult opponent despite my lack of age and experience. It's his way of saying I'm too much of a boy — too much like a man. Bitter gourds will move my *qi* and clear my heat, he advises, and then goes on to suggest I am weak-willed enough to succumb to the allure of molasses candy or dried fruit.

"I'll show you weak," I say, and leap back up onto the stage for more practice masquerading as entertainment.

This is what the crowd has been waiting for. They've watched my relationship with Wong grow as fast as steppe grass under spring rain, a month's worth of mentorship flowering in hours. Wong senses their interest and spices things up by demanding we exchange weapons. I am beyond uncomfortable with this. It is through the spear that I know the world and through the spear that the world knows me. It is my identity. In my hands the twin swords feel short and offer no role for my signature spiral, though as swords go, they are good ones—well-crafted enough so as to be indistinguishable one from the other.

As I swipe the air with them, Wong hefts my spear. He tests the shaft for springiness, and examines my modifications to the point: the extra width of the leaf-shaped blade, the straight iron guard mounted for trapping opposing blades, the stout pin holding it all together. The crowd soon has enough of the delay and starts clapping rhythmically. They want action.

"I'm going to thrust at you," says Wong, running his tongue across his top teeth. "I want you to pivot as you've seen me do. Use one blade to draw me past and attack with the other. Keep your elbow against your body so my force doesn't leverage you up and knock you over. I'll start slow. Figure out the footwork. Remember to shift and turn."

"I prefer my spear," I grumble.

"Using the swords will teach you their strengths and weaknesses. Knowing those, you'll have an easier time contending with them."

He moves in fiercely and I am back in the dance. My body feels strong and connected, my senses heightened, the air sweet with the incense of pine and the aroma of roasting pig. Hun whispers sweet nothings in my ear and I begin to appreciate Wong's wisdom and advice. I slide in along the length of the spear, using one blade to stay free of the point while slicing with the other. I tag his collarbone and draw blood. He smiles, withdraws, then comes at me again, his belly jiggling. He feints, dodges, and uses my spear as a staff down low, trying to break my ankles.

I soon realize that all I have to do is stay out of the way while I wear him down. I dodge and leap and roll. My antics exhaust him. There's an oak tree by the edge of the platform and I leap to it and scurry aloft, coming face to face with a troupe of golden snub-nose monkeys. They understand my predicament and rain acorns down on Wong's bald head, drawing huge laughs from the crowd. My legs wrapped around a horizontal branch, I dangle down from the tree, cackling along with them, swiping at Wong from above.

A slim man with a luxuriant ponytail and a double-handed straight sword slung across his back is watching. Disapprovingly, he mutters that I can't use footwork hanging from a tree and that Wong has the advantage of reach. As Wong closes in, the slim man leaps upon to the stage and unsheathes his blade. It's a beauty, black as the man's tunic everywhere but the bare cutting edges. He makes a run at Wong. Wong responds but the man is at once a mantis, a crane and a snake, erratic, unpredictable and tireless. He's so relaxed he appears almost lazy, yet he keeps the tip of his blade inexorably pointed at Wong's chest, eventually driving the fat man off the state and onto the ground. The crowd follows, as do I, as the combatants wend their way past the latrine pit, the pig roaster, the hanging peppers, and tables of leather goods. The slim man dances through the mud as gracefully as a heron; Wong's boots gulp like eels. At last, the slim man prevails, resting the tip of his weapon on my teacher's throat. Wong drops my spear, and the man shakes off his hood.

He has handsome, delicate features.

Really, he's just a grinning boy.

21

DURING OUR first autumn together, when the shadows were long and the night air cool, Lulu and I walked out onto the Santa Monica Pier, heading for the little carnival at the end, our fingers tightly interlaced. A Pacific storm was on its way to us but still far enough to rely on its harbingers, a wind gusty enough to snap carnival flags and a rain light enough to masquerade as ocean spray. I had things I wanted to say, but the reflection of the moon in the slick boards underfoot was so beautiful and the murmur of the waves so enchanting, I didn't want to ruin the mood.

An arcade barker, a kid with bad acne, called us in to try our hand at shooting and handed Lulu a BB rifle. My beautiful, exotic, and always surprising Chinese wife grasped it confidently, expertly even, the fingers of her right hand coming to rest easily inside the trigger guard, the battered wooden stock nestled against her cheek. She took a stance, cocked her hip, and squeezed off a burst of BBs, knocking down dancing ducks, hitting bullseye-bearing train cars, and setting metal disks spinning. The kid thrust a neon-orange teddy bear into my hand.

Lulu fired again, hitting all targets, left to right, top to bottom, as systematically as a machine. The kid produced a second teddy bear, bigger this time, and in more realistic colors, black with a brown nose and marble eyes. Lulu kept shooting until a loud gong went off and we became the proud owners of a giant stuffed dinosaur.

"She a cop?" the kid asked me.

"Not as far as I know."

"First date?"

"She's my wife," I said.

"Good for you, man. She's hot. Was she a soldier?"

I shrugged. "A sharpshooter, anyway."

"The way she concentrates is amazing."

"You have no idea."

"Can you guys quit now? She wins anymore, I'm gonna get in trouble. I'm not supposed to give away more than one bear per day."

I carried the stuffed animals back in the rain, sheltered as well as possible under my car coat. I wanted to give them to some kids we saw on the street, but Lulu wasn't having any of that. She didn't want to carry them herself, but insisted I keep them safe and dry and treat them with respect.

"You're so sentimental," I laughed, thinking she prized them as a memento of our day together, or maybe even of her shooting prowess.

"They're my ancestors," she said. "We must treat them with respect."

I searched her face but found absolutely no sign she was joking.

***

Colonel Ping's stare said she thought it was inevitable we would all end up here together in that hell of lead and water. Maybe she was right. Maybe we were just victims of that gravitational pull of souls.

"They won't shoot through the water," Dora shouted in my ear. "They can't be sure of their aim and if they kill us they won't get the information they want."

Leaving the hose a writhing dragon behind us, we pushed through the fire door. Once again, Dora stood poised to defend us and told me to run down the stairs. I protested until she drew a long and wicked knife, half a sword, really, and standing to the side, applied it viciously to whatever came through that door, a wrist, a foot, a shoulder. When the bodies piled up again, we took the stairs three at a time until we reached the ground floor and the alley.

Ping was there again, waiting, a futuristic black gun in a holster at her hip. Dora rushed her with a kamikaze scream before she could get it into play. I'd heard that knives were better than guns up close, faster to deploy anyway, but had never seen such a thing in action. Dora stepped to the side, grabbed Ping's arm, and locked it until shoulder came out of its socket. Ping screamed, the gun fell, and when it hit the ground discharged. A terrible red blossom appeared on Dora's side, growing through her clothes.

I shed my jacket and pressed it against Dora's wound. Distant sirens grew louder. I stuffed Ping's gun into my bag and slung Dora over my shoulder. As I ran out of the alley, her shoes bounced against the back of my legs and her hair cascaded over my chest. A garbage truck rolled past, then a school bus. The school bus stopped, backed up, came to a rest right in front of us. Its giant rearview mirrors curving backward from above the windshield like antennae. The door opened with a hiss.

I knew the driver was Lulu's brother the instant I laid eyes on him. The same slightly protruding lower lip, the same eyes, the same long neck, though somehow not quite as graceful in its masculine iteration. The only thing that didn't fit was his stature.

Where Lulu and Dora were both tall, elegant, and lissome, he looked like he had stopped growing at age 11. He flew down the stairs and put his head on Dora's forehead.

"How did this happen?" he demanded.

"Colonel Ping shot her. Actually, it was an accident. She needs a hospital."

I laid Dora down in the first row of seats and crouched beside her. Her lips were blue and her skin was clammy.

"Where is the colonel now?" the driver demanded.

"Wounded in the alley. You know she's just a cop doing her job," I said. "Even if she does want to send me to a place no flowers grow."

"Think what you like, but you're going to have to pick sides."

He resumed the wheel and we roared off. Dora convulsed again, her feet straightening, the insteps locked, toes pointing.

"Please," I implored. "A hospital!"

We actually passed a sign for one, but he kept driving. Another sign identified the Zhanshan district, an area with fewer houses and more greenspace.

"You're Lulu's brother," I said, not asking a question.

"Name's Bik," he said, lighting a cigarette while steering with his knees.

"Your sister's bleeding out, Bik."

"We're almost there."

I kept the pressure on Dora's wound and looked out at the dark city. I thought about the yin and yang of things that Lulu always described, the ever-changing balance between what we could see and what we couldn't, between light and darkness, between fast and slow, between life's glitzy, shiny moments and the dark shadows behind and beyond them. I tried to guess whether I was headed into light or into shadow.

"Where are we going?" I asked.

"A Taoist temple. Branch of the big one on Mt. Lao. I'm sure you know we're a Taoist family."

"Lulu told me. But Dora needs more than prayers."

"She'll be fine."

We arrived a few minutes later. The temple grounds were lush. Floodlights illuminated a group of turtles sleeping on a rock in the middle of a pond, the silhouette of a tall mountain loomed in the background. The moment Bik turned off the ignition, a troop of men arose from the seats behind me. My hair stood on end and I gasped. They'd been there all along, but I'd had no idea. There'd been sound, no smell, no movement whatsoever. Ghosts clad in loose black pants and black t-shirts, they filed past me and out of the bus. Two stopped, but only briefly, to lift Dora. Bik indicated I should follow and I did. We walked in the direction of a gate guarded by two stone lions.

"If you had soldiers with you, why did you let Dora fight the cops all by herself?" I asked.

"They're not soldiers; they're the family's bodyguards. We've employed their kind for centuries. They're part of us now. Some are even family members. Their role is as big as it ever was. Things happen in this world. Problems arise. They're schooled in old ways and in new methods and in this case, they were there to get you out safely. Dora trained with them for a while. She's very physical, as I'm sure you saw. They trusted her to get the job done. If they'd showed up at the hotel, it would have raised all kinds of questions. Too visible, you see. Too obvious."

That raised a lot of questions with me, but I was being rapidly and not-so-subtly trained to accept whatever answers I was given. We trudged up the steps. Joss smoke pervaded the grounds even at night, left over from constant ritual burning during the day. The curved, tile roofs cast haunting shadows on the ground. Brass lanterns with a green patina hung from eaves, grace points on white-and-blue tile designs. Small trees danced in the wind between rows of thick bushes, leaves soaked in dew. We headed for a main courtyard, while the men carrying Dora turned east toward another building. I started to follow but Bik put his hand on my arm.

"They're taking her to the monks. They're magicians with energy and flesh. You and I are going to the Hall of the Creator."

"You believe in one of those?"

"Not the way you do," he answered.

Heavy red ropes hung from brass poles delineating the central worship station, with kneeling pillows before it. Bik gestured at a large garishly painted statue flanked by a smaller one on each side.

"The great Hun," he said. "Source of all things in the world, master of the void and our guide through the chaos of life. Attended here by the god of Qingdao and the god of the sea."

We passed through the hall and out a carved wooden door at the back. Bik pulled a piece of cloth from his pocket and used it to blindfold me. "Take small steps and keep your knees slightly bent so you don't fall."

Bik spun me around to disorient me, then we started walking. I felt the slippery ease of the pine needles under my shoes. After sixty paces we veered left and onto a rocky, uneven surface. I stubbed my toe against a rock. After a time, I heard Bik working what sounded like a key in a lock. I reached out and confirmed the frame of a door. We passed onto unyielding steps and a smell suggestive of a subterranean passage. Bik kept a steady, reassuring finger on my elbow, lightly guiding me.

And then the blindfold was off, and I was in a kitchen with rough-hewn walls seeping drops of cloudy, mineral-rich water. Three people crowded around a Formica table set atop linoleum tiles that gave quarter, with little valleys and peaks, to the moisture underneath. Chongxian was one of the three, and responded to my nod with a look that said he was glad to see me, impressed I was still alive, and disgusted with me for leading Dora into danger. Present, too, was a rotund woman with outsized hands, familiar lips, tiny ears, and lustrous shoulder-length hair. I knew at once she was my mother-in-law. She glared at me, grasping a slender, foot-long knife identical to Dora's.

The last person at the table was the first to stand. When he did, I immediately perceived the origin of Lulu's height and grace, as well as the balancing influence of his genes upon his wife's: the thinning of her nose, the widening of the set of her eyes, and the imbuing of the preternatural calm that had so beguiled me that day on the beach in Santa Barbara. He wore crazy steampunk glasses of platinum and gold but balanced by a long gray beard growing straight down off his chin.

"You bring bullets to my girls, Solomon," he said. "Give me one good reason not to let my wife cut you into small pieces."

I thought of Lulu and her raised middle finger and terrible secrets. I thought about how much I loved her. I thought about all the twists and turns that had brought me to stand underground with this new, strange family. I remembered what Dora had told me about the god her family worshipped.

"Lord Hun gives and he takes away," I replied in my best Mandarin. "His work is not yours and it is not mine and often it is beyond our understanding."

My father-in-law grunted. My mother-in-law put down her knife.

22

THROUGH THE NIGHT and into the next day, the slender boy paints me a new world. His name is Fu Po, and when he is not fighting he is charming, funny, insightful, and seems to know me better than I know myself. Truly there is not one thing, not his flowing locks, not his elegant bearing, not the finery of his clothes, and not the Silk Road-market smell of him, that I don't find completely intoxicating. My brother watches us, shadows us as we walk in ever-widening circles around the festival grounds. I know he worries about me, but I think he worries more that his plan to use me as some kind of sex assassin might be lost if I spend more time with this enchanting boy. The thing is, I don't care. The only thing that worries me about the judgment of the people of Yidu Town is the chance they may deprive me of my liberty in their misguided sense of justice. I will not let anyone ruin my life but me. Besides, I think I know something about Fu Po that he wants to keep secret.

I warn him that we shouldn't stray past the festival perimeter as snow is coming, so he walks no further than the tree line.

"You're a Song prince in disguise," I say. "I'm sure of it."

He laughs and draws characters in the air with his sword. The message is "I'm no prince."

"Who but a prince would answer that way?" I ask.

He opens his mouth to answer and a dandelion-sized snowflake falls onto his tongue. I've never seen a larger one. He calls it a surprising taste of winter and I tell him that winter can never surprise us if we understand how cycles work and how the unexpected is built right into them. He wants to know if I'm a Taoist, since most diviners are. I tell him I'm no diviner. I don't want to mention the way Hun whispers things in my ear because I'm dancing on the tip of an arrow as it is with the great lord, currying his favor with the things I do, hoping against hope he can't read my thoughts and hoping even harder he will reveal to me the secret of his wasps.

"You say you're no diviner, yet you knew the snow was coming," he says.

"You knew it too. The density in the air, the smell of snow, the gathering of the clouds. You could not be the swordsman you are and have missed it. You're just teasing me."

We return to the tents, don furs, help cover cooking vats, bolster fires, and poke snow off the roof so it won't tear. Once their chores are done, the revelers retire to their sleeping quarters — lean-tos built against trees. Every group has their own hired sentry to protect them, not so much from outside bandits as from their own, for there are goods of value and there is envy, grudges, drinking, and, of course, beautiful dancers asleep and otherwise unguarded.

"In weather like this, sow bears give birth to cubs without even waking up," says Fu Po. "A bear can do that, and yet, we people spend so much time worrying about unimportant things."

I want to know what Fu Po considers unimportant. He tells me first and foremost it's what other people think of us. I look around for An Er, because he's the only one thinking anything about me right now. Then Fu Po asks me where I live. I tell him in Father's house. I tell him I'm sixteen and that Father is the mayor of Yidu Town.

"When I'm older, I'll rule my province like a queen," I say.

"I pity the fool who stands in your way," he answers.

My brother shows to glower at Fu Po. "Time for my sister to head home."

"Does she accept you as her keeper?" Fu replies.

That's all it takes for my brother to draw his sword. Fu has spooky skills but my brother has experience and speed and strength so I don't like the odds for either of them. I put my fingers on both of their blades.

"I want two days with him," I tell An Er. "We can talk after that."

Fu smiles, showing perfect teeth—clean white soldiers lined up in expectation of food but now in pursuit of truce. A few people drift by, girls in see-through veils and skirts, bare feet bright red in the cold snow, breath coming in clouds, eyes vaguely interested but thinking more about shelter.

"What makes you think you can trust him?" my brother demands.

"I don't," I say.

"You'll stay here at the festival?"

"I promise."

My brother nods reluctantly. "Two days," he says at last. "Then I return to collect you."

And just like that I am free and heading for the white and windy forest with Fu Po. He doesn't say where we are going. My teeth chatter and my breasts ache and my feet are numb. The ground sucks up all sounds until Fu quietly suggests we slip into the deep forest so the trees will cut the wind. He's a sorcerer there, seemingly able to see in the near darkness, slipping through the trunks the way a skilled butcher separates meat from bone. My fingers are red-crow claws around the shaft of my spear and my breath is a fog before me.

I hear murmurs and I see shadows. Soon, from an intersecting pathway, the former resolve into voices and the latter into giggling girls from the festival, all wrapped in furs. The golden-haired girl is there and so is the one with hair red as flame. The third girl has joined us, too—the one with brown skin and heavenly eyes that never leave me. They gather around us, cling close as vestments to Fu Po. They touch him slyly with their painted toenails dripping with frost and with their painted fingernails, too, lightly, on his cheeks.

Nobody says anything to me, but I am somewhat warmer in their presence as we walk together. I am warmer still when we reach our destination, which is a cave that smells of bear, but only faintly, and which offers a deep chamber just low enough to feel intimate and safe but just big enough to walk through, crouching. We climb inside and use moss and logs to seal the entrance against the wind. I lay down my spear and Fu Po puts down his sword and the girls sweep the ground with two twig brooms that have been left standing in a back corner of the chamber. Soon there is lantern light, as the red-haired girl nurses an ember beneath her cloak, and after the lantern light, there is fire. The smoke might choke us but for the cave's natural chimney, an invisible labyrinth leading the air aloft through shelves of shale.

***

What can I tell you of that night and the nights that follow? I can say that although I promised An Er it would be just a pair of moonrises before I saw him again, it turns out to be more than that. Will I tell you Hun is with me? I will because he is. I become aware again of the gauzy veil separating the worlds, the very thing I had first sensed while dancing with Mu, or perhaps even before that, when pulling away the papery cocoon that bound that old man to his master, courtesy of his winged, buzzing servants. This time, though, I am helped to see the world not through the eyes of fear or music or dance and not through the practice of war with my spear, but rather through the art of love.

I owe the most to Fu, not because his intimate touches are the most tender but because he is the one who brought us to this safe and comforting cave. After the five of us are there just a little while, the musk of the long-gone bear fades, replaced by fragrances of the flesh. Please don't think me too forward in my descriptions of those days—I promised my brother two moonrises only but I stole a few more—but instead understand what a relief it is to be removed from an ever-vigilant quest for survival and allowed to explore my proclivities, appetites, and most of all my secret desires.

The first time I experienced sex, it ended in murder. The second time was in a freezing lake where comfort was not on offer. This time, in the company of people who genuinely care for me, who answer my every want with kindness and my every need without judgment, I come to truly know myself. Have I ever thought of woman-love before? I don't suppose I have, for no voyage of self-discovery can take place when a person thinks only of killing tigers and collecting ginseng and rice while living on a hard dirt floor at night and during the day bears the burden of being a mayor's daughter.

So, no, I have not thought of lying with my head in someone's lap as my temples are rubbed and my hair is braided. Nor have I realized before that the very same sensitivity that applies to spearplay applies to love, including the role of gravity, momentum, leverage, and the all-conquering spiral. More, there is the quieting of the mind and the waiting for signals of movement and breath, even when the breath is not ragged panting but quiet gasping or, best of all, the momentary cessation of breathing that tell me everything I am doing, I am doing to perfection.

I've always considered landscapes in terms of usefulness, advantage, strategy, or threat. I've looked to climb trees for perspective or safety, for instance, or use them for cover. I've thought of rain and wind in terms of their effect on visibility and accuracy. Now I see bodies as landscapes, and as there is no threat and I am relaxed, I can use my eyes and ears and nose to scout the terrain for revelations of history. All flesh tells a tale, I learn, whether of hardship or ease, indulgence or abuse. I learn that the golden-haired girl, for example, has a body covered with scars and that each of these ties to a painful memory, an episode of loss, a bout of regret. I've learned that she uses both makeup and fragrances, precisely and artfully applied, to disguise her vulnerabilities and wounds.

The ease and intimacy of my time in the cave not only transports me through pleasure, it also allows me to hear and understand the world more deeply, and even to visualize far-off places. The girl with the gray eyes and the flame hair tells me of a land far, far to the west, a place whose name I cannot even pronounce but whose waters are azure blue by day and black by night, save for the reflection of the moon and the glowing trails of fish with fearsome teeth. She uses her fragrances — sweat and woman juices and oils she carried in tiny vials strapped to the inside of her intimate garments — to communicate moods, to say yes and to say no, to tempt and to betray, but only out of coquettishness and to heighten my wanting and Fu Po's, too, driving him to total distraction despite his poise and equanimity.

Both these girls share themselves with me eagerly and openly. The dark-skinned girl, however, is preoccupied with power rather than revelation. Her erogenous zones are her feet, and she commands me to attend to them and she rewards me for doing so in a way that leaves me wanting more. She is the one who teaches me that sometimes the use of power can be subtle, that I need not throw a dagger through an eye to claim victory. She is the one who urges me to get what I want from Fu Po by asking for it directly.

"I want to go to the city," I whisper in his ear. "Take me to the Song capital and show me more love and more music and more fragrances and more beautiful women and more beautiful men."

I expect him to smile and say he will do this, but instead he looks as if he's just seen a tiger.

He will take some convincing, but these nights in the cave teach me that convincing is something I can do.

23

I SPENT THE better part of half an hour telling my mother-in-law everything about my life with Lulu. How and where we met, how things developed from infatuation to love and then to marriage, how we happened to be on the freeway that terrible day, and then in the *barrio*. Why we were in two cars. The horn. The gun. The terrible time since. She barked questions without the slightest hint of warmth. It was business for her, like dishes or laundry or updating software, something she had to do, although at times I realized from the track of her inquiry that she already knew quite a lot and that this was some kind of test to see if I would level with her, if I was worth her time and trust.

When the facts were out of the way, we set to smaller talk, all the while knowing that Colonel Ping was looking for us, that the whole city was probably crawling with cops, that they had to know about the family headquarters in the temple if not about the underground bunker. I was expecting them, a strike force, an invasion, a trebuchet launching gas grenades, a full-frontal assault, all of it. All I wanted to do was keep my camera in play to record every moment so I could review the battle shots later, along with the family personalities revealed before the shit hit the fan, the way my mother-in-law so clearly ran the show despite her husband's sagacious mien. We made small talk while Dora lay on death's door somewhere above us, in the presumably capable hands of healing monks.

I wasn't comfortable with anything that had happened or was happening. Who would be? I deliberately conveyed that discomfort with my tone of voice, the way I answered things, the details I chose to share, my body language. I felt poorly used, distantly regarded, the brunt of secrets if not jokes. I felt like a pawn in a larger game, recognizing with resentment that a pawn's sacrifice represents skin in the game.

If there was one bright spot in the proceedings, it was that my father-in-law had a sense of humor. At one point, he juggled teacups and at another made a pomegranate disappear into his ear. Despite his initial ferocity, he was now trying to set me at ease by being friendly, a change I found quite touching. All the more reason that it took me a little while to summon the courage to tell him that Lulu had written, "I'm sorry Daddy." He took this news badly, turned away to wipe his eyes, and offered no further jokes.

I asked questions of my own and, in doing so, learned that when Chinese people find you gauche or are offended by your rough handling of sensitive subjects, they pretend not to hear you. What I wanted most was to ask about Lulu, but I couldn't bring myself to simply blurt that out. Maybe it was as simple as that I had so few cards that playing them all at once would leave me no future resource, no ace-in-the-hole, nothing up my sleeve. Maybe it was just that I was so very worried about Dora that my wits came and left like clouds subject to sudden winds. Maybe it was because I was afraid of what the answer might be.

"Colonel Ping was one of us once," Bik told me during the third hour of our conversation, as I helped him lay out the dough for pork dumplings. "Not a close family member but a distant cousin. And by the way, while rice predominates the south, we are all about wheat in the north. Dumplings are made of wheat flour and highly prized around here. The highlight of any dumpling dish is the stuffing, of course, but spicy dipping sauce matters, too. It must be as smoky as winter and as red as grape wine, thick enough to stand up to a small spoon and complex enough to look through, when lifted to the eye, after an evening of *baijiu*."

Before I could fully register my astonishment about Ping, a monk came into the room. I didn't hear him coming, didn't really know where the door was, given how I had been brought in. He went straight to my mother-in-law and issued a string of fast and quiet Mandarin into her ear. She straightened, nodded, reached back to fix the bun of her hair and then down to smooth her apron. I wanted to ask if she had received news of Dora, but somehow, I knew better.

"Hun power is female power," Bik told me, folding the dough into little pockets, then stuffing them with ground pork redolent of garlic and onions. At my first whiff of that filling, I thought about Lulu at the deli with me in LA, eating Jewish food and dreaming of home. The memory folded me over, elbows to my knees. Bik was solicitous. He wanted to know if I was all right.

"He is remembering Lihua," said my mother-in-law clinically, noting at my expression as if I might just be an animal in a zoo or a specimen on a slide.

"It's creepy the way my mother always knows what we're thinking," Bik whispered in my ear as he bent to help me. "But she's nothing compared this clan's green-eyed servants of Hun."

"Like my wife, you mean."

"Yes."

"About Ping," I said. "Was it a power struggle?"

"More like a betrayal," my father-in-law growled.

"She was one of us for twenty years," said Bik.

"Something I now regret," said my mother-in-law.

So there you have it. In just a few short days, I had come

halfway across the world and gone from drawing a complete blank on my wife's family to hobnobbing with gangsters, talking casually about the life and death of a Chinese police colonel, all in a secret compound somewhere under a Taoist temple on the north coast of China.

"And now Ping has it in for you? Is that it?" I asked. "Hell hath no fury?"

I expected the reference to be lost on them but it wasn't.

"Anything Ping does must be off the record," said my father-in-law. "That's possible for her because she learned from us how to create a loyal cadre, a cell within the department that operates with few limits."

"What did you teach her?" I asked.

"Blackmail," Bik answered. "She gets away with what she does because of what she has on her superiors. Corruption. Bribes. Lack of loyalty to the party. Pillow talk recordings. It's the same in every country. If you're not living with a dagger sticking halfway out your back, you have not yet gained power."

"We need people like her," my father-in-law interrupted. "This family has survived for eight hundred years by burrowing our way into the government of the day. Emperors, mostly, but warlords, too. They come and go. Things shift and change but we've become masters at quietly, mostly secretly, fitting in. The 20th century was particularly challenging, but we rely on people's vices and on their greed. We do business. We have our people inside the government structure, contacts, family members mostly, but sometimes long-term friends. We need them as our eyes and ears and advocates and protectors, and they profit from their relationships with us."

"So, Ping was one of those."

My father-in-law nodded. "She wanted more money, more power, more responsibility. We declined to give it to her. She tried to blackmail us with what she knew Lihua had done. When that didn't work, she tried to arrest her."

"When you talk about what Lihua did, what are you talking about, exactly?"

In response, my father-in-law focused intently on the dirty dishes in the sink while his wife found a spot on the linoleum so worthy of her attention it might have been the Hope Diamond.

"Let's go see Dora," said Bik.

"Please answer my question first. She's my wife. I have a right to know."

My father-in-law finally looked up from the floor. "Our family history goes at least as far back as the time before the Song dynasty fell to the Mongols. Scrolls and other documents have been lost to fires, conquests, thieves, and tomb raiders, but we know that much anyway."

"And were you always criminals?" I ask.

Bik groaned. My mother-in-law approached me with a cleaver dripping white tendinous strands of chicken. "We're rebels, not criminals," she said, poking me with the sole rounded corner of the knife, her English so cultured, the force of her breath setting in motion the red paper lantern hanging from the ceiling. "We reject the status quo. We reject authority. We find our own way in the world by seeking to understand the way things works and putting what we find to use."

"We're business people now," Bik put in brightly. "At least on the surface."

"What kind of business?" I asked.

"We're in a variety of fields," my father-in-law replied. "But whatever our enterprise, we are drive by a celebration of nature and a desire to return our country to a simpler, more sustainable, and more conscious state of being. We have products that improve health, programs that educate on being better stewards of the planet. Some of these run counter to the interests of powerful people who hold profit above conscience and responsibility."

"You work subtly," I offered. "Like your god, Hundun."

My mother-in-law gave me an almost-smile.

"…All of this takes influence," Bik interrupted. "*Guanxi*. Perhaps you've heard the word? Cultivating the right relationships? And sometimes we are branded criminals because of it, particularly because of the family history of sometime supporting emperors and dynasties that did not win their political struggles."

"Business is about people everywhere," I said. "But please tell me about Lulu."

"The Lihua we knew is gone forever," her mother spat. "What more do you need to know?"

"She was a special child," her husband added. "She had talents. Energies. School wasn't the right place for her. Rules. Other children. Teasing. Bullying…"

"Yet she succeeded as a scholar in a top American university," I interrupted.

"Not so successful now, is she?" said my mother-in-law. "Oh, she can focus when it's about Miao Zhen. She can think like a genius if it's about *that woman*."

"She does what she is expected to do," her husband countered. "Exactly what every woman born with the spear queen inside her must do. You know better than to speak of her this way. Hun always brings Miao Zhen back. That's how it has been, lifetime after lifetime. Our daughter had no choice but to receive him."

There was a subtle shift in power during this exchange. It was almost as if my father-in-law had grown in solidity, going from paper to oak, even his voice sounding more resonant. His wife glared at him but said nothing more.

"Life after life?" I repeated quietly.

"Reincarnation is a Buddhist idea," said Bik. "Maybe we should call it energetic possession. Green eyes go with it. Hun's beautiful gift to the ones he chooses."

Reincarnation? Possession? Was this a deluded fantasy? If not, how could the idea help Lulu wake up? Where did wasps fit in? Instead of that, I asked when we were going to help Dora.

"This dance with Ping is always a balancing act," Bik answered. "But like a pendulum, it never goes too far in one direction or the other, because if it did the price would be too high on both sides. We're well connected and if we chose to, could affect the operations she runs by drawing official attention to them in a way that could not be ignored. She knows things about us we prefer not be made public. She promises promotions and pays cash derived from her sideline operations. Some of her men are crooks in fake uniforms, some are real off-duty cops. Either way, their guns work and they obey her like she's their queen."

Suddenly, there was the distant thump of helicopters, more of a vibration than a sound as we were underground but even so we all stopped talking and listened.

"Sounds like she's here," I said.

"Yes," my father-in-law replied. "Time to go."

***

The kitchen exploded into action. Family bodyguards in black ran through the white room, assault rifles slung across their backs, on their way to meet the incoming threat. Bik snatched up his computer and propelled me and his parents in the opposite direction, toward a downward-sloping hallway illuminated by red bulbs. The farther we went, the fainter the sound of the helicopters became. At length, we arrived at a watertight door with a locking wheel. At our feet, a short dock led out to a vessel waiting silently, dark, and mostly beneath the waterline, a long, sinister-looking tube. I'd never been so close to a submarine before, never really seen one in real life, except a fat-nosed Navy vessel far off the coast of Baja that my father told me carried nuclear missiles. We crossed the hull to a hatch, and then descended a ladder into the control room. My in-laws were there, along with a crew of the black-clad men who had taken Dora off the bus.

"How long is this thing?" I asked Bik.

"Seventy-five meters," he replied. "Whiskey class. The Soviets built them in the 1950s and retired them in the early 1990s. They're a Russian version of a German U-boat. Eleven hundred tons, very dependable, but slow and noisy. They come up for sale from time to time. We've put as much money into refurbishments and upgrades as we did buying her. She runs much more quietly now thanks to prop and engine updates. We've also installed surveillance tech, electronic countermeasures, and turned most of the rack bunks into staterooms. They're not luxurious but they're pretty comfortable."

I was still trying to process the fact that I was now appended to a crime family that made dumplings in a secret underground bunker and had their own submarine when we began to move away from the dock. A dive alarm sounded and we were under water. Nobody seemed to mind me walking around so I did, looking at a bank of computer monitors that rendered the seascape outside the hull in videogame colors, the craggy rocks brown with the occasional streak of red, the sand below tropical white, the water ahead just blurry enough not to be taken for air. Objects I initially took for fish passed by in the water column but the screen showed them to be mostly trash bags. The sand below was largely empty save for what looked like a few refrigerators and the skeleton of a truck.

"What about Dora?" I asked after a few minutes. "We can't just leave her," I said. "She broke Ping's arm. They'll kill her."

"Nobody's killing anyone," my father-in-law said, but I didn't

YUN ROU

believe him because of the nervous way he was stroking his long beard. And not only because of that.

"Like Lulu didn't kill anyone?" I said, hearing my voice grow shrill. "Like she didn't kill all kinds of people?"

"Shut up," said Bik. "I mean it. Right now."

"Isn't there something you can do?" I asked the old man after a long moment, and this time much more quietly. "You can't just abandon her. Will Ping negotiate?

"What a foolish cowboy you are," said my mother-in-law. "They won't touch her."

"What if they do?" I pressed.

"Take it easy," said Bik.

"I thought of the *curanderos*, my friends from Baja, the old wise shamans who had their fingers on the pulse of a world I would never understand, seeing through eyes capable of beholding colors I couldn't see, worlds upon worlds spinning through space, connected like a stack of Frisbees with a pencil shoved through their center. I remembered them telling me, speaking as if with one voice, that the key to both good photography and long life was never to use force against force, to go with the flow, to just wait until everything lined up on its own.

"If they get rough with her and ask her what I'm doing here," I said softly, "she might just tell them about the wasps."

24

I MAKE a clean peace with An Er before I venture forth in the world on what feel like wings of love and wonder. He begs me to stay, to fight with him. I don't want to be dragged down by his ambitions and his rebellion and his dark, gray vision of the world, all conflict and blood. He tries to make me feel guilty about leaving our parents, tells me I'm moonstruck, drinking too much *baijiu*, lost in a fantasy that will never come true.

"You don't know anything about the world," he tells me, walking at a trot to keep up with me, because I'm just as tall as he is but my legs are longer, and I'm in a hurry to get back to the inn where Fu Po is waiting for me, his traveling cloak cleaned and his sword sharpened and a bag of coins and gems tucked inside his waistband.

"I know enough to have killed two men and to have lain with women and to wield a spear better than anyone you've ever seen," I say.

My frank confidence takes him aback, takes me aback too as I didn't know I had it in me, but realize now I gave birth to it in the cave.

"The capital's no place for you," he says. "You're just a kid. You'll be lost there, or, worse, you'll be found. You have no idea of the kind of men there are, the kind you'll meet, what they'll do to you even if you don't want them to, especially if you don't. You'll end up in some slave caravan going to the northern reaches, or to the west where the people are savages. This is total foolishness, Miao. A classic mistake. I have a bad feeling about this man Fu."

I stop on the single-track, standing between indentations in the mud that are broad from horse hooves and narrow from carriage wheels. Slowly, I lift my spear until it tickles his chin. "I told you before, I'm not under Fu's spell; he's under mine."

The petulant way he bats away the spear tells me this is as much about losing his little sister as it is about his ambitions and goals. "Just promise you'll come back," he says. "And make it a better promise than the last one."

"Hun tells me to follow the flow, not to plan, not to have any goal except to survive to follow the flow some more. Anyway, I'll probably come back."

"You know I could use your help. I was going to ask you to go to Li Quan's camp."

"As a whore."

"As my sister."

"A spy then. To gather information on your rival."

He tells me then that Li Quan is both his rival and his brother-in-arms, tells me they are both fighting to protect our no-man's land, and that he was hoping I would help him to convince Li to serve under him.

"By persuade you mean seduce," I say.

"I know you can be very persuasive when you want to be."

We keep walking through a grove of trees where some vendors have contraband for sale, away from the prying eyes of constables, soldiers, or undercover agents. Together we peruse the goods, weapons mostly, but also instruments of torture— tongs and picks and bone crackers and flesh twisters and limb locks and chains—along with sleeve daggers and hairpin needles. My brother picks up a few of these things and examines them, clearly awash in ideas. He is nothing but resourceful, no doubt the reason he and his little band of men have survived against such long odds.

Fu Po wanders up to the table. Without acknowledging us, he chooses a sword-breaker made of that marvelous, folded steel from Baghdad and hefts it, sliding it in and out of his cloak. An Er grabs his wrist.

"You're taking my sister to the capital," he says.

"She asked to go."

"And your intention?"

"To keep her safe and to please her."

The weapons vendor hawks a wad of spittle onto the mud, coughs, does it again. When this ugly bit of nose weather is over, Fu Po asks for a price. They haggle. At the next table, a shy teenage boy is selling a few combs, some buttons, and a finely-wrought flute, all made of elephant ivory. I pick up the flute, noticing how smooth and warm and beautiful it is. The boy watches me carefully then asks if I like it. I say I love it but can't pay for it. He closes my hand around it. I reach up and touch his cheek gently in thanks. He blushes.

Back at the weapons table, Fu Po and my brother are still arguing about me.

"She has her own ideas and appetites," says Fu. "They're fine. No problem."

"What if they are," my brother presses.

"Do you not yet know she cannot be denied?" asks Fu. "You can try, of course. Control, incarceration, whipping, even torture, but it won't really work. There is no domination possible other than by death, and neither of us wants that."

"Finally, something upon which we can agree," my brother sighs.

Annoyed at being discussed like I'm some stubborn goat, I return to the flute table only to find that the boy has gone off somewhere. I blow a few notes, just to clear the air.

***

The flower of roads leading to the capital is shaped by the topography, the Great Bay, the Grand Canal, and of course by concerns about Mongols attacking from the west and Jurchens from the north. The flower is missing half its petals now, and as such is tired, dusty, dirty, and misshapen. Even this one petal, this road we're on, is no longer well-formed or fragrant, although I suppose you could say it is still colorful. The white of snow and the verdure (a word Fu Po teaches me) of evergreens lend some of that color, as do the gold and purple flags flown by the retainers of some minor lord, whose caravan passes us, heading north. Sometimes, right before I fall asleep or as I'm waking up, I think I catch a glimpse of red crows at the edges of a canopy of oaks, though I'm not really sure they're there.

There are also monks in saffron-colored robes on the road. When I ask where they are from, they tell me a land far to the south, a steamy, jungle place where a spear warps in one single rain during one single night, sandals disintegrate after a week in the mud, the stinging bugs are the size of hummingbirds (my wasps!), and rice grows mold after dinner. They are eager to get home because their Lord Buddha is well-celebrated there, and they've had enough of the cold wind and the cruel, savage people up here in the north, people they say will eat their own kind if there is no other food available.

I can't say I've heard of eating men, even in war, even when the Mongols shut off cities and the only rain was flaming arrows and throats grew so parched people could barely speak and hardly swallow. These Buddhists know nothing of Hun, have never had him whisper in their ear. Of course, Lord Hun's words are not the only thing I hear, for there is the wind and there are the sloppy slurping sounds of wagon wheels in deep furrows in the road and there are the belches and farts of men who think being on the road gives them license to behave as beasts and to smell like beasts, too.

Not Fu Po, of course. My man floats like a cloud above the road, impossibly resistant to fatigue, not much for chattering, of course, which is one way he preserves his *qi*, but even so, the way he walks keeps even the hem of his long robes from showing any signs of dirt or mud. Do I fear bandits while in his company? I am reluctant to admit I fear bandits at all times, but with him by my side, I fear them less. Fu Po is generally quiet, but the closer we get to the city, the more agitated by my presence he becomes. I wonder if he has changed his mind about me, or perhaps is worried that An Er will hunt him down if I do not eventually return to Yidu safely. In the face of his growing frostiness, I busy myself with finding patterns in the happenings on the road.

I'm well prepared to notice such things. Did not Grandmother teach me to watch bubbles rise in tea water? Did not Mu teach me rhythm with his thrusts in the frozen lake? Did not Li teach me about quick responses and Gui about taking advantage of opportunity? Did not the cave girls teach me to be sensitive with their arched backs and kneeling, their flutters and gasps? Did not Hun teach me to predict events, teach me that there are always openings whether in love or war. Do I not know that rain and clouds whisper messages about the state of the land and sky? Do I not know how to avoid getting lost in the borderlands men and their gods? Do I not know that sometimes it is better to be in bed safely dreaming of killing and fighting than it is to be fighting and killing and wishing I were home safe in bed?

Despite all this preparation and knowledge, I am still a young girl who can be distracted by hunger and desire. Even when I shouldn't, I reach for Fu Po even when I know he will bat me away. As we grow closer to the Song capital and his preoccupations appear like small storms on his brow, I am left to my own devices, trudging along as I practice my ivory flute. My discordant notes, my initial lack of subtlety with tones and breath, drive Fu Po to wave me off. Sometimes, he just looks at me and puts his fingers in his ears. Have I mentioned his fingernails, though long, are always clean? How he keeps them that way on a journey like this, where I can smell myself despite the dips I take in creeks and ponds along the way, is a mystery.

I like my own aromas, as any woman should, and I am coming to like the feel of this flute in my hands, too. It is like a cock with extra holes, but one that does not flag. My lips warm it and it warms them, and my breath finds the restriction and discipline of the reed challenging but agreeable. And I make music! This is not something I've ever done, not something I knew I could do. The melodies I create are as random and chaotic as the unexpected gift of the flute from a boy who wanted, I think, to give something of value to a beautiful girl, once in his life, and be able to say that he did. I know now that the lack of music in my early life — the seriousness of training and tigers and poverty and war — all exactly *prepared* me for music, for how else could I relish it so?

And relish it I do, not just for its pure beauty, for the startling clarity of the notes as they issue from the flute and meet the cold, morning air or the still, nighttime fog or the sun or the stars, but for the way music enables me to create my own mood, to swap desire for melancholy, for instance, or bring brightness to sorrow. Why am I concerned about sorrow? Why, in these early days away from home and on the way to the most exciting capital in the world in the company of my strange, strong lover, would I worry about sorrow more than I worry about tigers along the road, or being kidnapped by rapacious men?

I don't know.

But Hun tells me sorrow is a thing to come, and so I watch for it.

25

My physician father saw the entire world as measurable and quantifiable, whereas I saw the world as a mystery to be plumbed. He was always wanting me to be precise, to hit the target I was aiming at, whether in school or getting a girl or a job, whereas I was content just to score in the general vicinity so long as it felt right. In his view, accuracy was the way in which we impress ourselves upon the world. We can't be sure we exist, he once told me, if we don't cause something in the world.

One time, he tried to teach me and Bryce to shoot air rifles at a local orchard redolent with citrus. While I watched, he shot a beautiful, brightly-colored hummingbird out of the air as it zoomed from one orange blossom to another. I was horrified. It was enough to hit a piece of fruit by projecting power with barrel and pellet; killing was something else. Bryce acquiesced and tried to please my father by shooting anything that moved. I refused.

Despairing of my pacifism, my father bought me a bow and arrow. He told me it was more artistic and organic than a gun, and much physically harder to shoot, though cocking a spring-powered air gun admittedly took muscle. There was the drawing of the bow — naturally, my father chose a large one better suited to a man than to a boy — the holding the apparatus steady with the string by the cheek, and the uncertain business of aiming, far from the clear cut post-and-notch business offered by the rifle. My efforts were half-hearted, though I didn't have the balls to rebel outright. Thankfully, Bryce stepped in and gave archery his all.

One afternoon, I found my brother practicing in the narrow swale in front of the house, land that technically belonged to the city of Palos Verdes Estates as an easement to fire hydrants and such. The target was a traditional item in bow sports, a round, straw pack the size of a dishwasher mounted on a wooden frame, concentric, multi-colored circles marking the target, solid red at the center. Amazingly enough, no neighbor complained, perhaps because the arrows were innocuously blunt, though more likely because even at a tender age (and despite the mischievousness that led him to lock me in the closet that time) Bryce evidenced the winning gregariousness that led him to become a successful sports agent.

I came outside to tell Bryce I'd found one of his pet desert tortoises upside down in the fountain, alive but clearly traumatized, likely the victim of a feral housecat. Finding him concentrating so deeply, I kept the news to myself and watched him work. He started at just a handful of paces from the target, drew the bow, shot the arrow at the center of the target, hit it, and moved back a few paces. He was following my father's method, which was precise and logical and controlled. The trouble came at about twelve paces, at which he simply couldn't hit the straw circle at all. I wasn't quite sure whether the problem was his inability to steady the bow due to fatigue, or whether there was something wrong with his eyes. The latter seemed unlikely, as he has never, even to this day, worn spectacles. Seeing clearly, it seems, runs strongly through our family tree.

He didn't know he had an audience, as I was quiet and stayed behind the low border wall of our property, surveilling him from a prone position like a little-boy sniper, peeking out just far enough but no farther. Over and over, Bryce walked up to the target, shot, hit it, and retreated until he didn't. The distance at which he missed the target entirely seemed to diminish as he grew angrier. Finally, I stepped up from behind the wall. My objective was to distract and amuse him, for I understood what he was going through, just plain knew, even at that tender age, that he was wrestling with my father even more surely than he was with the bow.

"I can do it," I said, laughing.

He knew perfectly well I was a far poorer marksman than he was, so he thrust the bow into my hands. "Go ahead, little man," he said. "Knock it out of the park."

What made me do what I did next is not something that to this day I can explain. My best guess is that it was a crazy impulse, likely intended to make Bryce laugh. Holding the bow aloft and whooping like an Indian wearing tail feathers and carrying a tomahawk, I ran across the road to Mrs. Goldstein's yard, then past the Geeserman's two-house compound. I might have stopped there, because I'd already made my point and Bryce's junior bow, with its thin string and easy draw, could surely not generate enough arrow velocity to hit the straw target from that distance. But I didn't stop. I kept going, putting four more houses' worth of atmosphere (the Kinder's, the Becker's, the Applebaum's, and one other I don't remember) between me and my brother, who stood gaping at me, stupefied by my crazy Apache run.

The last house had a topiary fence, carved smooth by the same Mexican gardeners who took care of our own yard, and behind the topiary, a star fruit tree favored by a colony of escaped conures—chattering, brilliant, little parrots with yellow bodies and red-and-green wings. Their colony peppered the crown of the tree, but I needed a vantage point from which I was visible to Bryce and him to me, so I risked nearly-certain soiling to dash through the break in the topiary and climb the tree with the bow and arrows tucked under my arm. Standing with one foot on each side of the first V in the trunk, I took aim at the target as Bryce scampered out of the way.

"Wuyia!" I screamed like an action-film star, taking my impossible shot.

What I now figure must have been the God of Chaos carried my arrow through the ether in a series of impossible spirals, turning it this way and that, threading the space between a moving van and a parking sign, lifting it on rising air currents (it was summertime in Southern California and the day was as hot as a cookie sheet fresh from the oven), and bringing it zinging and winging, first across the tarmac, then the opposite sidewalk, and at last that insulating no-man's land, the green strip. The arrow hit the target dead-center. So dead-center that my father, later assessing the feat first with a measuring tape and then with a micrometer (a micrometer!), could find no meaningful deviation left to right or top to bottom.

That was the beginning of the Solomon-as-Superhero myth, one that my sister, Ginger, colored mystical and shamanic when, later in life, I became interested in the Baja *curanderos* and their spells. Bryce did not throw a tantrum or grab me by the scruff and throw me in someone's root cellar. Instead, he froze, stared at the arrow for a time, and then slowly turned his head to gaze at me.

What can I tell you about that gaze? That it cut me to the quick for having diminished his efforts in what started as a joke but became a scythe of sorrow? That it haunts me even now, when Bryce and I have long since grown past it? No. What I can tell you is that it was a look of fatal grace, a deciding moment in both Bryce's life and mine, a time when destinies were determined and we both became the men we are today.

As the submarine moved silently away from the temple, I wished I were the superhero my brother thought I was back then, able to burst out of the hull like a missile or shoot out of a tube like a torpedo, overcome Ping's army, scoop up Dora, and fly her to safety while my in-laws applauded. Instead I just waited patiently as the captain brought the boat to a halt just off the coast and cautiously raised the periscope. While he walked in a circle surveying the scene, I asked if someone would please tell me about the wasps, where they were, what was special about them, and why Lulu had sent me to China to retrieve them.

Nobody seemed inclined to answer, so we just hung there in the frigid water column breathing recirculated air pulsing with ozone from the CO_2 scrubbers. It felt like a game of chicken, each side waiting for the other to crack and say something. My opponents were Chinese with a thousand-year history of overcoming obstacles and suffering unimaginable deprivations, so I lost.

"Do any of you read science fiction?" I asked.

The family looked at me blankly.

"Sometimes," Bik answered at last.

"Do you think the voices in our heads are aliens communicating with us? Manipulating or guiding us all through the ages, but unrecognized and unknown?"

"Such voices are gods," said my father-in-law.

"The great Hun speaks to the women in our line," said his wife.

"Well, the great Hun is telling *me* we should go back for Dora. "I'm getting the message loud and clear. That's what he wants us to do."

"You're mocking us," said Bik. "You don't believe any of that."

"Not mocking," I said. "And as for believing, after all I've seen, I'm not sure what I believe or don't, other than that Dora was injured before Ping came and is probably worse now."

"We'll get a report in a minute. Just be patient."

As if on cue, one of the family soldiers appeared. "The colonel and her men have departed," he said. "The team has taken a couple of men to the hospital."

Before I could ask why the soldiers were going to the hospital but not Dora, the captain broke in.

"I see no activity at all at the temple."

"May I go get her?" I asked him.

"We can't risk surfacing just yet. Ping has been known to use drones. We need to keep this boat a secret."

"She saved my life," I pleaded. "Fought and bled to get me to safety. The least I can do is help her now. If you move this thing close to the beach and come up almost to the surface, I could swim in and get her. Bik said you have all kinds of anti-surveillance on this thing. Can't you tell if anyone's out there?"

"I don't see anyone and there doesn't seem to be any drone activity," said one of the men sitting at a screen.

"He's willing to swim," said my mother-in-law.

"He doesn't know how cold the water is," said Bik.

"I'm from California," I said. "I surf. Cold water's no big deal to me."

There was another one of those silent interludes, this one long enough for me to go to my bag and grab my camera and take some photos of the family in the eerie wash of the lights from the screen. I don't know why I did it, other than that those shadows were so very compelling. Maybe it was just what I remember a psychology professor calling displacement activity – doing something else when you could not do the thing you so wanted to do. In any case, I didn't have time to frame and snap more than a few images when my father-in-law finally cleared his throat.

"Let's go," he said.

***

They put out a rubber boat with an outboard engine. Bik went with me. We made it to the beach in five minutes. It was rocky underfoot and awash in empty, white, shoe-sized laundry-detergent bottles. Bik told me to go look for Dora while he tried to determine if the underground lair had been discovered.

"If they found it, wouldn't Ping's men be all over it trying to figure out all your secrets?" I asked him.

"Remember that she's acting on her own. This wasn't some kind of police operation. She already knows a great deal about us. The submarine is a relatively recent addition and if she finds the dock she'll guess we have one, even if she didn't have a way to find where we'd sailed off to."

We parted company and I ran toward the central temple pagoda. I made it all the way to the entrance to the monks' quarters at the east end of the courtyard. I entered the building and tiptoed over the sticky ground, breathing air that smelled like blood. The first thing I saw was a dead monk lying next to a giant brass cauldron, his feet oddly splayed, his shins coated with incense ash. I'd only seen one other dead person before, the grandfather of a friend whom I found cold and still on his recliner, the TV playing loudly. My friend had cried and I had taken a picture, which started a row from which our relationship never recovered. I don't blame him for thinking me heartless and ghoulish, but I just couldn't resist. I looked at the image over and over again for weeks, trying to understand what was missing, what piece separated the dead from the living.

I closed the monk's eyes and unclenched his fists, finding his fingers still pliable. Why I did that I can't say. It just seemed the right thing, that a person who pursued acceptance and peace should not, at the very end, be left in a posture of hostility and anger. I wouldn't have taken the time to do this had there been any scary sounds in the hall or any sign of action at all, but the place was quiet. Assuming that Dora's absence meant Ping had taken her, I ministered to the rest of the dead monks one at a time. I photographed some of them, but not all, and then took views of the hall as a whole, because I somehow thought there should be some record of the scale of the massacre.

I did not find Dora, but she did find me. Wrapped and bandaged and looking even fresher than the day I'd met her, for she'd still been jetlagged then, she emerged from one of the giant cauldrons in response to my sobbing. I believe she may have been watching me for some time, as I was intent on my task.

"You came back for me," she said.

"I can't help Lulu without you."

It was a terrible greeting, and to this day I regret it. A flicker of sadness passed over her, left to right, ear to ear, not so different from what I'd seen in her father.

"Well, Ping's gone."

"Why would they leave all these bodies?"

"That's Ping. She's used to blaming everything on us."

"But helicopters and gunfire? Won't someone call about all that?"

"Call whom and say what? Call the police to say the police were here? Nobody will know it was Ping and her goons borrowing government assets, calling in favors, running their own operation. Sooner or later it will fall apart for her but she's the kind of person who pulls stuff off for far longer than anyone would believe possible. My mother says it's because she has dirt on higher-ups, but we don't really know. Eventually someone will say something but we'll have the monks buried before the curious start showing up."

"The same monks who saved you."

She nodded sadly.

"You lost so much blood. I thought you were dead."

"I've seen them do magic setting bones and prescribing potions, but in this case they just sewed up a wound. I'd still be in the hospital if not for their stimulant herbs, though I'm running on empty right now."

I gestured at the cauldron. "Did they not look for you in there?"

"False bottom," she said, sitting down on the temple floor and drawing her knees into her chest. "It might not have fooled them forever but it was a bloody fight and our guys sent them packing."

"Not without a lot of casualties, I'm afraid. There were no monks to help them so a lot of your men are in the hospital right now."

"Oh, no," she said quietly, surveying the carnage. "This is such a terrible loss."

I sat down next to her and told her about the submarine and how I had convinced her parents to let me come back for her. "I don't know where we go from here," I said. "But it's time for you to tell me about my wife. Everything. All of it. It's time I understand what's going on. Bik came with me. He went down to the tunnel but he'll be back soon."

Moments went by. Breaths were captured and set free. Her fingers played on the tile, moved over to me, touched my hand briefly, and then retreated. She swallowed. She shifted. She gathered up her thick, indigo curtain of hair, took it off her neck, then let it fall again. She worked the odds and angles as I watched, and finally turned to look me full in the eye. The force of her gaze was no less shocking the cold, dirty ocean had been, pinning me like a butterfly to a board as she searched my face. I didn't know what to do, whether to take her hand, touch her cheek, say something reassuring, or to look away. In the end, I just sat in stillness until finally, finally, she began to talk.

26

BEFORE GRANDMOTHER taught me that a stick could be a cudgel, arrow, or spear, she taught me that it could be a tool for exploration. Together in the forest, during special times I now miss so much, we used sticks to probe for roots and herbs and to unearth the astoundingly-ordered complexity of an anthill, with its tunnels, trails, granaries, and lofts. I learned that small things with apparent limits could belie vast depths, could spread out *li* after *li* across and below the ground underfoot. I learned that as it is for the empire of the ants, so it is for the skin of the mind, the outermost layer we wear against the world. What seems compact, delicate, and sensitive may actually be infinite, impermeable and hard; what seems unchanging may in fact be as temporary as a wave; what appears meaningless at first may in fact provide a fount of wisdom down the line.

The Song capital shows me a side to Hun I've not seen before. It is simultaneously quiet and loud, stinking and fragrant, dangerous and abundant, wild and tame. Hun is the Lord as Jester here, not the grand creator of sunsets and snowfalls but the mischievous imp who can lend lasciviousness to the rolling, white ring of the eye of a donkey, billow an aristocratic woman's dress with the power of a fart, lead a braggadocious sword master to impale his own foot while showing off for a commanding general, and reveal a toe-sized pearl to a larcenous orphan looking for no more than a chewy spurt of salt as he cracks a stolen clam. Such fascinations are all the sweeter after the travails of a trip, during which we penetrate hard borders, bypassing roving soldiers, and checkpoints and posts.

As the whole region is unstable, various factions vie for control as the city prepares for a siege. Officials have handed out swords, and those who didn't get one have sharpened what they have: scythes, shovels, rakes, anything. The mood is so somber, I wouldn't be surprised if the local squirrels have socked away poisonous peach pits just in case starvation makes life too bitter to endure. Fu Po, however, makes my visit comfortable. Passing through the city gates, he laughs with guards about preferring lovemaking to swordplay, and brandishes talismans, papers, and scrolls that lead them to kowtows. Magistrates wave at him and, unlike me, the dirt of the road does not show on him. He radiates such happiness and promise, I have no reason to suspect he is about to completely change.

I can see, however, that he is in a rush to get home, and when we arrive, I understand why. I have never imagined a residence so grand. Not even my hometown magistrate, who, for all I know, has his constables looking to apprehend me for murder, lives like this. Indeed, not even the richest person in Yidu has a compound this extensive, with stables and pagodas, sentry towers, and high walls.

Back in his domain, Fu Po immerses himself in the details of his home. Everything from the position of each table and chair to the way pots and pans hang in his kitchen, must be just so. His cape must be cleaned, his bag unpacked, his bedclothes laid out, his supper prepared in the customary way, the garden pruned to please his eye, the courtyards raked so that the lines in the dirt are all perfectly parallel, and joss sticks of varying fragrances—

each with its own unique effect on physical and emotional wellbeing — set to burning in just the right corner of each room.

When it finally occurs to him to give me a tour instead of having me follow him like a tail, it is his collection of landscape paintings that he wants me to see first. Each of these, he explains, is a representation of the structure and *qi* flow in the human body. Everything is tightly organized in these renditions, the waterfalls flowing just so, every outcropping balanced by one on the other side of the scroll, all the little tiny people tipping their hats in the same direction against the imaginary wind, the mountain showing just a hint of the scales of the dragon of mortality coiled at its base.

And then there is the jade collection. It started with his father, but Fu Po has taken to growing it with great passion and it is now of sufficient significance to be known to even the Crooked Chancellor himself. He knows of the stone's varied origins — the tropical south, the windswept north, the dangerous west, and the eastern seacoast, where the stones are polished by the action of waves. He tells me that its patterns are as unique and varied as the veins of a woman's breast, that the feel of it against the flesh can bring a courtesan to tears, and that its colors — greens, yellows, reds, whites, purples, and blues — are varied and lush enough to make a poet's heart swoon. He has a sense for which stones should be left in their natural state and appreciated for their energy and which beg to be carved into images of Buddha, Guanyin, or Maitreya, the messianic Buddha of days to come. He tells me of pieces that, by the dint of their natural twists, evoke dancing Taoist deities. I wait for some mention of formless pieces that bring Hun to mind, but none is forthcoming.

He offers me a jade necklace as a gift. At first, I think it renders a tiger and am sure I will not wear such a thing, but when I turn it vertically, I realize that it is not a tiger but a wasp. Not just any wasp but a smooth, green, life-size rendition of the special wasps I know so well.

"Where did you get this?" I ask him, astonished. "Was it in your father's collection?"

"My own acquisition," he says proudly. "A man sold it to me while we were on the road. You were sleeping. The jade is very fine."

"What kind of a man?"

He shrugs. "Why do you care? A merchant."

"What was his name?"

"You think I asked?" He was hunched over and old. I saw him a few times while we walked, going the same way. He commented on your beauty. He was selling some things. He said I should give it to you, said the green precisely matched your eyes. He was right."

I ask for more details, suspecting who that old man might be, but all Fu Po wants to tell me is what a good acquisition it is, how he paid so little that it amounted to theft, how the seller had no idea how fine the carving is and how extremely fine the stone. I bow inwardly to Mu and thank him for the gift, for it is surely he who has given it to me.

All these possessions seem too sophisticated for Fu Po, not that he isn't slick and competent and self-possessed, but because he is barely older than I am. A conversation with the bath maid confirms my intuition. The house is Fu Po's only because his father died a year ago, victim of a kick to the head by a horse gifted to the family by a nomadic prince with whom they once traded. The murderous horse was then gifted to the greedy current leader of the dynasty. Gifting a dangerous animal to a ruler is a prescription for family erasure by torture, but no one I meet is concerned. Clearly the Song capital runs on influence peddling, power brokering, family hierarchies, and political subtleties that this spear girl from the countryside may never understand.

I understand a good bath though, the finely carved gazebo walls filtering the torchlight, the osmanthus petals in the water lending a beautiful fragrance, the steam softening the twinkle of stars above. I lean back against the block of pear wood carved for necks and let the bath maid run her fingers through my hair and across the tops of my shoulders, dragging the flower petals here and there in swirls and using twigs to tickle my senses. I hope Fu Po is watching the proceedings, but find he is not. There is in me a great resource of energy and creativity, ideas for moves and techniques he has never even imagined, and yet he seems to be slowly losing interest.

The bath maid's name is Ti and I can tell by her pitying glances that she takes me for a young and tender rube and that she has seen her master bring in girls like me before. As she gently wipes me clean in the water and the clatter of horse hooves signals courtiers arriving for a meeting, I lean back and bring my lips to her ears.

"I'm not like the other girls," I tell her. "You don't need to worry about me."

***

Ti is from the Middle Kingdom, the old state of Ch'u, an area overrun by refugees from raiding nomads, and birthplace of the Taoist sage, Laozi, a friend of Hun and the celestial master of yang and yin. She has a lily's voluptuous proportions and she smells of something she calls vanilla, which comes from the seed pod of an island flower known as an orchid. She tells me this orchid plant climbs as a vine and was all over the trees where people first lived, before they came to ground in ancient times. I tell her I am descended from these tree people myself, as I prefer to be aloft.

When we sneak out together at night into the city, Ti warns me that Fu Po's tastes are strange, his behavior erratic, his commitments to women notoriously fickle. I explain to her that Fu Po has not, as she assumes, broken my heart. She thinks I'm lying, wants to know how it's possible to desire a man passionately enough to leave home in order to be with him, only to have him slip away day by day on the road until, upon arriving at his home, I am as a leaf turned yellow on the tree, ignored and left to fall where I may.

"I'm no dead leaf," I tell her. "And I don't cling to him in any way. I'm as interested in other women as he is, and in other men, too. He was my way to the city, that's all, and now that I'm here, I'm as happy to see it with you as I would be with him."

Ti cannot fathom my reaction. She thinks less of sensual adventures than of the stability of employment and the protection Fu Po's house affords her. She feels, as a woman alone, that she is constantly in danger of abduction or abuse. Lacking my skills, she is fascinated by the confidence I derive from my spear. Indeed, she is fixated upon the spear itself, taking it for nothing so much as a long, wooden phallus. She strokes it as we walk, playing her fingers along it the way she did my hair and, no doubt, as she does on Fu Po's manhood when she bathes him. She borrows it from me to stab at hanging lanterns. She makes monkey noises as she hops around with it when we cut through alleys, and she attacks shadows with it as she hangs from scaffolding in the old part of the city by one arm. She is wild, this vanilla-scented girl, a forest creature if I've ever met one and poorly suited to this cold capital.

Ti's first-stated mission is to give me a tour of the whorehouses. She deems this essential because, in her view, I need to understand the dangers of Fu Po losing whatever interest he still has in me. Without him, my life will spiral down to degradation and despair. She does not know of my background in the rural north, nor of my keen acquaintance with the rough world of men and the men of the rough world. Intent on showing me how bad things can get, she takes me to the pleasure quarter of the Song capital on this, our fourth night together and our very first out on the town.

Unlike my dry and windswept home, this city is defined by the vast network of canals pervading it. Most important of these is the Grand Canal, which links many lesser towns and cities to the capital. Barges ply it, some pulled by oxen on the banks, and others propelled by sailors' poles. The smaller canals weave in and out of all quarters of the city, smelling of flowers in the rich areas and of shit and garbage and rotting fish where the less fortunate live. The pleasure quarter is just off the Grand Canal, making it easy for rich gentlemen to reach it. We get there by footpath, for we are girls of no consequence and we have no boat. Ti knows the place well because she is frequently there with Fu Po, not as a participant herself (this surprises me) but as the one to watch over him when he drinks too much and bring him home when he is tired, always on his own junk, the term for sailing boats in this great city.

I don't ask how it is that Fu Po does not travel to the pleasure quarter with a bodyguard but chooses his bath maid instead. I don't ask because I understand right away why he does so. His sense of his own skill would never allow him to ask another man to protect him. In this, from what I have seen and felt myself, he is not mistaken. Also, a man in the pleasure quarter would be easily distracted and thus unreliable. In this, too, Fu Po is correct. Ti's focus would be ever on her master. Her sexual disinterest in girls is something I seek to remedy, but I await the right moment.

"Cinnamon Forest," Ti tells me, steering me to a pagoda with flapping yellow curtains at the entrance. "Master Fu's favorite house."

It starts to rain just as we duck in, and I wipe the shaft of my spear on my cloak. The madam is there to meet us and greets Ti warmly.

"Your master?" she asks.

"Not tonight," says Ti.

"On an errand then?"

Ti nods solemnly.

"Looking for new ways to please him?"

"That's right," says Ti.

The madam eyes my shining hair, my high cheekbones, my energy and carriage and, of course, my jade pendant. "And this beauty with the animal eyes?" she asks.

"Master's new favorite," says Ti.

"Then perhaps *she* should do the choosing."

"Perhaps she should," says Ti.

I drift through the house's winding halls, which are clearly designed to create the illusion of a treasure hunt for men. Sounds of passion seep through closed doors, the tinkle of pipas, the whisper of flutes, the giggle of girls, the groans of men. I grow excited. My breathing quickens. I hear Ti behind me and I duck into one of the rooms and close the door behind me. I am filled with a sense of adventure as Ti passes by, calling my name. The room is empty and the incense burner is cold, but there is grape wine in a carafe on the table. The bedclothes slip through my fingers as smoothly as pig-greased peas. I breathe in their history, which is rich with perfume and opium and, beneath that, the faint trace of sweat.

I lay down my spear and take off my cloak. I remove my leggings and tunic and slip under the covers. A great fatigue takes me, a bone-weariness I had not realized I felt, the hammering tiredness of weeks on the road, the dull ache of being abandoned by my lover. I hurt at the idea I could possibly bore him. There is nothing boring about me, not now, not ever. I fall asleep listening to the music of my growling stomach, suddenly loud, then soft, persistent, a melody whose message is that it is time to satisfy all my appetites.

Things happen outside my door, but I am away in a dream.

27

"It started when we were seven years old," Dora told me as we trudged along Qingdao's waterfront, the soles of my shoes still sticky with blood. "Lihua killed a bird by throwing a chopstick at it. The weird thing was the stick didn't tumble like sticks do, but flew straight as an arrow. I thought it was some kind of trick. I felt bad for the bird and told my parents everything. They didn't seem to care but Lihua gave me a black eye for being a tattletale."

"So, you didn't get along?" I asked, trying to distract myself from the cold feeling growing in my belly.

Ignoring the question, Dora kept walking, eyes forward. In the distance, the lights of the city blinked out as a brown dusk debuted.

"About a year later, I woke up during the night," she says at last. "Lihua and I shared a room and a bed and the window was open and snow was coming in. My teeth were chattering. I was freezing. I said something to Lihua. When she didn't answer, I got worried. I reached out for her with my foot and found only a pillow. I opened the door and looked down the hall but she wasn't there. I checked the bathroom but it was empty. I tiptoed around the house. It's a nice house, the same one my parents have now, up on top of the hill in town, not so far from here."

"And then what?"

"I was sure she'd be in the kitchen but she wasn't there either. I went back to our room, closed the window, and snuggled under the covers. There was a giant old red oak growing right outside. It was there before the house was and my father still trims it. When I turned out the light, I noticed that the branches, rendered in shadows on my wall, were moving. I went to the window and saw Lihua in the tree, chasing a housecat with a stick. The cat was scared and kept moving out to thinner and thinner branches and Lihua followed it. I was afraid she would fall but she was amazing out there, like a monkey. The way she moved, it wasn't normal."

"What does that mean?"

"It was magic," she said. "Supernatural in some way. She got close to the cat and then stabbed it with the stick. The cat screamed but it didn't fall and it didn't die. Instead, it jumped with the stick in its chest. She went after it by looping her legs around the branch she was sitting on and letting go with her hands so she could grab the cat on the branch below. She squeezed its neck and it screamed and scratched her and then she gave a hard twist. I heard the cat's neck break. She sat there smiling and then threw it on the ground. My heart was hammering and I went back to my bed and cried under the covers. In the morning, there was blood from her scratches all over the bed. Lihua told my mother we'd had a fight. Even though there was no blood on me, I admitted to it."

"You were afraid of her," I said.

Dora nodded. "That was the first time I realized it. And things got much worse. A couple of years later, right around the time we reached puberty, she started doing things at school."

"Doing things?" I repeated tightly.

"In the locker rooms before physical exercise class. Sometimes, in the trees, at the back of the school building. My sister loves trees."

"Tell me what kind of things."

Dora turned to face me. "Are you sure you want to know all this?"

"I need to," I said. "Every detail."

"Sexual things, then. Some of the girls said she was nice about it, most of the boys said she was mean. She forced them. There was a terrible scandal. We had to leave the school."

"You, too?"

Dora gave me a horrible smile. "I look just like her. People couldn't tell us apart."

"But you still don't think she's a serial killer."

"I told you, we never use that term," Dora said. "Lihua doesn't go looking for trouble and isn't excited by danger, but if someone stops her from satisfying her appetites or curiosity, bad things can happen. Anyway, can we get something to eat? I'm starving."

We walked into town. It was a long walk and every step of it felt alien. Even the sidewalk was different, not the crystalline composite I had slid down outside of the deli in LA, but a dull, smooth concrete over which my bloody soles slid too easily. Dora told me there were all-night snack bars in China that were the rough equivalent of donut shops at home. We found one. Inside, the place reminded me more of an interstate truck stop without trucks and truckers. We were alone there, save for a man in a rumpled railroad uniform and a thin teenager, a girl with a bad cold sneezing into a paper mask, her hair amateurishly streaked blonde.

We slumped into plastic chairs across from each other at a Formica table. As beautiful as she was, Dora looked pale, drawn, vaguely blue, and exhausted. I remembered how much blood she'd lost and brought back an assortment of food from the counter: cold noodles with a foil pouch of soy sauce, a flakey pastry with yellow custard inside, a platter with shredded pork and chicken feet and oily slices of roast duck with skin that had once been crispy. She ate hesitantly at first, eyes on me, but then hunger took over and she devoured the lot. I dabbed some grease from her chin and she gave me a shy smile.

"She killed her boyfriend when she was 21," she went on. "He was a nice guy, a violinist in a government program for musical prodigies. He was so gentle and quiet and kind, I personally thought she didn't deserve him, but the whole family liked him and hoped he would straighten her out, loving her the way he did. He liked fantasy movies. Fairytales. I watched them with him sometimes. Lihua said he assaulted her when he was drunk and that it was self-defense. The way he worshipped her, nobody could believe it, but he actually *was* drunk, which itself was weird because he was so conservative, none of us had ever seen him touch a drop. Nobody ever saw him lose his temper either. She hit him so hard on the side of the head with a beer bottle, she sent fragments of his skull into his brain. He died right away. A neighbor called the police."

"She didn't go to jail?"

"Ping was still one of us back then, a local cop who grew up up with us, like an older cousin, came around, ate my mother's dumplings. She was on the case and helped us get my sister released from jail. Everything went quiet after it happened. We turned into a family of morticians. No laughing. No talking at meals. The only loud noise was Lihua's chewing."

"She's not a loud chewer," I said.

"Back then she was. Anyway, the denial drove me crazy. The silence. And it stayed like that, the not talking about things, until the next thing happened."

I watched Dora eat. I should have been hungry myself,

couldn't remember when I'd last had anything, but it didn't occur to me to get anything for myself. I was too busy listening to the train wreck my life had become, too consumed by the need to know everything that had been kept from me, what the next chapter might be, where it was all going.

"After the animals when we were kids, starting when we were old enough to feel things, it was mostly about sex," she said, pushing her empty plate away. "A confusion between love and hate, tenderness and violence, like something wrong in the brain where the wires aren't connected properly."

"I never saw any of this," I said quietly.

"She became a prostitute," Dora said, looking me straight in the eye.

"Stop," I said.

"Not a common streetwalker. We don't have those here like you do in the States. The police don't allow it. Prostitutes have to be employed by a house. Lihua was and men paid her for sex. Women, too, according to Ping. That was her specialty. They called for her service, to be discreet, because our society is not so open about such things. When they called, my sister went. Certain women, they like to be..."

"Dominated," I said.

I don't know why I said it. Lulu was not like that with me. Things were always measured. Even. Passionate, yes, but in retrospect perhaps choreographed. Love really is blind and I'm glad it is. Later, things can bubble up as they did that night with Dora. Realizations. Truths. I chose that moment to take out my camera and aim it at the woman who looked exactly like my wife, the wife I had before the bullet, the wife I *thought* I had. I saw the sadness in her eyes and realized it was for me. The tears that started as I photographed her head-on, adoring her, setting up the shot just so. I had thought she was crying from happiness at what we had. Now I realized she pitied my lost innocence and perhaps regretted the way she had used me.

"I don't believe in laws against consensual sex," I said.

Dora looked around, got up slowly to stretch her body, locked her knees, and put her palms flat on the floor. It was a spontaneous thing, a release. Telling me these things was having a physical effect on her. The man behind the food counter stared. I remembered her martial moves against Ping's men, against Ping herself.

"Tell me the rest," I said.

She nodded and sat down. "At first, she just beat her clients. Hurt them worse if they tried to hurt her. She used her fists and feet, and a stick she always carried as part of what they expected from her."

"You mean like a dominatrix' whip or something?"

"Or something. Anyway, nobody called the police then. There was too much face to lose. Ping discovered these early things after the fact, when she went back with vindictiveness because of what happened later."

"She killed someone else?" I said.

"Lihua herself never saw them as murders. I talked to her about every one of them. She might as well have been discussing a game of mahjongg or, better, Go. She was out adventuring in the world. Experimenting. Testing others, gratifying her appetites. No sense of right and wrong about anything, although she did understand legal consequences and worried about being caught, judged, tried, convicted. Mostly about the judging. She pushed back about conforming, about being like everyone else. She defended her right to do as she wished."

Blowing her car horn and lifting her middle finger to the gunman made more sense now, but other than that our entire past together was shrouded in mystery. I wanted to believe Lulu loved me as I loved her. I wanted to believe in the intimacy, the peace, the world we made for ourselves and each other. I still wanted to believe all that was real, that with me she had finally found some peace.

"I know what you're thinking," she said. "You're wondering if she could really change or if she went looking for victims whenever you left her alone because you were studying late or visiting your parents."

I looked around the restaurant. The juxtaposition of these pedestrian surroundings and the horror of our conversation was not lost on me.

"You've described a psychopath," I said. "Someone who doesn't care what anyone thinks and goes looking for violent sex the way vegetarians forage for mushrooms. How many victims were there?"

"I don't believe any of them were premeditated, if you think that makes a difference. I have a feeling they were just encounters gone wrong. I think some rejected her or didn't want to do what she did, either giving or receiving. She didn't act the way most people thought a woman should and she didn't care for those prejudices. In her own way, she's a feminist. A tomboy, even. She would probably still insist nothing that happened was her fault."

"How many?" I asked numbly.

"We'll probably never know exactly, although once Ping figured out what was going on, tying it all together became her obsession."

"More than ten?"

Dora's face gave the answer.

"More than twenty?"

Again.

"More than thirty?"

"I don't think we should keep talking about this."

"And what did she do to them?"

"Does it matter?"

"It does to me."

"Most of the damage was with knives of one kind or another. Puncture wounds, slashing. I always knew when she'd done one because she'd come back and speak in numbers. It was a fixation, like yours right now."

"Speak in numbers? What does that mean?"

"12. 4,076. 111. 66,915. She'd just speak them. Totally random. Totally chaotic. And only after someone died."

"Chaos," I said. "Like your family's god. Actually, I heard her do that sometimes. Not after anyone died, though."

"As far as you know. You weren't with her every minute, right?"

"That's nice. Thanks for that. Look, your brother said something about her being the reincarnation of someone famous."

"The spear queen," Dora nodded, using a chopstick to idly push the remains of a chicken foot across her paper plate. "Her name was Yang Miao Zhen. She's the number one disciple of Lord Hun. She reincarnates over and over again to do his bidding. Of course, all that didn't start with Miao. No doubt there were many others before her. We just don't know their names, but they were all in our family line. Right back to the beginning, and only women."

"You have to know how crazy all this sounds."

Dora looked up at me with her beautiful eyes. Lulu's but not green.

"I know you're in pain, Solomon. I can't even imagine how much. But don't be that way. Like I told you back in LA, there's a lot about our family you don't understand."

I took her picture with that expression. I didn't want to forget what compassion looked like when it was directed at me. I checked the image on the screen, then put away the camera and picked up my phone. I hadn't turned it on since I waited in my hotel room before the fight with Ping. There was a long string of text messages there, most from my sister, but a few from my parents too. They wanted me to call them. Lulu's condition had changed.

Hector-The-Bullet was on the move, and Dr. Granate was in a mood to chase lead.

28

In my dream, I'm back in the Yidu market with Father. He holds my hand as we walk and he has a bounce to his step that I know comes from loving me so much. He's proud of my beauty, and even more for me killing the tiger, but protective when men look at me. As Father asks a Sogdian vendor about a cooking pot for Mother, I slip away to look at targets for spear practice. Apple paper is here, as well as paper made from oak bark and from the pressed, dried shit of oxen, which is full of grass fiber but washes white and clean for painting and calligraphy. My favorite mulberry paper is here, too, and I slip some quickly into my tunic. Mu said Father was the one doing the stealing but I cannot bear that thought now, the idea that such an upright man, a mayor, a man with a golden and devoted heart and a character of the finest jade would do such a thing just for me. I slink away with the paper but it is a dream so I don't have to cross the town nor even exit the market. Rather, I find myself instantly in the forest, in my beloved glade, where my birch trees wait for me. I hang my paper targets and prepare my spear. As I do, there is a crack of thunder.

I wake up. The thunder is the slamming of the door to the room in the brothel where I have been luxuriating in fabrics as soft and fragrant as at Fu Po's house. It is not the wind that has slammed it but a patron, a visitor who, by the expectant look on his face, takes me for a whore. I take my time deciding what to do with him. I stretch my arms above my head, swivel my hips, yawn, bat my eyes. I show a stretch of my smooth white belly and the undersides of my breasts as well. Thus distracted, this patron doesn't notice as I reach for my spear, which lies at the side of the bed covered by the blanket that has fallen from me in my nighttime gyrations. Anyone who has ever shared my bed knows I am no dainty sleeper. I am wont to explode into combat inside my dreams, sometimes fighting big cats, sometimes fighting with otherworldly monsters baijiu-born.

He is a man of some finery, this client — a good cloak, a deerskin satchel — but he has a weak chin and his left knee supports him poorly. The way he enters the room tells me he wants to play emperor because he worries he is a worm. I can tell this by the way he licks his lips, not lasciviously as the boy Gui did when trying to talk me into the hayloft but as a result of trying too hard to relax. I control him without saying a word. I wonder how long silence will reign.

He sits on the side of the bed and reaches for me. I slap his hand away. His eyes fly open in surprise. He starts to say something but I put my finger to his lips, which are chapped and rough like Father's hands. He makes to stand but I yank him back down. He sees the spear peeking out from beneath the bedclothes and can't seem to take his eyes off it. I stand before him and slyly remove the clothing from the bottom half of my body. I hear noise outside the door. Worrying we might have an audience, I go and close it firmly, then bar it with the shaft of my spear. We are trapped in the room now, this trembling man and me.

His tongue appears. He touches himself. I slap his hand again, not allowing any of that. He gasps at the pain, for my slaps are born of training and are not intended for this environment, this bedroom, this whorehouse, this strange and unexpected sanctuary in which I am suddenly as confident and in charge as I was back in my birch forest.

The door to the room rattles again.

"Miao!"

It is Ti's voice. She's found me, worried, she's been looking for hours. Not all night or I would not have this visitor.

"Go away," I call. "I'll stay here a while."

"You can't! The Master is coming!"

Her voice is full of fear. Clearly, she doesn't know Fu Po as I do.

"If he does, tell him I'm busy. I'll come back to the house when I'm ready."

Ti wails.

"Go now!" I yell. "Leave me in peace."

I hear her shuffle away. It sounds as if she's sobbing. I return my attention to the man with the weak chin. I ask him what he wants. He drools a little bit, regards the spear barring the door, regards the patch between my legs. I wonder how it is that I have drawn this simpering eunuch to my room instead of a stallion come to lose himself inside a woman. I would lose myself too, right now. He takes down his pantaloons and shows me what he has. He is no eunuch after all, although he apparently has no interest in me.

"You came to command a lover," I say.

He nods, his eyes cast down.

"But commanding is not what you really want."

He says nothing.

"You don't know what you really want. You're lost."

He looks up at me hopefully, pleadingly. Suddenly, I do not feel like a teenage girl anymore. Suddenly, I feel like I might be an empress.

"I saw you when you came into the house with the girl who knocked just now," he says. "I like the way you carry yourself. Your self-possession and strength. I like the way you walk coolly through this place while every other woman cringes and bows and acts diffidently. I *love* that you carry a weapon."

"Your clothes say you're a rich man. Why are you timid? Don't you have plenty of concubines? What's your name?"

"Long Long."

Double dragon? The name hardly fits. I choose not to make this point. Instead, I rummage for my flute. When I find it, I close my eyes and invite the memories in. When they come, I blow them through the flute. First there is Grandmother and her strong fingers and the way she squatted to dig for herbs. I play the kindness of her smile and the way we walked together like soldiers, me struggling to match her steps, fearing nothing in a world of tigers and men, our spears always at the ready, her long supple one and my tiny version of the same. I play the big cat, too, and the sound of its paws cracking twigs. I play the terrible darkness that descended from nowhere that day and how it turned the terraced world of trees black, silencing chattering magpies and jays. I play the sanzuwu and their beady eyes and their extra legs. I play Mu reborn and I play, with great tenderness, my ecstasy with the cave girls. I play the joy of training my weapon in my secret glade, especially as snow fell, and I play fighting fat Two-Sword Wong with his rasping breath and his deceptions. I play my mother and her disdain for my practice.

My music is spontaneous, seductive, mournful, and so personal it cannot but be unique. It drives Long Long to madness. When he is spent, he folds like a broken reed, panting, drooling, crying, declaring his slavish devotion to me even though he does not yet know my name.

"Your Master," he says. "Will he sell you?"

"He doesn't own me," I say. "No one does. I'm a free woman. I travel where I like."

He digests this, lying tucked against me, his wet chin in my armpit, the corner of his eyelash a butterfly on my shoulder.

"And who is he?"

"He's called Fu Po," I say. "He's a boy, really. But rich like you."

Long Long shoots from the bed like a celebration rocket, his face suddenly red, his breath coming in gasps. "Fu Po, son of Fu Gow?"

"I don't know his father's name," I say. "I know he collected jade and art, though, and that he died recently."

Abruptly he is up and struggling into his clothes. "And he's coming here?"

"And what if he is? Are you in his employ? An adversary in trade?"

Long Long shakes his head.

"But he knows you."

"If he sees me here, I'm finished," he moans.

I wonder about a feud between rich families. I fantasize about men in brocade sipping tea and arguing over jade. I imagine them fighting for their fetishes at a market, competing for the purchase of a landscape by a famous painter, carefully carved *ding*, or beautifully written poem for their collection. They are new to me, these people of means, and I can't help feeling their wars are trite and precious, a diversion to keep alive the spirit of those who have the most to lose as the steppe tribes close in, soon to confiscate pretty things and chop heads. I finger my jade pendant. This city life, with its idle preoccupations, is a fantasy. We are all little mice living in the safety of shadows of our own making while all the while, the hawks are circling.

***

People shout in the corridor outside my room. I recognize Ti's voice and those of the thick-armed, bowlegged men who surrounded the madam when I arrived at the Cinnamon Forest. Someone bangs on the door. I tell Long Long the quality of the strikes mean it's Po, that he doesn't speak much when he is angry, but he cuts plenty.

"I need to hide," he says.

Together we rearrange quilts and pillows, moving the mattress to create a narrow space beside the wall against which he can press himself. Once this is done, I dress, remove the spear from the door, and feign wiping sleep crust from my eyes as I open it to admit Fu Po. I'm shocked by the way he ferociously grabs me by the throat with both hands while Ti cowers, begging him to be merciful.

"I never said you could come here, you whore!" he roars, his spittle spraying my face.

I cannot answer, of course, as I am gasping for air and my throat is drawn tight in his fingers. I lift a knee hard into his groin. I am, at that moment, not thinking about what effects injuring him there will have upon my pleasure over the next week or two, I'm just thinking about breathing. My move has the desired effect and he drops his hands. When he does, I kick him soundly in the head. He goes down, comes back up, and draws his blade. Ti screams at him to put it away. The madam appears in the doorway and says something, gently, about not liking swordplay in the house. It's obvious she doesn't want to offend a rich patron but is trying to avoid the need for a cleanup. Her bodyguard pulls her gently away.

There is scant space in the room for spearplay, but I pick up my weapon anyway. I try to reason with Fu Po, wondering if drink has poisoned his mind. I tell him there is nothing in our time together that suggests I need his permission to do anything at all. I apologize for hurting his feelings if I have done so. My words appear only to enrage him further. His fearsome black blade turns the room to tatters. I worry as much for Long Long as for myself. Something of the shredded furniture might land on him. Despite this worry, I am careful not to give him away.

In his rampage, I notice a change in Fu Po's sweat. It's not a sudden thing; rather, I've noticed it since we arrived in town. My impression is that it signifies some shift in the balance of his yin and yang, something out of kilter with his *qi*. I wonder if he wants for challenge or meaning because the death of his father has left him with so many options and so few cares. I wonder if this is the smell of someone who knows his privileged life will soon enough end against the edge of a barbarian's sword, his skill notwithstanding.

In his attacks, Fu Po has the advantage of strength, and his sword is better than a spear in these close quarters. He is so angry it seems he is really trying to kill me. I think back to when he used the same skills to save me. As I pant and parry the dizzying thrusts of his blade, it occurs to me that I don't really know him and never have. I am now alone here in the Song capital in a whorehouse, and there is no retreat to my brother's tent or my father's house. I cannot even skip back to Fu's private pleasure palace. His blade catches the lobe of my left ear, shearing off a tiny sliver. It stings and hot blood runs down my neck. Ti screams for him to stop. He pays no attention. His rage is an animal all its own, not a tiger though as tigers are cool and calculating and kill from hunger more than malice. Perhaps Fu Po is a lion. I've heard of them but never seen one. Perhaps, and this is most likely, I think, he has been overtaken by the spirt of a wandering weasel. Weasels, I know, smell fetid and are given to frenzies of violence in which they kill more than they can eat. That's it, I decide, as he presses me to the wall. A weasel has Fu Po.

Recognizing this gives me an idea. Weasels arch their backs before they leap. They are also good at sinuous, sideways movements, bringing their jaws into play in slashing fashion. Amazingly, these are characteristics of Fu Po, something I've never noticed until this moment. I do what I would do if Fu Po were a giant weasel, I drop to the ground and roll beneath him, not between his legs but beside them as he thrusts. Coming up behind him, I grab him by the neck and yank as hard as I can, stepping out of the way as he falls to the doorway. Ti helps me there by pulling on him as I prod him out with my spear, all the while staying out of range of his blade. The instant his feet pass the threshold, I slam the door shut and block it once more.

Alone once more, I survey the damage. Candlelight hides a great deal but the crack in the wall opposite the bed is clear. I work my fingers into it and feel cold air. It's an outside wall. I hiss at Long Long to get up and help me. Together, we work apart the wooden slats until we have a view of the alley behind the Cinnamon Forest. Fu Po is back to banging at the door, which is starting to give way. It's our turn to be weasels now, Long Long and I, as we try to slip through the crack we've opened in the wall. My fingers are bleeding from the effort, and his are too.

"I never expected this," I say as I move the bed in front of the door and retrieve my weapon.

"In that case you are as naïve as you are ferocious," Long Long answers.

Outside, I look for a way to make use of our head start and disappear but we are trapped in an alley. that runs along a fetid canal and has no outlet because all the houses are sewn together against flooding. This seems a fire hazard to me, not to mention a challenge to privacy, but I really know so little of city ways.

Before we get very far, I hear the distant sound of Fu Po breaking through the brothel door, and this time I hear his voice call my name.

"He hated his father," Long Long tells me as we jog along. "That's the root of most of his problems. The old man belittled him. Judged him and criticized everything he did. Appreciated only his swordplay, which is why he's so good at it but refuses to teach or use it for any good purpose. Be thankful you yourself weren't sired by a rich porcupine like that."

"My father is the best man I know and he loves me," I huff as we run. "And Fu Po wasn't like that when I met him, or if he was he didn't show it. He was so funny. So sweet."

"I'm sure he was adorable," says Long Long, the first time I've heard him be sarcastic.

That's when I hear Ti shriek in terror. I stop. Even before Fu Po yells his threat, I know what he's doing. He knows I care for her and he's grabbed her and is going to kill her if I don't come back. I stop running and turn. Long Long grabs my sleeve. I jerk away and the fabric tears. I don't have to say anything about needing to go back. It's obvious. Long Long's eyes go wild. He cannot afford to be recognized and wants to run. I whisper a third option in his ear, telling him to hide and wait for me. If I fail, no one will know he was with me. If I succeed, I'll be right along to protect him.

Fu Po drags Ti into the alley, coming right for me. I charge him as if he's a tiger. Ti encumbers him but he can't let her go until I'm well and truly in range, and range for me is greater than it is for him because my weapon is longer. In the room, he had the advantage; out here, with space to move, things are different. I lift the spear high and try to smash him on the head. He dodges, but holding on to Ti slows him down. I hit his shoulder and he cries out. He describes what he will do to Ti if I don't put my weapon down this instant. He tells me he will cripple her, torture her, make her life a living hell, make her wish she were dead. I speed my thinking and slow my breath. I think about what I've learned about him since that first day when he seemed such a deft and magical dancer, such an elegant and unassailable boy. Furious, possessive, vindictive, and spoiled — those are the words I would use to describe him now. Possessed by the weasel or not, I know how to beat him.

I throw the spear.

It's a frightening gambit, for if it misses its mark, I am without a weapon and totally at his mercy. Still, it's a risk I'm willing to take, for success will end the conflict utterly and completely. After all, I killed a tiger with a stick when I was but a child, and I have spent thousands of hours throwing my spear at targets far wispier and more mobile than a slender boy with a fearsome sword. I have pierced paper dancing in the wind and done so with my eyes closed. I know the way spears fly, and I know the way men die.

I do not miss.

29

THERE WAS a shopping mall in Westwood, not far from UCLA. Whenever Lulu left our apartment upset, I knew to look for her in a shop quietly tucked away in a corner of the top floor, far from the brand boutiques and outfitters selling skateboarding shoes, backpacks, watch caps, and hoodies. Like any other stationery store it carried pencils, pens, and greeting cards, but the main emphasis was on a great collection of fine writing paper from around the world. The first time she took me there, Lulu's fascination with exotic paper was obvious. She grew visibly calm and serene while handling it, a wistful, far-away expression hijacked her features, and she swayed on her feet as if she were on a moving train. The more primitive and less finished the paper, the more she liked it. She pointed out the grain of the paper for me, and always demanded I run my fingers over the surface like a blind man reading braille, looking for the tiniest bumps and ridges, feeling the thickness and resistance to creases. That was the biggest thing for her, the way the paper felt to the touch. Certain papers had soul, she told me, and for some strange reason, I came to believe her.

Lulu also liked the video arcade at the opposite end of the mall. The arcade actually occupied three floors and offered games we had to pay for with tokens we purchased from strategically-positioned vending machines. I told her it seemed stupid to pay when she could play opponents around the world for free on her computer. She told me she understood my point intellectually but still loved the lights and sounds of the place. I guess she wasn't alone in that, because we were never there when there wasn't a crowd of kids and adults waiting in line to shoot aliens, jump wildly on a pressure pad, drive a go-kart, or fly a spaceship. Lulu's favorite game, in fact the only one I ever saw her play, involved wielding a sword against virtual opponents: an axe-wielding giant, a slender girl in a lime-green kung fu pantsuit, a jut-jawed ogre with a club, a gray-bearded monk with a staff, and finally, if you were good enough to get that far, a wide-eyed boy child dressed in rags and wielding a spear. Lulu never left the arcade until she defeated every enemy and thus the game.

Lulu loved exercise, loved staying fit, and even when she played her kung fu game drove her avatar to martial victory with white-knuckle intensity. All the same, I never saw that violence in her any other time, not when she was angry with strangers, not when she was angry with me, and not when she was angry with friends. In truth, she really didn't have any friends. There was the roommate she had in Santa Barbara before she met me, a black bodybuilder who waited tables at an Italian restaurant in town, but I never saw them argue.

Violence has always made me uncomfortable. Long before Lulu received that bullet in her brain, I came to understand it as the lowest common denominator of human interaction, the thing we do when we are so frustrated with the world and with ourselves that we don't know what else to do with our feelings. Thinking of Lulu doing the things Dora said she did, I could only imagine she must have been in terrible pain.

***

"And how come you sent her to America? What made you think she wouldn't kill people in Los Angeles and end up in some American jail instead of a Chinese one?"

The words came out in a jumble. I'd been holding everything back just trying to get Dora safe. First thing's first. That's how things were with me back then. Linear. One step at a time. At least when I was thinking clearly. We were out of the snack restaurant and back on the street, fearful of cameras, keeping mostly to alleys, slowly heading inland, with Dora leading because I had no idea where to go or what to do next.

"She went on her own," Dora replied angrily. "She never told any of us she was planning to leave, never said a word about where she was going. We were as much in the dark as you were. You know all about her ability to keep things to herself, right?"

I took a deep breath. "I deserved that. I'm sorry."

"Never mind," she sighed. "There's been so much for you to process in such a short time. Let's talk about something else. Tell me about your family."

"You know I have a sister. A brother, parents, and a nephew. We are ethnically Jewish. The rest of my family eats smoked fish and chicken liver but I'm vegetarian. We used to spend a lot of time in an RV. My father's a skin doctor and my mother's an artist. We follow sports, in fact my brother is a sports agent, but we don't play them much. My mother still believes in an all-powerful old man with a stick watching us from the clouds and sending down a lightning bolt should we shoplift or masturbate. The rest of us are agnostic and irreligious."

She took my hand. "I can see why my sister chose you."

Right from the start—her casual offer of sex in her rented LA apartment comes to mind—Dora and I were easily intimate, a fact I ascribed to her being my wife's twin. All the same, I was suddenly embarrassed by the the heat of her body and her just-wounded-and-nearly-killed vulnerability. I asked her where we were headed. She countered by asking me to tell her about my love for her sister.

"Right now, it feels curated, directed, produced, and manipulated," I said. "That's a terrible feeling."

"I understand why you would doubt her for lying to you the way she lied to everyone, but I wouldn't doubt her love for you or yours for her because of that."

"Why not?"

"Because she's able to separate such things."

"Maybe she can, but I can't."

We both knew everything changed the moment I made that admission. We were quiet for a while.

"Perhaps it has been that violent spear queen acting through her all along," Dora said at last. "Maybe none of what she's done is her fault."

"Well, a neurosurgeon is about to go fishing in her skull," I said. "And neither of us is there for her."

"I think I know who to ask about the wasps," she said.

30

So as not to have it catch me by surprise, Grandmother often told me to live in perpetual expectation of reversal. It always comes, she said, and often when you least expect it. Even though I was far too young to know about men at that time, she said I would find reversal in them more often than in the weather, and more violently, too. In the years since she has been gone, I have found this to be true, and I await Long Long's treachery with interest. So far, however, he has done nothing but complain how badly the Song capital suffers by comparison to the old capital at Kaifeng, what with Muslim-style buildings popping up everywhere.

I run better than Long Long does. Perhaps this is because he is spent and I am not. Men sleep after they spend their seed, requiring a reinvestment of their energy to make more. Women don't, so I run better and faster than Long Long does and have to keep stopping to wait for him. We use alleyways between shanties and dark, narrow waterfront paths. It is on these that I realize how uncomfortable I am with so much water. In the lake with Mu I feared nothing because it was so shallow and the entry was gradual and, even though it was so terribly cold, I could walk into it and feel ground beneath my feet, mucky as it might have been. Here, the water is deep enough to swallow an army.

I hear Ti's distinctive footsteps behind me, her quiet off-balance gait. I learned it the first day at Fu Po's house, anticipating her approach to the hot bath and her soft hands on my neck. I beckon Long Long into the shadows and we wait for her. When she comes, I leap out and cover her mouth and whisper in her ear that she should leave us and go home.

"I'm going with you," she says. "But we must be careful. There are many eyes along the canals and not only those of turtles, fish, and frogs."

We zig and zag until we reach the bay. The water glistens in the budding dawn. I cough and Ti tells me that's from the salt cleaning my lungs. I let my eyes relax to the flat and distant horizon, to the line of light making the fog glow. Something shifts inside me. My mother once told me that her first look at the sea changed her forever and now I understand why. We huddle out of sight beneath a jetty built for barges and ferries. The water rushing away pulls the gray sand so hard, the stanchions moan. Ti tells me this is the tide working the will of the moon, and that it flies faster than an eagle. I see crabs gasping in their little holes and wonder at such a life, helpless in the face of the forces of nature. Unsurprisingly, Hun has something to say about this and does so promptly, loudly, in my ear.

You are no different.

Long Long produces a bunch of jarrow grass from his cloak and breaks the stalks so the great Zhou-I, the instrument of divination, can guide our next move. He works purposefully, slowly, with great practice. Father did this too, when I was a little girl, but I haven't seen him do it in years and he never did it with the precision Long Long does.

"Number forty-six," he says at length. "Shêng. Pushing upward. Your small, consistent steps toward your goal will take you there because you are not rigid in your intentions."

"You asked about me?"

"Of course he did," says Ti. "You are the glue that binds us all, the reason we are moving away from where we were and toward wherever it is we're going. This says you will achieve your goal because you don't push for it."

"I want to live," I say. "I want to fight and I want to love. Are those goals?"

By way of answer, Ti smiles and gently touches my face. Long Long opens his deerskin satchel and withdraws a dark cassock with a white collar. It flaps, unfurling in the wind. He exchanges it for his cloak. "We go to Zhoushan," he says, his dimpled chin quivering.

"Five Pecks of Rice!" Ti breathes.

***

Somewhere deep inside, despite all the rafts and junks and barges I've seen since arriving in the capital, I still consider boats to be something for people other than me. Not that women of my common station don't deserve river transport or even to make ocean voyages, but depending upon a bucket of wood to support me precariously atop water is an idea I find disturbing. When I find out that Zhoushan is actually an island and we must take a boat to reach it, I worry. To calm myself I lean back and close my eyes against the growing light. I open them again when distant voices come across the roaring tide. A ferry trailing a coracle nears the jetty and a few people have gathered at the shore, including a boy with a monkey on a leash and an old man with one white eye, bent over a cane. Ti wipes sleep from her eyes and I gather her hair for her. I ask what she meant about the rice.

"A Taoist sect," she tells me with a secretive smile. 'They have a temple on the island. Long Long is a priest there. They practice public shaming for offenses. Sex is a big offense."

I understand Long Long better now. He decided to stay and help me because if I were caught, the truth about his visit to Cinnamon Forest might come out. I share this conclusion with Ti. Her laugh awakens Long Long. He sees the ferry and leaps to his feet, bidding us to come quickly. We board with him. I try and stay away from the monkey, as his shit has already perfumed the deck. The ferry is a small one and it wobbles. I feel my heart in my throat. I put down my spear for balance, driving the handle into a gap in the hull.

A moment after we push off, there is a commotion onshore. A group of men wearing the uniforms of magistrate's men bursts out of the tree line. Seeing us on the boat, they yell at the ferryman to turn the craft around. The old man comes alive and shoves the ferryman off the boat. Long Long leaps to the oar. Holding their swords high, two of the magistrate's men jump into the water and scissor kick toward us, screaming commands. The monkey boy looks around dumbly, clearly confused. The monkey, too, appears agitated and Ti strokes its head reassuringly. Long Long has no skill with the oar and the swimming men close in. I'm too frightened of falling in and drowning to fend them off. My breath comes in gasps. My hands sweat. My grip on my spear slips. Another official jumps into the water. He's such a fast swimmer, he reaches the boat at the same time as the other two. The old man tries fending them off with his cane but quickly tires and fades.

Ti screams my name. I collect myself and pierce the nearest swimmer with my spear. His blood blossoms into a red line, his eyes white and wide. The fast water takes him and a moment later he's gone. The second man grabs the gunwale. I put my spear through his throat and he disappears under the boat. The third man yanks the old man into the water and Long Long dives in to save him. The ferry spins, rudderless, nobody rowing. Ti grabs the oar and holds it out to Long Long. The third man hauls himself onto the boat and charges me with his curved blade. It's a common blade nothing like Fu Po's elegant black straight one. Water from his slashing attack lands on my lips, a salty taste of impending death by drowning.

The boat rocks violently. The monkey screams. Out of the corner of my eye I see Ti struggling with the oar, with Long Long, with the poor old man. My attacker is fast despite being waterlogged. I work the spear in spirals, continually deflecting his thrusts. One moment he makes me promises of clemency if I will simply surrender and reveal who put me up to killing Fu Po, the next he details the horrible way in which I and three generations of my family will die once he has my eyes burned out, stripped the skin off my body, and ground up my bones to feed pigs.

There's something in his voice that alarms the monkey. Animals can be that way, sensitive to things humans choose not to see, aware always of the workings of Hun, even though they may neither know nor speak his name. He beats the golden hair on his narrow little chest, furrows his wrinkled brow, balls his black fists, pulls furiously on his little red root, grunts, and shrieks. An arrow thuds into the deck by my feet. It shivers, its feathers black and shining. My attacker waves at his troops to stop shooting, obviously lacking confidence in their aim at this distance, with our craft turning and the two of us dancing back and forth. The message is received, but not before one more arrow flies.

It lands in the monkey's head, dead center, protruding from his crown point as if dropped from heaven. Despite being stone dead, the little creature continues to stand, mouth agape, mane ruffled, lips showing teeth. The sight distracts everyone on board and I slap the official's sword from his hand. An instant later, the monkey's boy slits the man's throat from ear to ear. Seeing this, the archers on shore loose a new volley of arrows. There is no place to hide. The ferry and the coracle become pin cushions. Everyone but me dives overboard and uses the overhang of the gunwales for shelter. On deck, I dance in the barrage like a butterfly dodging raindrops. It is not until a fire arrow hits the deck that I howl in anger more loudly than that little dead monkey ever could.

It must be my screams that summon them, those impossible three-legged crows, either that or it is Hun. The *sanzuwu* materialize not from trees along the bank nor from the low-lying mist but, as their name suggests they should, straight from the sun. They are as silent as they were when standing sentinel around Mu's cocoon, even with their wings beating, and the sheer density of their flock makes aiming or firing an arrow past them a sheer impossibility.

I want to say that some of the men try shooting them down, and perhaps they do, though neither falling crows, trails of flame, nor the hiss of arrows hitting the bay provide evidence for it. I alone recognize my patron at work and so I take his silent cue and move silently myself, past the bristling monkey to the gunwales, from which I haul everyone aboard, first Ti, taking just a moment to clasp her to my breast, then the old man, Long Long, and the monkey boy. Everyone whispers, awestruck, about the propitious intervention of the birds. Long Long tells the old man and the boy to take leave of us in the coracle. They do so, but only after the boy has removed all the arrows from his pet's body and taken him to his bosom.

"They saw my robes," Long Long says. "They'll look for us at the monastery."

"We need help," says Ti. "Perhaps we can find it there and move on quickly before anyone comes?"

"I can think of no better plan," says Long, though he doesn't sound happy about it.

I take the oar and steer us along in the current.

31

FASTER THAN any academic, corporate honcho, or student of architecture could, I discovered that while things in the West were always designed to impress from the outside, things in China (at least until globalization took hold) were designed to hide treasures on the inside and keep things low-key on the surface. While an underground bunker, armed men, and a submarine certainly suggested criminal activity, in another country and under different circumstances all that might have been nothing more than tight corporate security. While Lulu's family didn't exactly seem like corporate types, they did seem to own as much of Qingdao as some emperor of old might have.

In the whirlwind days after the escape from the temple, I discovered that family had been hugely wealthy for centuries, had preserved the lion's share of their fortune through the upheavals of the 20th Century by keeping a low profile, and had continued the family mission of making people more sensitive to the natural world by resurrecting traditional Taoist values. I learned they were in the art business, for instance, and had galleries that featured traditional Chinese landscape painters, often supporting the artists themselves in material ways that went beyond selling their paintings. They were looking, Dora explained, to have a certain vision of the world seep into the general populace.

That seeping wasn't just aimed at the sort of people who bought art. There were health food products that offered alternatives to traditional choices, turtle jelly that wasn't made from turtles, for instance, and grocery bags made from ubiquitous, fast-growing bamboo free of chemical processing instead of milled hardwoods from trees that take decades to grow. There was sustainable agriculture, humane management of livestock, and an abundance of subtle-but-powerful spiritual messages that relied on aphorisms, vocals, and visuals that were compelling. There was even a company that manufactured oils and scents based on traditional Taoist formulas aimed at encouraging relaxation, clear thinking, compassion, and ease.

It was while visiting that latter company's factory that I realized the family was, if not completely accepting me then at least becoming accustomed to my presence. My new equilibrium left me feeling comfortable enough to call my parents regarding Lulu's pending surgery. As I spoke on the throw-away phone Dora had picked up for the purpose, Lulu's parents watched me carefully, not only listening to my end of the conversation but also trying to read my expressions.

The neurosurgeon hadn't made his move yet, but they said it could be any minute. It wasn't clear whether there would be any long-term benefit to Lulu's mentation through the removal of the Hector-The-Bullet — the medical staff continued to dismiss the notes she'd written as either a fiction or a fluke — but the feeling seemed to be it would let Lulu's body survive longer by restoring some missing functions. This was important because new scans showed the twins developing normally and well.

"Of course, if they survive, you'll have to parent them alone," said my mother. "Lulu obviously won't be in any condition to help."

""So you're suggesting I tell the hospital not to try to take out the bullet and save them?" I asked.

"You have to think about your life," said my father. "You're still so young, so much in front of you. To be saddled this way...."

The moment I hung upl Dora took the phone and smashed it on the floor. "Even burner phones can be traced if Ping has her eye on the numbers she thinks you will ring. One call per phone is all you get. So, what's the latest news?"

"They'll do the surgery soon," I said. "Nothing to report beyond that."

There were a few nods but no questions.

The energy of the Yang family was as steel wool to the edges of reality. Frustrated by my inability to capture that quality with my camera I left the office for the factory floor. My camera found much worth capturing there: amusingly phallic bottles filled with herbal decoctions, glass jars filled with multicolored medicinal pastes, and a panoply of faces. I asked and discovered that the workers were Han Chinese, Philippine, Burmese, and Lao. They were all dressed in street clothes rather than uniforms or smocks and chattered and laughed as they executed their tasks with speed, accuracy, and precision.

My father-in-law followed me around while I shot, either because he was curious or because he didn't trust me. He was intrigued by my portraiture of people and enjoyed it when I showed him the results on the camera's screen, complimenting me on how well I captured expressions and feelings and how well I framed the shots. It was a nice moment, perhaps the first simply kind words I'd heard from him.

"You should go back to Lihua," he told me after a time. "If she wakes up after the surgery, she will need you."

"You should go with me."

"The general cannot leave the troops during battle," he said.

"Lihua is in a battle, too," I said.

"Yes, but that battleground is not accessible to me."

"She can hear you when you speak to her," I said. "They say she can't, but I'm sure she can."

"Travel isn't so easy for me," he said.

"If everything works out, you'll have grandchildren," I said. "Even if the surgery doesn't help Lihua. But somehow, I think her best chance lies with the wasps."

"Wasps," he muttered.

"Do you know where they are? Where I can find them? The ones she asked for in the note she wrote?"

Dora joined us. "I think I know how we can find them," she said to her father. "The food company. The honey."

He looked startled for a moment, then gave a slow nod. "Maybe," he said.

"Will someone tell me what's going on?" I implored.

"Lord Hun is aware of what violent monkeys most people are and how much they damage universal balance."

"Because we don't see things in terms of deep time," my father-in-law puts in.

"Deep time," I repeated.

***

My father kept a late 1960s Angelman Sea Spirit docked at Marina Del Rey. *Skin Hook* was a 33' ketch with a long, low cabin, in good shape but worth no more than a battered farm tractor. That should have mattered to him—he was obsessive about his possessions and their values—but strangely it didn't. Maybe this was because he had received it in lieu of cash when an expired insurance policy denied him payment for the removal of a myeloma from behind a patient's knee. Manna from heaven, he called it, a celestial intervention that allowed him the peace of the Pacific between the coast and Santa Catalina Island, a foray in which he took great and frequent delight.

His boundless enthusiasm for sailing outstripped his skill as a sailor, but as children festooned in life vests, the three of us accompanied him on his day trips, sometimes with my mother and sometimes without her. I remember every one of those rides, the bright ones where the strong sun burned the skin of my ears so badly it crisped and peeled off to leave raspberry flesh beneath, the ones where we huddled inside against the fog, listening to the screams of gulls and holding on for dear life while my father guided us inexpertly through the waves and my mother attempted sketches on the galley table, still life portraits of a sea that was anything but still: a sunflower-yellow cup dangling from a hook, a cross-woven blue-and-green potholder beneath a stained coffee cup, the blow-hole of a dolphin seen from the top down, wrinkled like a little old eye. None of these sketches were very good, they couldn't be with the ride ruining her lines, but her artistry improved over time.

As he aged, my father sailed less often, although he came to have a more sensitive hand on the tiller and to be better at reading the sea, wind, and weather. He became, in the end, such a good sailor that none of us blamed him for holding on to the old boat so long, refurbishing it as necessary but rarely putting very much money into it. My mother took his attachment to the old tub as a sign of loyalty to her, to their marriage, and to all the commitments he had made in his life. She saw it as his way of saying he would stick by us all forever. I read it differently. I didn't see my father as the kind of man who could feel he owed anything to a boat, even if that boat had often taken good care of him and his family. Instead, I thought it was about ego. I thought my father wanted to feel superior to other doctors who spent fortunes on expensive boats but never really learned how to sail them. I felt he wanted to prove it was all about the man, not the vessel. He wanted to gloat about the money he saved and the skill he had developed.

My mother developed vertigo and lost her tolerance for the sea. Bryce was in New York and Ginger's boy, Nash was too rambunctious to keep safe on the boat so, in time I became the only one who went sailing with my father. Our standard arrangement, barring bad weather or a school exam, was to go out together on the second Sunday of the month. Those outings stopped when I moved to Santa Barbara but my father continued sailing alone. When Lulu and I returned to LA, the invitations resumed. I went with him when I could, and in truth, I got along with my father best when we were out on the water. The demands of the sails kept his mind busy and off such topics as what kind of living a photographer could make in the digital age, wasn't photojournalism dead, could any image really be trusted, and wasn't it clearly better to be a practical money-earner than an artist? I'd had a lifetime to learn his moves, and those of the boat, so we sailed well together.

We always went to Catalina for lunch at a seafood place in Avalon. My father had the same Shrimp Louie every time: crisp iceberg lettuce, a mix of cocktail sauce on the shrimp and Russian dressing with dill on the greens, so many lemon wedges squeezed over everything that every bite contained a seed, with celery stalks and carrot sticks for crunching. I had baked beans and a potato. It was a ritual, my father clucking about what a waste it was to take a vegetarian to a seafood place, and that I should at least try the oysters.

Lulu never went with us. At first, I construed her refusals as a desire to avoid spending time with my prickly father but as months went by and she was never available, I began to worry something else was going on. Her explanations, the things she said she had to do — spa care day or extra time at the library — seemed odd for Sundays. I didn't suspect her of any kind of infidelity, I considered our relationship far too new to worry about anything like that, but I had the nagging feeling she was being dishonest with me about something.

What that something was did not come to light until the weekend we flew together to Catalina in a friend's Cessna. I had known Abdul since grade school, and he had always wanted to be a pilot. Bad eyesight kept him from working at it professionally, in fact he was far more suited to his job as an accountant with a big LA firm than he was to being behind the stick of a plane, but it was a dream for him. He went to flight school and we talked on a regular basis and he let me know he had received his license and purchased a share in a four-passenger airplane. In a show of support, and because Lulu thought it would be great fun to see the city that way, we went up with him one night. We circled the downtown area, flew low over the Hollywood sign, went out over the sea and up the coast, then circled back over the desert to land at the general aviation airport in Santa Monica. I was being particularly impressed by Abdul's ability to handle the airplane even while talking incessantly to air traffic control. We were comfortable flying with him.

Abdul mentioned flying us to Catalina that first night, telling us it was probably California's most dangerous airport. He also told us he wanted to conquer it. When we flew there with him a few weeks later, we assumed he had practiced the run, worked it on a simulator, done whatever preparation any pilot would do to assure a safe landing. It was a beautiful morning, the second Sunday of the month, and Lulu and I were optimistic enough about the flight to bring a café mocha along for me, a sweet chai tea for her, and a double shot of espresso for the pilot.

We took off with the sun behind us and the glittering ocean below. Lulu sat up front with Abdul; I sat directly behind her, snapping photos out the window. After twenty minutes or so, the crags of Catalina drew close. Abdul located the 1,000-meter concrete landing strip and we descended for it with a series of right turns to scrub off altitude. The sharp brown rocks drew into focus. Seabirds rose on thermals. We seemed to be coming in at an odd angle, too low. When I mentioned it. I got a mutter in return, something about the first half of the runway being set on an incline.

Abdul worked the flaps, the engine, the rudder. If something was wrong, Lulu did not appear to notice, but sipped her tea and looked out the cockpit window. In previous flights, I had noticed how things became very quiet right before touchdown, something about feathering the propeller and cutting the engine, Abdul had explained. Not this time. Instead of silence, I was treated to a screaming engine as a gust of wind pressed down on us like the hand of a god, directing us right into the face of the cliff.

Lulu screamed. I braced myself with one hand and raised my camera with the other. Abdul desperately yanked on the yoke. The veins in his hands bulged and his biceps shook. The edge of the runway loomed above us rather than below. I snapped a shot of it just before we went nearly vertical. At the last moment, the Cessna's little tailwheel touched the ground. I suppose that pivot might have flipped us over backward, but because of our flap angle and the pull of the engine, it brought us down instead.

It was a hard landing. The airplane slid sideways down the runway but Abdul managed to keep enough control to bring us to a stop. When he switched off the engine, I saw he had a cut over his eye. Lulu stepped out of the airplane and took a few steps. I climbed out after her and found her all right. Abdul vomited into the dusty ground. Some people appeared from the airport restaurant, carrying first-aid kits. They talked to us, put a bandage on Abdul. He arranged for a mechanic to look over the airplane while Lulu and I went into Avalon on the local bus.

Meeting my father for lunch was supposed to be a surprise, at least insofar as I had not reminded Lulu it was sailing day. It wasn't. She greeted him without much enthusiasm, listened to him chatter about what a beautiful sail over it had been. I mentioned our rough arrival. He told us we were welcome to return with him. I said, of course, that we would. Lulu ordered a huge buffalo burger with bacon and cheese. My father watched her with some fascination as she ate it ravenously, grease dripping down her chin. Other diners watched her, too. People nearly always watched Lulu. After the meal, we went down to the boat. I helped my father with the lines. Lulu stood on the dock. When it came time to cast off and leave, I jumped aboard and offered my hand.

"I'm flying back with Abdul," she said. "I'll see you at home."

She trotted off before either of us could say anything. My father looked at me. "What was that about?" he asked. "You two fighting?"

It might have seemed she didn't like my father. It might have seemed she liked to fly. Without knowing the precise truth, that was the moment I began to suspect, on some level beyond any conscious awareness, that my wife not only had a past, but a fear of water.

And many secrets she was keeping from me.

***

Dora and I headed for the huge northern port of Tianjin, site of the family food company and the fourth largest city in

China after Beijing, Shanghai, and Shenzhen. It would have been fast and comfortable to take a bullet train but we would have been exposed to police surveillance in the service of Ping so we stowed away in the back of a truck from the cosmetics factory. Huddled between huge crates of product, we sat on blankets atop the cold metal floor. I asked Dora how her bullet wound felt. I couldn't imagine that with all the running and hiding we had been doing it wasn't bothering her, didn't it need at least a change of dressing. She thanked me for asking, lifted her blouse, showed the hole in her side. It was still angry and red, but also small and clean.

"Our monks know things you can't imagine about such injuries," she said. "They come from a world of swords and spears and harnessing energy. They see the body differently. It's not a material thing to them but waves of *qi* flowing across a sea of emotion, intention and unfolding. If they can align their intention with the waves, they can guide them to heal, to grow, to repair."

I had the sudden urge to rub her feet, so I took off her shoes and did so, chastely. She closed her eyes and offered no complaint. The six-hour ride was bumpy and seemed longer. The only real break in the monotony was when we ate some of the food we'd brought along, and, using crates for privacy, employed a corner of the truck as a toilet. Much of the time we lay with feet entwined, a default position mandated by the space we had but maybe by more than that. Dora slept while I thought about Lulu. I tried to visualize the surgery. I had researched all kinds of surgical entries into Lulu's brain during those first weeks of her coma, so I was easily able to envision Granate removing the top of her skull, reaching into the folds of her brain with his forceps, and teasing away layers of brain tissue in pursuit of Hector-The-Bullet. I imagined that just as Granate cleared the pathway,

Lulu pushed the bullet into his hand by her explosive force of will. That was the way I saw my wife — as capable of just about anything.

I told Dora that I felt I understood the chaos of the universe better now than I had before meeting her and her family, that I'd been thinking about her comment about deep time. I told her that I was beginning to accept that I could neither control nor understand the world and the life I was caught up in, that I doubted that human beings would ever really understand why or if a god had sent a bullet to a brain or brought about the creation of twin children. In return, she told me more about her family, told me that if I hadn't already figured it out, her father was the innovator and the dreamer while her mother was the organizer and business person, though she had an unexpectedly green thumb and soft touch with the animals she was bent on saving. Dora also told me that while they were both devoted to Lord Hun, they were also very serious about preserving and protecting the family's mission and good works.

In addition to details of the family interests, she also told me about the history of Tianjin. By the time we arrived, I knew that the independent spirit of the place that had started a thousand years ago and persisted through the Boxer Rebellion of 1900, when local thugs protesting foreign influence on the country conspired to throw out the forces of the imperial west. I didn't get much chance to suss out either the city or its people, though, for the moment we entered the Tianjin Port Free Trade Zone, we got another ride through the vast industrial landscape directly to the family facility. It was a gigantic place, and a retinue of factory bosses and supervisors gave us a royal reception and followed us single-file as Dora led me to a little enclosed electric cart.

"The indoor greenhouses go on for acres," she said. "We're better off riding than walking. There's so much to see. My father based this cart on a little German Messerschmidt three-wheeler from the late 1950s. He had a model of it on his desk. We didn't really need it, we could have used a golf cart, but it's just so cute. This one is made of superstrong, lightweight materials. Gives off no pollutants that might be taken up by the plants. Not even from the tires. And it makes no noise. My mother believes plants can hear."

"Thus the background music."

"It's Chinese opera. You wouldn't believe the arguments about that. My father wanted Bach, And the cage around the cart? It's because all the plants and the high humidity can lead to indoor showers in here."

"You're saying the facility has its own weather?"

She smiled as if she was a high-school student at a science fair. "Fog, too. From the sprinklers. We're beyond state of the art here. We're breaking totally new ground."

I wasn't sure which was more impressive, the greenhouses where the family grew the herbs that could substitute for animal parts in medicinal plants or the processing plant that turned the plant material into faux animal bits with convincing size, color, and texture.

"Do you market these things as animal products or as animal product alternatives?" I asked Dora as we cruised through what seemed like miles of production lines, again staffed by seemingly cheery workers, not robots. "I'm not exactly clear how you go about selling the stuff."

"Alternatives," she said. "There are some diehards who are just never going to give up the real thing and try something new, but there is a whole new generation that is more sensitive to the environment and more aware of animal suffering, yet still wants and needs results."

"Fantastic," I said. "But I'm here for Lulu. What does all this have to do with wasps?"

Her answer was to steer the cart toward a big black button on the wall. She got out, pressed it, and a steel door in front of us slid open on tracks. We drove through, and the door closed behind us with a thunk.

32

ZHOUSHAN'S pine-scented air banishes the stress of the ferry fight almost at once, cleaning me from the inside out, bones to skin. Ti and Long Long seem eased and in better spirits, too. We hide the ferry deep in reeds along the bank, tie it to a thick tree so even the fast breathing of the tide will not disturb it, cover its deck with branches and twigs and leaves, and follow a dirt path up a steep and rugged coastline to a lookout. From there, in the morning light, Long Long shows me that there are other islands close by. All are mountainous and look as rough as the one on which we stand. He explains why the Taoists are here, that the *feng shui* of the watercourses weaving through the land masses with their forests and peaks creates a powerful spiritual energy for devotees of nature and its beauty and power. What he does not say, but what I am able to immediately divine, is that such an intricate landscape must contain many, many places for people in trouble to hide.

Through all this, Ti holds tightly to my hand. She does not have to tell me that she feels fearful and adrift, her life irredeemably changed through her association with me. I yearn for a way to reassure her, but in fact have none. We follow Long Long trustingly. On the water, the light was flat, even at dawn. Away from the water and in the shadow of mountains and trees, it is murky, changeable, and moody. I see the interplay of yang and yin and think about my brother. I wonder how his campaigns fare against the Jurchens. I wonder if he is well and safe and enjoying the support of his men. A jellyfish of regret stings me sharply. I might have listened more carefully to his reservations about Fu Po, but I realize that one way or another, I had to leave Yidu Town. I wonder if my mother is terribly lonely without me there to fuss over and chastise.

I miss Father.

What surprises me most here is the silence. Everywhere else I've been, even my beloved birch forest, had a rhythm and pulse I could detect as easily as I had the crab eyes in the tea water I prepared for my grandmother the day she died. This place is different. It is hidden from me. It neither takes energy nor gives it. Sound is invisible here. There are only Ti's feet crunching dirt and Long Long's strained breathing rising, gradually, up and back into the forbidding light. I feel something new and strange and recognize it as a cousin of something else I felt the day of the tiger, the day my childhood came to an end. I'm afraid, but I don't know what I fear.

Long Long chews herb twigs. Ti hums tunelessly. The air becomes thick enough to cling to my hair. I let it down and shake it to be free of the damp. Long Long says we'll be at the monastery soon, but his sense of time is different than mine, because we do not reach it until late afternoon.

The buildings are nestled against a mountain, positioned to align with the notches of the surrounding mountain peaks so that the light percolating between those peaks illuminates monastery walls painted orange in tribute to the hues of sunset. Once inside, we follow Long Long's increasingly slumped and halting gait through beautifully-tended garden. Miniature trees are everywhere, each one deliberately stunted to never create too much shadow, branches trained with wires and sticks into shapes dear to the Taoists: snakes, turtles, characters for longevity, qi, the Great Stillness, and the interplay between yang and yin.

Above us rooflines sweep upward gracefully up like the prows of ships. The roof tiles are blue, indicating the liberal use of the expensive stone lapis lazuli, a thumbnail-size chip of which Father once gave my mother and which she treasures. The pillars and beams of the walkways and halls are of a dark wood whose name I don't know. Weathered by sun, wind, and rain, their diameter dwarfs any birch, pine, or oak. Brightly painted statues of Taoist gods watch us pass and the fine murals on the ceilings, replete with trigrams and characters, look to have been painted by masters. The place is old and busy, though far neater and tidier than other crowded places I've been. All the same, I can see playful flicks of Lord Hun's finger in the the stains of bat shit on statues, in the roof leaks that create stains on the floor, in the nests of pigeons and in the bone-and-mouse-hair owl pellets on the ground. All the men wear the same robes as Long Long does and their feet bear the same sandals. These men don't stink as most men do. Long Long tells me that this is because they all bathe daily in the cold, pounding, white stream of a waterfall a few steps up the mountain.

My arrival at the Song capital went utterly unnoticed but my appearance here causes a stir. First, Ti and I are the only women in evidence. Second, Long Long has been missed and elders are waiting to speak with him. We proceed to the central hall in which there is only one shrine, this one to the local forest god — large, gilt in gold, and lit by torches fastened to the walls. A line of white-bearded elders have questions for Long Long. Listening to his answers, I discover that the priest was not in town only to indulge his appetites, he was there on a political mission. I try to understand the sides, the points of view, the core of the conflict — where there is politics, I have learned, there is always conflict — but it is all beyond me.

"The Song court is run by a man called the Crooked Chancellor," Ti explains, whispering.

"My brother mentioned him," I say.

"He eats only rabbit grass and manipulates the emperor, who is a child. Fu Po's father was his friend but the common people are not. Genghis Khan is coming. Our armies cannot stand up to them. When they fall, the dynasty falls, men are slaughtered, women raped, children enslaved, granaries plundered, treasures stolen forever, and our cities burned to the ground. The chancellor negotiates with the Jurchens and their Jin dynasty, with rebel groups, with anyone who will side against the Mongols, but these priests feel his judgment is poor and his alliances are shaky. They seek to wrest control of the court from him, to install their own minister and generals who they feel are more likely to preserve us. Long Long was speaking with people about these things in the capital. That is how he knew my master."

Ti's eloquent recital makes me dizzy. I know little of city politics, have only heard whispers of such intrigue, and share everyone's fear of the Mongols, even though they remain some distance off and I have no personal experience with either their ferocity or their misdeeds. I have been hoping this place would offer refuge for me, that I could be myself here, away from tigers and men who would hurt me, free to enjoy the company of my friend, perhaps have new adventures in love and nature. Instead, I find myself back in the same stew I left in the north. Despite the serene beauty of their mountain monastery, these scentless men in robes are no different than anyone else I have met; they are schemers despite their avowed worship of natural law. They are, by their nature, no friend of Hun. I feel the pickle of sweat in my armpits. Despite my stubbornness, determination, and conviction that I know what is best for me, I feel despair.

And that is when I see him.

He has such presence. He's tall and broad and his arms bulge through his yellow raw silk uniform. He stands while the monks around him sit. He feels my eyes and returns my gaze. His eyes are slits, his lips move but not to say anything. Ti nudges me. I kick her. I go to him. She tails me, grabbing at my hand. I shrug her off. His eyes go to my spear.

"You can use it?" he asks, pointing with his chin.

"I can."

He nods. "Your language. North?" "Yidu."

He laughs. "The new capital!"

"No such thing. Just a small town."

"If the lord lives there, it's the capital, yes?"

"No lord there," I say.

"Have you not heard the name Yang An Er?"

"I have," I say cautiously.

"Then you know he ran the Red Jackets."

"Against the Jurchens and their new Jin dynasty," I say. "Not to be emperor."

"That's what I thought," he says. "I was wrong. That's why I'm here, not there."

The blood rises to my face. I demand to know why he makes such a jest and he unfolds himself and stands a bit straighter— now I can see that the top of my head is no higher than the middle of his chest—and assures me it is no jest at all, that he, too, comes from Yidu, that he knows An Er personally, that he has also had some involvement with the Red Jacket brigade, though now he fears they have lost their way.

As he speaks, I sense the presence of Hun, and with him, his minions, Grandmother, and Mu.

You know him.
Everything is right on schedule.
You met the Five Pecks monk for a reason.

"You're Li Quan," I say, interrupting his narrative.

He recoils. His hand goes to his sword. Mine goes to my spear. His blade comes out. Ti gives a cry. It is not so subtle nor reptilian as Fu Po's dark menace, but it is oversized, a blade that could only be handled by a man of his size, and it appears red in the torchlight. I can tell by the shift of his footwork that he is looking for my throat, if not to pierce it then to threaten me into telling him how I know his name. I divine these things because each meeting I have with a man, particularly a man good with a sword, lifts me to a higher level of sensitivity. I am better at sensing deception, too, and I sense none of it here. In fact, I sense something else.

Round and round goes my spear, deflecting his movements while pulling him inexorably toward me. He thinks I am yielding, or perhaps that his attacks are more than I can handle. I want him to think exactly this. The council of monks cease grilling Long Long to watch us. Someone grabs Ti and yanks her clear of the fracas. Li Quan presses what he thinks is his advantage. I see an opportunity to put my spear through his foot while avoiding his blade. The opening tempts me, I would be lying if I claimed it did not, but something keeps me from it. A few seconds later, there is another opening, this one to pierce his left shoulder in such a fashion that he would never wield a sword so proficiently again. This time, too, I let the opening pass. I know I smile, though I try not to, and I know he sees it and it infuriates him. His temperature rises, I can feel his heat. That's how close I have let him come to me, that is how successful my spirals are, my bending, twisting, and jumping. May I say I take joy in it?

May I say that, while those present fear for my life, and Long Long in particular appears ready to vomit, there is something unaccountably erotic in the exchange for me, which is why I take my time before I let him have his way.

When I do so, it is with the utmost artifice. If he is to believe it, if I am to continue the weaving of the spell, he must believe I have lost my footing. There is no way, at this point, that he would not suspect me if I seemed to misjudge my distance. I make it about a spot on the floor, one I identified when approaching him, although I had no plan for all of this at that time. I make the slip tiny, but it is enough for him to get past my spear point and put his sword to my throat. He uses the edge, not the tip, which is how I know he does not intend to kill me.

"Don't," I say, dropping my weapon and putting hands gently on his. "I am your lord's sister."

There is a moment of confusion. He frowns. Then his eyes go wide.

"Miao Zhen!" he breathes.

33

THE ROOM we had stepped into looked and smelled like a zoo. One wall was lined with cabinets and drawers made from plastic containers of the sort a busboy might use to clear a table after a big party. The other walls bore lavish bird cages replete with fantastically plumed inhabitants hopping from branch to branch. In the center of all that, just the way a courtyard might be in a house, was a lush stand of tropical plants, broadleaf jungle varieties of the type my mother always tried as houseplants—bird-nest ferns, *Pothos*, *Spathiphyllum*, lobster-claw *Heliconia*—though they never thrived either in our air-conditioned home or outside in the dry Southern California air. Brightly-colored lizards skittering through that foliage, and in the middle of that miniature jungle, in a clearing barely big enough to clear the three legs of a wooden milking stool, sat a woman the size of a leprechaun.

I knew from what the family had told me that this was the repository for the world's most endangered creatures, but in all that valuable wonder what struck me as the rarest of the rare was the tiny woman herself. Wizened and ancient, with stringy hair, brown skin, penciled-on eyebrows, and gnarled hands, she watched our approach without blinking an eye. Dora got out of the cart and kowtowed to her, knocking her forehead on the floor as I had seen supplicants do in movies. I managed my own theatrical flourish, with one hand behind my back like a sommelier pouring wine. She smiled at Dora but only acknowledged me with a nod.

No smile, though, and no word of greeting either. Rather, she rose unsteadily and lead us to the racks and slid out a gray bin. Inside was some bright green moss. She reached under it and pulled out a small turtle with a café-au-lait shell and a bright yellow head. She pointed. "Chinese box turtle from Hainan Island," she said in Mandarin difficult for me to understand, mostly because of her missing teeth. "Species extinct, la. Last male alive. Need to find a girl for him. I have my feelers out."

"She has a worldwide network," Dora whispered in my ear. "People who run computer hunts for her, hobnob with collectors and aficionados, and put boots on the ground wherever the species in question comes from."

The tiny woman closed the drawer and moved on to another. Inside was a startlingly blue butterfly. The color was cobalt, but washed out and delicate as fine old china, the edges fading to brown and then fine white hairs. I recognized the bug. My mother had done a watercolor of one. "Palos Verdes Blue," I said. "But they've been extinct for years!"

"Everybody think so but not true, la," the woman smiled, showing only a single tooth in her upper gum and another, off center, in her lower. "Rarest in the world. They breed like roaches for me."

Dora pointed to a door nearby. "There's a conservatory in there," she said. "She succeeds with breeding other rare species, too."

I produced my camera. Who could resist photos of such a thing? The moment she saw it, the old lady shrieked and batted at it. Dora put her hand in front of the lens. "No photos in here," she said.

I put the camera away. "I didn't think it would look like this. Your mom's project, I mean. It's so high-tech, so businesslike, and right next to the factory."

"What counts is the results, right? We have more species here than you could possibly imagine and Shu Chun runs it all from her little stool in her little jungle here. My mother may have the knowledge and the drive, but Shu Chun provides the magic. She has this amazing gift. She understands the needs of any living creature. She can raise anything, Solomon. After all, she raised Lihua and Bik and me."

"She was your nanny?"

Dora nodded. "You would never have guessed, right?"

"Honestly, she seems, um, an unusual choice."

"But a wise one. My parents met her in Singapore decades ago, right after they got married. She's very spiritual. Pure. Intense. Her mind is utterly unclouded by artifice and unpolluted by culture. She lives in service to Hun and always understands what's going on. She immediately sees right to the heart of everything. She tells it like it is. There's no arguing with her because she's always right. The problem is, she feels everything so intensely that what happened with my sister, what she became and what she did, broke her."

"What do you mean, broke her?"

"The first murder, the boyfriend? Shu Chun refused to accept it, even though she had scolded Lihua for what she did to animals so surely she had some inkling something bad was brewing. She went wild screaming and scratching when she heard about it the boy. First, we put her in a hospital, but she talked too much so we had to bring her back home. My mother gave her a pet, a little monkey. She carried it around like it was a baby. Cooed to it. Fed it from her teeth. I know, I know, but she had more of them back then. Most monkeys get wild after a while but she had a way with that little guy, a natural gift with animals. We would never have known about it if Lihua hadn't started her craziness. A silver lining, I suppose."

"Don't say that," I said. "There really isn't one of those."

Shu Chun opened another, larger cabinet. The back side of it was mesh and so was the top. Inside was a y-shaped branch. I had the odd thought it would have made a great crutch for the old woman — it was about the right size. I didn't immediately see the inhabitant in the dim light, but when it turned its head and opened its giant yellow eyes, I did. It was about the size of a squirrel, with a pink and pointed nose, silver fur, and a long tail.

"Dwarf lemur from Madagascar, la," the old woman cooed. "Nosy Hara island race. Most rare primate on planet."

"Look at those testicles," Dora murmured.

Indeed, the animal was formidably endowed. If a man were similarly proportioned, he'd be wearing grapefruits. Shu Chun clapped her hands, laughed again. "Famous for that," she cried. "Small balls small price, big balls big price. So much value is why there are no more. I get them going, though. More and more babies, la!"

The show went on: a naturally-mutated python from Borneo, snow-white albino but with gold-and-blue eyes, already sold to a breeder in New York City who would sell its babies for a fortune; birds Shu Chun claimed were Carolina parakeets, American birds thought to be extinct since 1918, but instead secretly bred in a Hong Kong billionaire's aviary; a primordial New Zealand reptile called a *tuatara*, with an eye on the top of its head, and many more. We were with Shu Chun for hours, and despite the fascinating creatures, the pressure to know what had happened with Lulu's surgery was finally more than I could bear.

"I have to call home," I said. "I have to find out how Lulu's doing."

"I don't have another disposable phone right now," said Dora.

"What about using one of the factory phones?"

She stomped the floor in frustration. The reaction was so Lulu, it took my breath away.

"Don't you get it? Ping is listening to everything now. She knows about these facilities. Every call to your family or the hospital will be monitored. Call your mother, your sister, your brother, she'll know in half a minute exactly where we are."

"What about Lulu's doctor?" I said. "Or the hospital itself? There are so many extensions, there's no way she could cover them all."

"The stakes are too high. There's nothing you can do anyway. You just have to wait."

Suddenly, the little woman was tugging at my jacket. The look on her face made me wish I'd had that last conversation with Dora in English, but it was too late.

"Who are you?" Shu Chun asked. "Who is Lulu?"

Looking down at the ferocious expression on that tiny face, her very gaze a spear, I suddenly knew that everything Dora had told me about her was true. There was no lying to this astonishing person. That's when I decided to tell her everything. Lihua had fled to America. She had become Lulu. We had fallen in love. I was her husband. We lived together in City of Angels, California, land of the free, home of the brave.

Despite the fact that Dora was shaking her head violently and begging me to stop, I knew that I had to do what I was doing. I was not there for show and tell. I was not there to make friends with Lulu's family. I was there to find those wasps and bring them home and save my wife and save my children. Despite the little woman's disbelieving expression, I kept right on talking. I told the Shu Chun exactly what had happened to Lulu. I told her about the shooting. I told her about Hector-The-Bullet. I told her about the upcoming surgery, and that I needed to see the honey right away because somehow the honey would bring me the wasps and I'd been sent to get those wasps, whatever the hell they were, and goddamnit I was going to do just that. I was going to bring them home.

When I stopped talking, Dora was plainly furious, disapproving of my plan and probably having a better one. The little woman, however, was far beyond disapproving and far beyond furious; she looked like she was going to explode. Her eyes bulged and her breath was loud and raspy and her finger pressed into my chest.

"I don't believe what you say," she cried. "Not one word, la."

Hearing those words, seeing my chance evaporate, I did the one thing I had not done since I arrived in China. I unbuttoned my shirt, reached inside it and withdrew the thing I'd kept closest to me since I'd arrived in China, closer even than my feelings for Dora. I wrapped my fingers around it and pulled it out. I peeled off the taped-on tissue I'd wrapped around it and thrust it at the face of the tiny, toothless sprite.

"What about now," I hissed angrily, presenting Lulu's jade pendant. "Do you believe me now? See these flecks of red? They're Lulu's blood! My wife's blood."

Far from being in any way gratifying, the effect on the old woman was grotesque. Her face twisted until its curves matched her spine's, pathological, dysfunctional, harsh. She let out a shriek that stopped dead every living thing in the room, a sound that made Dora cover her ears and avert her eyes. Then she began circling the room rapidly, running in front of the cage and trays, knocking things over, her body vibrating, her torso nearly horizontal, her breathing labored. It was an unforgettable display of personal anguish and sorrow, of feelings held so long, they had disfigured her, transformed her into another person, another creature entirely.

I was instantly sorry for what I had done but I knew I'd had no choice. This wasn't about me, after all, nor about the old lady or Dora. I was here for Lulu. I needed to know if she was still alive. It might make no sense at all, might be a fool's errand in ways utterly beyond my own comprehension, but I still needed to do what I told her I'd do.

I needed to bring back those wasps.

34

WHAT BROUGHT the big man and I together in that hall of monks? On the surface you could say I was looking for refuge and he was in search of allies, but down deep it was Lord Hun, who uses chance like an aphrodisiac and coincidence the way I use a spear, though far more deftly Maybe, if I practice for the rest of eternity, I will become half as good at cuts and parries and thrusts as he is, a fraction as able to bend the world to my will while recognizing how shallow my ambitions and intelligence really are. I have been a leaf in the wind, willfully naïve regarding the politics of my time and the grander forces threatening to extinguish my family and my people. Perhaps this is because my childhood was so brutally ripped open. Perhaps it is because I was born with a galaxy of spirals within me. Whatever the reasons, I am grateful to be here, with Li Quan.

You might not imagine a monastery to be a romantic haven, but I have learned that if there is any religion in this large world that celebrates the joys of human union as the full flower of natural law, it is Taoism. As such, the monks are forbearing, amused, supportive, and even forthcoming with techniques to help us deepen our pleasure. Though we begin with sword against spear we end up in each other's arms. When it comes to true love, the spark that ignites must come first, then the flaring into heat of kindling twigs, then a breeze to turn the flame into an inferno, and finally, forged in all that heat, something ineffable that will last and last. Accordingly, the revelation of my identity was followed immediately with small talk. Li Quan wanted to know how long I had been afield and what path brought me here; I wanted news of home, to hear the town was safe from marauders, to know the details of how my brother came to anoint himself monarch.

My parents were well, at least as far as Li Quan knew. He had heard that my mother was delighted by An Er's desire to establish hegemony over the region. Her opinion seemed to be that, despite my brother's youth, his personal magnetism and strategic brilliance entitled him to the highest position in the land. Why be a mere rebel-leading general if the forces against which one was rebelling were themselves the fragmented and disorganized remnants of a dynasty defeated? Why not capitalize on one's local roots—a father who was a mayor, for instance— and sow the seeds of what might, dare she suggest it, become a new dynasty? Why not, in short, lead people who needed to be led using the support of those who already did?

According to Li Quan, Father saw things differently. He had always been torn between his love for his son and the recognition that my brother, while a very good fighter, has what is perhaps an insupportably high opinion of himself. The word was, he had reminded An Er of his humble beginnings as a saddle salesman, a fact no self-proclaimed lord bandied about, particularly in heated fashion in front of a lieutenant. I wasn't surprised by Father's reaction to An Er's regency any more than I was by my mother's. Others may bow down in obeisance but Father did not, not even to the governor who appointed him mayor, and certainly not to his own son. I found myself hoping An Er would listen to Father, and would follow his counsel as any king might a trusted advisor.

The monastery's Taoist garden bears a feature I have never seen before. Large rocks, placed according to the most sublime *feng shui*, dot the paths like sentinels. According to Li Quan, each has been found in precisely the form in which they appear in the garden. Their shapes evoke miniature mountains, replete with chasms and peaks, and gives the stroll we take together the feeling of a spiritually uplifting montane journey, a climb to the realm of the immortals. It is in this sacred space, this ode to nature's beauty and proportion, that Li Quan shares his own opinion of my brother's action. Later, I will come to know that the big man expresses his deepest judgments rarely and with reluctance, for he is of the mind that a cultivated person ought to be able to discern things without judging them.

He tells me An Er is wrong to have anointed himself as he did. To be lord of a small, autonomous region is to be a meaningless monarch. It demonstrates the sort of hubris that will only invite attention and ultimate ruin. He confesses that he has offered my brother's men a different vision, an alliance with the south that will legitimize the ragtag militia and give them legitimacy and resources. He is willing to work with my brother, even work *for* him, but he wants them both to be part of something greater.

"An Er won't have that," he says. "He is too blinded by the way everyone kowtows to him now. This is a shame. I would have worked with him, would have even served him, but now I'm here to meet with the Crooked Chancellor and these influential monks are going to help me. I'll put together an army bigger than your brother's, and when his little empire rots from within, I will step in and protect the lands I love from what I know is to come. I can only hope you don't hate me for this, for I know blood is thick and that you are surely a good sister to him."

I walk next to him as we speak together. Another woman

might stay a few paces behind and even shield her face modestly with a hood, but I am not she. As he goes, his hips roll easily and his feet remain planted, despite the twists and turns of the path. His battle sword, slung diagonally across his back, barely stirs. He moves like a mountain and feels like one, too. When our arms brush together tiny human lightning erupts at the point of contact. I know he notices. Later, when we return to his quarters, it appears between our lips. I ask him if he would like Ti to join us. Because he does not yet know of my appetites, he takes this for a test and says no.

It is not a test.

Do I run too quickly to men? Do I give myself too easily? Certainly not. There are a hundred men, a thousand men — women, too — who want me and whom I ignore. But when I see what I want, when I see whom I want, I do not hesitate. He is a man of war, not love, and while I am certain he has been with many women, he has never been with anyone like me. I enjoy looking up at the line of his chin from below, at the fluttering of his hooded eyelids, and at the way his fists clench and unclench as I do what I do. At one point I caress his knees and he reacts as any warrior would, twisting his thickly-corded muscles to protect such a vulnerable spot. from there I see the swell where his back meets his thighs and am reminded again of a horse by the bulge of his thickly corded muscles.

When I sit astride him and proclaim my ownership, he laughs. It is not a demeaning laugh like other men I have been with, like that first night in the tent with the treacherous soldier, Liu. That seems an age ago and a different world. No, it is a laugh of delight, a sign that a bond has already grown. He puts his feet flat on the bean mattress supporting us and rises and falls, rises and falls. I touch his cheek at the edge of his eye and trace a line to his lips and then to his ear. I whisper his name and he whispers mine.

"You came all this way to meet monks," I say.

"I came all this way to meet you," he answers.

"Lord Hun works in mysterious ways," I say.

By way of answer, he reaches above his head and fusses with something below the line of the mattress. Later, I will learn he asked the head monk to put it there while we were in the garden. I pout. I want his hands back where they were. Then, suddenly, he lifts them in the air and throws something. The warrior in me would ordinarily react defensively, but I am beyond such things with Li Quan. What he throws is a cluster of dried flowers. Gardenias from the southern lands, something he has encountered in his time in the Song capital among the generals there. They rain down on us, mostly on me. They land in my hair. The wall lantern singes a few, but even burned, they smell like heaven.

I start to cry. He kisses my tears. I pivot around and grab his ankles and move differently to pleasure us both. His hands are warm on my haunches. I feel myself slipping away. Where I am is beyond passion. It has happened impossibly quickly, but where I am is in love.

And then I hear my wasps.

35

WE COMFORTED the old woman as best we could, but even with Dora's strokes and kisses, it was a quarter hour before she stopped gasping and shaking, and more than that before a factory employee finally brought me a clean phone with which, against all protestations, I called the hospital about my wife. It was 3:00 AM in Los Angeles and I couldn't reach Dr. Granate, so I rang the nurses' station on Lulu's floor. When I said who I was and inquired about Lulu, they refused to give me any information. My mouth went dry with dread.

"Is Coraline working?" I asked, half afraid of the answer. They told me she was, but it took a few minutes to get her on the phone. When at last she answered, her voice trembled, sounding weak and distant. My dread increased.

"Solomon," she said. "Are you still in China?"

"Yes," I said. "With Lulu's family. Please tell me about my wife."

"She's alive."

"The surgery?"

"Yesterday. The bullet is out...."

"The babies?"

"They're fine. Actually, Dr. Granate ordered a series of scans of them over the last few days and they show no developmental abnormalities. He's astonished, as you can imagine."

"Tell me about Lulu."

"She came through with flying colors. The surgeon's a wizard. I've seen him work before. He kept the incision above the hairline and at the back of her head. You can't see anything at all from the front. Her MRI shows a reduction in inflammation. It's almost as if her body was willing it out. I think that's why it was moving, the bullet I mean. But look, I don't want to get your hopes up, Solomon. Granate wants to be the only one who talks to you. Lulu's still in a coma, still in that terrible posture, but I do think her spasticity is improving. It's easier to move her arm than it was before, although I can't tell you whether that means anything. When will you come back? Has to be soon, right? I mean, I sit with her twelve hours a day, but I'm not you."

"I'm working on the wasps," I said.

It took her a moment to remember what I was talking about.

"Ohhh," she said, slowly. "Right. What she wrote to us. There hasn't been any more of that. No more moving her hands. I've been watching."

"Thank you for all you're doing," I said.

"You really should be here."

"I will be soon."

When I hung up, I told Dora everything. Shu Chun listened, too, but seemed confused, so Dora gave her a fuller explanation in Chinese. Then, gently, Dora reminded her about the wasps. The old woman shuffled off into her tropical garden. When she came back, she carried a stretched-out plastic shopping bag in one hand, and a paper sack in the other. She pulled a jar of honey from the plastic bag. I didn't immediately recognize it as such because it was bright, raspberry red, but when she unscrewed the cap (I had to tap it on the floor to loosen it, first), I saw the sticky consistency.

"Taste with finger, la," she said, offering me the jar.

I put my pinkie in, an artist's affection I suppose, and brought it out dripping. I twisted to catch the threads of honey and brought it to my mouth. My lips went instantly numb. Dora saw my look of surprise and nodded encouragingly. It was when I licked the honey with my tongue that things began to happen. I'm not sure I will ever really understand them, ever be able to explain the sensations much less the mechanism of action in pharmacologic terms. What I *can* say is that my heart hammered in my neck, that I felt pressure behind my forehead, that I found my eyes blinking uncontrollably. I can also report that I began to see things. My hallucinations where not of monsters, nor did I experience flashbacks as I had when doing acid and mushrooms and even mescaline, once, with the curanderos in Mexico. Instead, I suddenly seemed able to perceive that discrete objects were not discrete at all, the empty space between them, the contents of the laboratory and storeroom for instance, not empty at all but rather filled with fine, shimmering, beautiful tendrils that wove everything into one continuous fabric.

Dora stuck her thumb into the honey and put another portion in my mouth. I grabbed her hand and held onto it, sucking her thumb like an infant at the nipple, running my tongue over her flesh. She looked with concern at Shu Chun but the old lady only smiled. I looked at the wisps surrounding Dora, surrounding Shu Chun, too. I saw that these wisps were expanding and contracting, reconfiguring, detaching, and fixing again, all in time with Shu Chun's breath and Dora's, too. When Dora finally pulled away, the plants in the old woman's jungle called to me. I stood in their midst and watched the tendrils in the air between them—I say in the air but I realize now that the emptiness of air is itself an illusion—and discovered that the plants were breathing, too, the tendrils between them shaking and moving in chaotic but beautiful fashion.

"Hundun," I heard Shu Chun say, but faintly, as she was some distance away.

I reached out to touch a spider plant, the sort with slender white-striped leaves. The plant's tendrils turned toward me. Without actually touching them, I waved my hand back and forth. The plant tendrils followed, apparently eager for connection. My hand grew its own tendrils and when they touched the plants they meshed. Somehow, I understood I was seeing energy and was so inspired by the realization that I watched it until the effect of the honey began to slowly fade and I could see it no longer. Afterward, I sat down on Shu Chun's milking stool and put my head in my hands. Reality seemed lacking. Sterile. Lonely. It was as if a beautiful symphony I'd been listening to had come to close and the hall in which I'd been listening, with the orchestra now silent, was filled only with echoes of a glorious past.

I wept. I couldn't help it. Was it the news that my children were apparently healthy? Was it the news that Lulu had survived the surgery and might even be improving? Was it the gift of the honey, the revelation of the true nature of the universe? Yes and yes and yes. Dora and the old lady came to comfort me. I felt their hands on my shoulders. I looked up and started to ask something. I can't remember what it was and it doesn't matter because Dora put her finger on my lips. The old lady took my hands and turned them palm up, side by side in my lap. She produced the paper sack, opened it solemnly, and shook its contents into my hands.

If I hadn't just experienced the honey, if I hadn't been so drained and empty, inspired, transformed, and barely able to think straight, I know I would have leapt up in fear. In my hands were twenty wasps. Although they were perfect in every way and showed no evidence of being dead or dried out, they were utterly and completely immobile. Some lay on their sides, others on their backs, and others looked like they were in mid-crawl. They were the largest I'd seen, identifiable only by their narrow waists and torpedo wings, their oversized stingers, and their striped, green-and-orange bodies.

"They won't sting?"

Shu Chun shook her head.

"The honey is from them?"

"What you had wasn't honey," Dora answered. "Honey is from bees. Bees gather pollen from flowers. These are wasps. Predators. The serum you had was what they use to fly long distances and hunt and kill other insects."

I stared at the creatures in my hand. This is what I had come to China for, I thought. Somehow, despite their dramatic coloration, they seemed small in my hand. I thought about what I'd seen. I looked at Dora. She was so beautiful, Lulu but not Lulu, even with the air around her free and clear and clean of her visible connections to the universe.

"Is it the nectar Lulu needs?" I asked.

"I don't know. Maybe."

"Necklace," said the old lady, reaching for it.

I took off Lulu's jade pendant and handed it to her. She turned it over and over in her hands, threading it through her fingers the way a magician seduces a coin, humming tunelessly. After a while, she thrust it into my empty palm and closed my fingers over it. She watched me closely then. Time passed and when I tried to shift or move, she grabbed me and held me still.

"Is something supposed to happen?" I whispered to Dora.

"I have no idea," she whispered back.

The old lady took my hand in hers. She waited. I waited. Nothing happened. She took the pendant from my hand and put it back around my neck. She seemed sad to do so. Disappointed.

There was no narrative to go with any of this, just her expressions and movements. She sighed.

"Kiss her," the old lady commanded.

"What?"

She pointed at Dora. "Kiss her," she repeated.

Dora's eyes widened. I leaned in and gave her a peck on the cheek. Shu Chun snorted. "You understand kiss, yes, American boy? Kiss her, la."

I felt a tremendous blush coming on. Dora turned to her one-time nanny. A flurry of Chinese ensued. A barrage, really, for it went on for a while, back and forth, and the best I could do to follow it was to turn my head back and forth as if I were watching a tennis match. Dora blushed during it too.

"Someone want to tell me what's going on?" I asked, trying unsuccessfully to interrupt.

At last, the exchange came to an end. "It's about the wasps," said Dora. "They do something special. She's trying to activate them, to get them ready to go with you."

"What does that mean, activate them?"

"Wake them up. She tried to tap into your connection with Lulu by using the pendant. She says it should have worked. Would work if...."

"If what?" I demanded.

She spread her hands.

"Kiss her," Shu Chun said again.

"Is this okay with you?" I asked.

Dora closed her eyes and nodded.

This time, I did better. I was shocked by how readily she parted her lips, and perhaps even more shocked by how quickly I parted my own. I hoped Lulu could forgive me, especially for noticing that not only was there more to the kiss than I had ever expected but more, in a different way, than there had been with

Lulu. I hated myself for the desire I felt, and almost as much for letting guilt interfere. There was a world in the touch of our tongues, so much that, at first, I did not notice the wasps moving in my hand, tickling my flesh with their tiny legs, shaking their wings, then leaving my palm.

In the air, they issued a low-pitched, rumbling sound, louder than any insect noise I'd heard before, including an apocalyptic invasion of the Palos Verdes Peninsula by cicadas when I was a teenager. I felt them circle my arm but I was too interested in Dora to look. Neither of us was willing to break the kiss, but Shu Chun was, and she did, gently, by shaking us and pointing at the wasps. Their intricate flight pattern had bound our interlocked hands in a cottony, gray cocoon. I hadn't been aware of it during the kiss but afterward I felt its light, tickling presence. It grew thicker and thicker as we watched, fascinated. The line of gray began creeping up our arms.

"You wait too long, you end up inside," Shu Chun declared.

Without further ado, she produced an unmarked spray bottle and aimed it at the wasps. I heard the hissing of gas but smelled nothing at all. "Carbon monoxide, la," she said.

The wasps dropped out of the air and she collected them carefully from the floor. Dora and I stripped ourselves of the cocoon. We could not look at each other.

"Dead?" I asked Shu Chun.

"Not dead," she answered. "Sleeping, like before."

Then she looked at the two of us, raised her index fingers, and brought them together in a pairing.

"You two, yes," she said. "Lihua, no."

It was at that moment we heard gunfire.

36

WHO CAN SAY what place my wasps call home? Are they in every birch forest, every pine forest, every oak forest, every tall tree, near water, in all the land, always ready to come forth like a loud, humming spear when summoned by true love? Do they live in heaven with Lord Hun and rain down, like tiny arrows of tiny wings and striped, slender bodies, to alight upon the target of the great lord's favor? What I can say is that Li Quan, despite his strength and stature, fears them. Any man would, for any man knows well that next to the great beasts of the forest, the tigers and lions and elephants and buffalo, nothing can kill its prey more surely and painfully than an angry swarm of wasps. Still, I shush Li Quan with my lips and wrap my legs around him to keep him still and make him feel secure. I draw his head to my breast to protect his eyes. I cover his ears with my arms. I rock him like a child while the wasps make their magic around us.

The inside of the cocoon is different than I could have ever imagined it when I first saw the tall one standing in the forest clearing with Mu inside. I expect it to be dark as a moonless night, but the wasps spin a rainbow of comfort, their threads as warm and soft as a woman's tongue on a man's root. The whole cocoon pulses with Hun's heartbeat, each contraction long and slow. Because it originates from the lord who understands all unfolding from the beginning of time to time's end, it is a rhythm to soothe the world. Rocked by Hun, we fly to other worlds there, together, one body. The big man whispers to me that he has wanted me ever since he saw me at the market, when he was just a boy and I just a girl. He had longed to ask Father for my hand but had worried the offer would be seen as no more than a way to mend bridges between him and my brother. He couldn't bear the idea anyone would think this, especially me. He tells me that the hardest thing about his feud with my brother was the wedge it drove between him and my family, making it less and less likely by the day that he would ever have me.

I marvel at these words. I wonder how I could have missed him as a boy, as such a beautiful man, how I could have been completely oblivious to his love all these years. I suspect Lord Hun in this and, specifically, his agents, my grandmother and Mu. How many times, I wonder, did my grandmother distract me from Li Quan to avoid a family feud? Did Mu lightly mention him to simply plant the seed in my mind for our future meeting at the monastery? I ask Li Quan about my grandmother and he tells me she once applied a poultice to his knee when he fell from the monastery wall. Another time, after my brother yanked him clear of a Jurchen arrow, she reset the joint.

"She was a powerful healer and my brother is a mighty warrior," I say.

He nods and tells me he has never seen better on either count. He tells me he knows Mu, too, the old man with a crazy, toothless grin and a wild cackle who sits perched in a tree and never comes down to take a bath and smells like a shit pit. He confesses to have sat at the base of Mu's tree and listened to his stories of the animals of the forest and the coming of rains and floods and dry spells and droughts and the rustling, subterranean battles inside the empire of the ants. He says he sometimes talked about war strategy with the old man. He says he heard Father talk with him sometimes. This makes me think Father knew of my destiny with Li Quan and, for this reason, never pressed me in the direction of another man, even though the whole town spoke of my beauty and the fact I was still unwed.

Does it sound strange that we would converse while making love inside a wasp cocoon? If it does, I say there are no rules that apply when Li Quan and I are together. We shatter every boundary as our juices run together and our flesh melds as one. Beginning as two, we become one, and with Hun there, we become three. Inside the cocoon, all bodily functions besides lovemaking are suspended. Free of need for food or drink or toilet, we remain coupled for three days of perfect bliss. During all this time, no monk disturbs us and even Ti, ever hungry for reassurance and conversation, manages to keep her distance. Near the end of that special time, and despite what I know of men's universal vanities, I confess to Li Quan that I let him best me with his sword, that as good as he is, as good as my brother is, I am better. I do so even though I realize he already knows this. I tell him I want not even one tiny secret between us.

Not now and not ever.

***

Is it an earthquake that tears the fabric of the cocoon and brings us crashing back to earth from heaven? Is it a strike of lightning from the hands of Lord Hun or a fire consuming the monastery? Is it my friend Ti's growing and unquenchable fear of the future, of what will become of a bath maid whose master was murdered by the very woman with whom she has fled the scene of the crime? It is none of these. Rather, we are exposed to the world once more by the slender, pale, lady-like fingernails of one Monk Long Long, who does the deed, driven by the news that the magistrate's men are at the monastery gate.

"Our boat broke free of its mooring," he explains, so panicked and breathless that he barely glances at our naked bodies. "It floated to another island and they went there first. That's why we've had this much time."

"Lord Hun," I mutter, thinking of the action of currents and tides that lifted our ferry and deposited it somewhere else, thereby commanding magisterial attention.

"But they're here now," Long Long moans.

"How many?" Li Quan demands. I know he needs this information in order to formulate a plan of either battle or retreat.

"Twenty-five," says Long Long. "They are afraid of Miao."

Li Quan smiles. He can't help himself. "And what rank is the most senior commander?"

"Captain," says Long Long.

"Not high enough," Quan mutters. "If he were a general he would be more confident in beating a strategic retreat at my request."

"I won't have you endanger your position," I tell him. "You have important work to do."

"I wouldn't dream of letting them have you," Quan says. "I will die first."

"Nobody's going to die," says Long Long. "There's a tunnel. But we must be quick."

"You, me, and Ti, then," I say.

He nods. "We are the three they seek. They don't even know General Li is here."

I will always regret that Li Quan and I couldn't spend more time in the cocoon together. A week would not have been enough. A month would have been better. But I strip myself of the last of the cocoon, grab my spear, and kiss Li Quan in a way that plunges Long Long into a fit of coughing.

"The birch forest," Li Quan says.

I look at him, not immediately understanding.

"Please," the monk wails. "We must hurry!"

"Your special place," Li Quan continues. "Where you train. Not this full moon, for that is tomorrow, but the next one. I will be there."

"You watched me...."

"Many times," he says. "Mulberry paper."

I marvel that I could have been aware of so much and yet not of Li Quan, that I could have been so very sensitive to all the workings of the world but have had a blind spot where a big boy, a big man, lurked. I know that Li Quan's passion will deliver him to me where he says it will and when. I turn and follow Long Long out the door. Ti is waiting outside in the corridor and I can hear her heart beating from ten paces away. Her face is stained with tears.

"I missed you," she cries, and runs into my embrace.

Yet this is not the time for reassurance; this is the time for action. Long Long runs better here than he did through the back alleys of the Song Capital, presumably because this is more familiar turf and he knows just where he's going. The tunnel is behind us in the mountain and we serially ignite the torches on the wall as we go. There are cobwebs and large, white cave spiders. I can't hear the magistrate's angry men talking with the monks, but in my mind's eye, I see their peaked black uniforms and austere expressions, their segmented staffs and halberds, their rigid sense of Confucian certainty despite their Taoist vows, their dedication to the letter of the law, regardless of the fact that it was Fu Po who broke my trust and treated me like chattel, and it was the same spoiled child who beat Ti when she failed to kowtow to him at the baths. Taoists can be so... practical.

I know Li Quan will be stalling the capital's enforcers, demanding an explanation for the intrusion, wanting to hear the details of the case. I know he will get the answers he seeks because he holds the rank of general, and because there is no way to link his name to mine. Because I'm thinking so much of Li Quan, indeed I am still thick with the scent of him and memories of our union, I am distracted. As such, I am surprised when the tunnel ends in a cave where a pack of wolves with pups are wintering.

Wolves are territorial. I know this from the birch forest. They tracked me there, and I tracked them, too. I knew where their dens were and they knew which was my favorite trees and the glade I favored for my practice. They chose their dens carefully there and I am sure they do the same here. They will not whelp when people are around they will certainly not whelp in the presence of bears. Since they are here, and the canine stench and piles of scat say they have been for a long time, I know the monks have not tested their escape route in months, probably years. The low growls and the glare from their yellow eyes tell me nothing will go well here.

Ti is terrified. She cowers behind me. "We should go back," she whispers. "Better taking our chances in court than being torn apart by these creatures."

Long Long is too afraid to speak a single word. I take a step forward. The wolves growl more loudly. I take another step and they rise up onto their long, tall legs, their necks angled down, their hackles up. I lift my spear.

"Too many," Ti wails.

She does not know what I know of wolves. I head straight for the largest male, the dominant animal, the leader of the pack. He snarls and lunges at me and I pierce him all the way through. I feel my sharp tip grate past his ribs, feel the drag of his thick heart muscle against my spear point, fight his jerking as he leaps in one last spasm of rage. I grab the shaft of my spear well forward of center and with some effort, lever his body off the ground until, dangling and dead, he issues a stream of urine that sets his followers cowering.

"Quickly now," I whisper.

Long Long and Ti rush past me. They make it out of the cave. The wolves gather around their fallen leader. I regret what I've done. I wish I could have used my Hun-like wiles to beguile or deceive rather than kill, but there is nothing for it now. I pass through the cave just as a cauldron of bats drops from the ceiling. They surround me, flapping and fluttering, their high-pitched cries a shrill serenade for my escape into the night.

I find it is early evening outside, just after dusk, and the moon is low and full and bright and the air is heavy with the promise of rain. I see a path before me but no sign of my companions. I follow it downward off the mountain and toward the water. I dare not call out, I just await our reunion. I come around a bend in the trail and find Long Long and Ti standing in a grove of giant trees. These trees have a presence, an intelligence, the ability to bear witness to what is about to transpire. I can sense this, and I know, too, that they are the giants from which the thick, dark monastery beams are made.

Ti and Long Long are not alone, sadly, but in the company of half a dozen men in tall red hats and black cloaks. They are the magistrate's men, for sure, but more senior than the ones I encountered at the ferry.

"They found the tunnel," cries Long Long.

One of the men smacks him on the head and his eyes roll up and he slumps forward. Ti cries out in dismay. Two men take her arms and pull her roughly. They tell me to drop my spear. When I do not comply, they put a sword to her throat. She screams at me to run, says not to save her, says we are all dead anyway if they catch me. For the second time in a week, I throw my spear. The point is still drenched with wolf blood so red drops trail its flight. It pierces the first man's neck, passes behind Ti, and catches the second one the same way. Both men drop, Ti breaks free, and I yank my weapon free.

Four men are left and two have Long Long. They drop him to surround me. These are better fighters than the ones at the ferry, older and seasoned, with rumpled clothing and grizzled faces. I would rather fight younger, faster, fitter men because such men are always in a hurry and thus always make mistakes. These men know time is on their side. They don't care about retrieving Ti, who runs into the forest ahead of us. They don't care about what happens to Long Long, who lies unconscious on the ground. There will be no more hostage games with them. They will capture me if they can and kill me if they must.

But for the noisy breathing of one man with a damaged nose, it is dead quiet in the center of this circle of swords. Taking small, shuffling steps, working together as if all eight of their feet are under the command of one mind, this highly-trained band of enforcers closes in. I hear a monkey chatter. A seed pod falls to the ground from a nearby tree but the men are not distracted, don't take their eyes off me for so much as an instant. Another monkey gives a call and throws something else, a handful of scat this time. The scat hits one of the magistrate's men on the head. He cannot but wipe it away, as it is foul and it drips down his face. Even so, he maintains his gaze. Truly, the concentration of these men is formidable. Even monkey shit does not distract them.

But the change in the moonlight does. At first, I think it is a cloud passing over the face of the turgid moon, but there is something in the feel of the forest, something familiar, which tells me it is not. This is not a cloud. I know it and the animals know it, the birds, the monkeys, the insects, the tigers. I wonder if the men know it though, because they seem discomfited. Even though they keep their swords steady, they shuffle slightly in their stances. They work their jaws. They say nothing, but I can hear them swallow. The moonlight fades even more, its cold whiteness giving way to a dense, disorienting darkness.

I have shifted the moon into the rising shadow of the world for you. Now go!

Hun is repaying me for what he did to me the last time he manipulated the alignment of heavenly bodies. The darkness brings back memories for me, and with those memories, an idea. I leap straight into the air. My hand closes around the branch above me — the other hand keeps hold of my spear — and I swing myself over it. I feel the edges of sword blades whistle past me, blindly because in such darkness, the men can only guess where I might be.

It has been years since I have moved through the top of trees. When I last did, I was a little girl. The thin branches of a tree's crown can support a little girl but I'm a woman now. Thankfully, this particular type of tree is the source for the massive beams at the monastery and as such would hold up an elephant. More, it is commanded by Hun to nurture and guide me as I climb higher, as sure of myself and my footing as when I was aloft with a sharp stick, cavorting in pursuit of squirrels.

Now it is dark again, as it was on the terrible day I lost Grandmother. This time, however, I will not lose hold of my spear. Instead I use it to break off four branches and use the edge of my spear point to sharpen them. As the silver edges return to the world, as the moon glow reappears, I swing across the branches in search of pointed red hats. I find that the men have lost each other in the darkness so that each presents a clear and unencumbered target.

I do not aim at the hats themselves, for stiff fabric can deflect such sticks. Instead, I hurl my little arrows at the medical point Jian Jing, on the gallbladder meridian, at the well of the shoulder, on the side of the neck. I know from Grandmother's teaching that if I pierce it deeply enough, I will reach the artery below. This is what I do, to one magistrate's man after the other. They fall as silently as Go stones in wet sand, each hears nothing of the other's demise. After the last one is gone and the moon is back in her palace, I say a quiet prayer of thanks to Lord Hun and climb down.

I call for Ti and I find her. She shakes and sweats even in the cool night but I warm and comfort her. Together we attend Long Long, or at least we try to. When we find him, we discover that he has left this earthly plane.

"They went back for him when you took to the tree," Ti tells me. "They were so very angry, they snapped his neck."

I mourn for my friend. I salute his loyalty. I feel rage rising within me. I turn back toward the monastery.

"You can't," Ti pleads with me, sobbing even harder. "We have to go. You've done enough. You have to save yourself. You have to save *me*."

She is an anchor around my leg as I trudge back toward the temple. The more steps I take, the harder she grips me. She will not be deterred, even when her chin is in the dirt and pine needles pierce her cheek. She will not let me go, even when the side of her soft body scrapes against bark and roots hard enough to make her cry out. She will not release me, even when I try to kick her off me.

"You would kill one friend to avenge another?" she moans, looking up at me. "You would hurt one who loves you just to let your anger run free?"

At last, her patience and devotion calm me and my hot rage abates. I set down in the dirt with her and cradle her. Together we weep for all we have been through, all we have lost, and all that is still to come. Most of all, we weep for our fallen friend.

Then we make our way to the water and we hail a passing barge and make our way back to shore, leaving behind our pursuers.

Leaving behind my truest love.

37

THERE WAS security at the factory, not merely aimed at corporate espionage, but specifically because of the family feud with Colonel Ping. Even so, Ping came in forcefully, and there was little the facility's security officers could do to stop her from entering the premises with her armored car parked outside and her heavily armed force of a dozen officers. We didn't see these men, with their riot shields and their bulletproof faceplates, until they were already deep enough into the factory to have breached the container that protected the door to Shu Chun's inner sanctum.

I will always wonder what bit of influence peddling the family used to get Ping to break off her deadly hunt for me and Dora back in Qingdao, and what measures she took to contravene that influence. I will also always wonder what broke the truce or stalemate and how Ping found us. Perhaps, as farfetched as it sounds, the hell-hath-no-fury blood feud between the colonel and my family really was too virulent to contain for long. In any case, I had to assume that once she was after us again, Ping surveilled all family holdings, monitored every telephone line, and pulled in data from facial recognition software nationwide. Then again, perhaps it was never about Ping versus the family at all, but more about the way the colonel herself had represented it to me; they were the parents of a serial killer who had taken lives on her watch and she was determined to bring that killer to justice.

Events that unfolded later pointed more to the last explanation than the first, but when bullets are flying, battering rams are in play, and a voice is calling your name through a bullhorn, much of this speculation is either idle, moot, or both. I'd like to tell you that Shu Chun was of some use, that her quasi-shamanic control of the wasps made a difference in the battle, that she used them to sting our way to victory by awakening them once more and sending them winging toward our aggressors and under those thick plastic visors they wore. In point of fact, the old lady vanished at the first sign of trouble. One moment she was there and the next she was not. I never saw her again.

Dora had a completely different reaction. "Really, this has to stop," she said.

I suppose I should have read between the lines on that one, but I was neither familiar with feuds between police and criminals nor did I know Dora that well. I construed her words to simply mean she was sick and tired of running from Ping, that she felt the vendetta against her family was unjust, and someone should just promise to extradite Lulu to China once she was well enough to travel. Whatever she was *thinking*, what she *did* was to run to the tool section of the room and came back with a hammer and a Chinese version of a Louisville slugger. She thrust the bat into my hand, then dragged me a few feet to a padlocked cabinet on the wall. I assumed it contained a first aid kit, but when she smashed the lock with the hammer and the door swung open, I was surprised to see a scuba-tank-sized canister inside, along with two over-the-head gas masks. She pulled out the masks, thrust one into my hand and donned the other. Then she yanked out the canister.

"Nerve gas," she said before I had a chance to ask. "Things happen in zoos. Creatures escape. Cages break. You haven't seen what's in the other rooms. We have tigers. We have venomous snakes. We have to be able to shut the whole thing down if it all goes to hell and have time to regain control."

"Control means killing everything?"

"Not killing. Paralyzing. We might lose some delicate little creatures but not many. And if we needed to use it, that would be an acceptable price. It's a fail safe."

"Effect on people?"

She answered by pointing at the mask. "Put it on," she commanded.

The valve atop the canister looked like a miniature trumpet with a lever below. Dora moved to the entrance the room. "They'll send in a drone first," she said. "Your job is to smash it the moment it comes through."

"Consider it smashed," I said.

Despite my confidence, the drone appeared so fast, I barely had time to wonder how Dora knew to expect it. It was a flying sphere containing propellers and a camera. The moment it headed for the ceiling, I hit it with the bat, sending it crashing to the floor in pieces as promised. Dora not loosed a cloud of colorless gas as policemen poured in. They fell to the ground almost instantly, all in uniforms, guns forward, hands and feet splayed, eyes wide.

"Oh boy," I said.

"They'll be all right. Like I said, it's paralytic but not fatal," she said, her voice wavering as she tried to keep up a brave front.

It took us a little while to find the colonel. She was hiding inside the little covered cart. Apparently, she had been bringing up the rear, had seen her men crumple, and deduced what was happening just in time to jump in and close the door behind her.

It wasn't a perfect solution, as the gas had still gotten to her, but she saved herself from a higher dose and was weak and slow but awake. She tried to raise her gun but Dora opened the car and took it from her.

"Lihua is dying," she said. "There's no point to this anymore. My parents are willing to forgive you. To forget everything. They ask only that you let it go."

Ignoring her, Ping turned her head to me. It was clear the move took massive effort, and when she spoke she did so slowly, the words slurred and burdened with far more accent than the last time she spoke to me.

"Where no flowers grow," she said.

Dora looked at me questioningly.

"She still wants to punish me," I said. "To send me to a freezing, windy prison where I'll die alone."

Dora's shook her head. "My sister is a monster, but in your own way you're just as bad, Ping. Do you really think her tally is greater than your own? I doubt it. If she has a demon inside her, then so do you."

Without knowing any of the specifics, it occurred to me that Dora's words explained so very much about Ping's obsession with my wife. There is nothing we judge so harshly as our own flaws manifested in others. I felt such gratitude to Dora then, such a debt on so many levels, that I went and embraced her. We looked at each other and I know a thousand things went through my head. I suspect a thousand plus one went through hers, because as many memories as I had of Lulu, Dora had more.

I am sure it was because we were so deep in those memories, and in the thoughts that accompanied them, that we didn't notice Ping produce the second gun. All cops have backup weapons, at least they do in the movies, so we no doubt should have been more careful. I was the one who noticed her movement first, saw the dull black object rising toward Dora. I had no time to grab for it and no time to push her out of the way, but I did have time to kick shut the door of the little car. She fired. The sound of the shot was muffled by the cabin. Later I found the mark where it hit the titanium door brace and ricocheted into Ping's throat, just above her bulletproof vest.

I'd like to say the colonel died instantly, but the truth is wide-eyed gurgling and twitching came first. If she had been able to speak, I'm sure Ping would have cursed me to hell and back and promised to come back in the next life to wreak vengeance on the entire family. I'd never watched anyone die in such violent and bloody fashion and the fact that she could still be thinking about revenge as she went to meet her maker startled me, driving home just how twisted the rogue officer really was. Hun, lord of chaos, twists, and turns, had probably intended intended this end for Ping all along.

Dora and I made our way out of the factory. Dora explained everything to the factory manager and suggested he leave Ping's men to awaken and clean up the mess. He wanted to know what do do with the animals if Shu Chun didn't return.

"Oh, don't worry about that," Dora told him. "They're all she has now. She'll be back."

Out of the building, we stayed in the shadows, watched the road as if we were eagles, the horizon as if we were storm chasers, the skies as if we were mice. Before we left, however, I collected the wasps.

38

BACK IN THE Song capital and heading north, we find the city full of smoke from lightning fires. I know this is Lord Hun's work, because the fires distract everyone, drawing all available men to man bucket crews along the Grand Canal and leaving so many alleys and streets empty for our safe transit. The smoke provides good cover, and with new fires constantly erupting it seems unlikely the magistrate will spare men to chase us. After all, in such times of crisis, important officials have better things to do than chase girls as a favor to spurned lovers, no matter how rich those lovers may be.

Although our passage through town is easy, it is hard to breathe with acrid ash and the tiny bits of people's lives— including their flesh and their bones—floating through the air. Ti and I hold patches of silk over our mouth and nose but the fine fabric becomes rapidly clogged and we have to press more and more pieces of our undergarments into this surface simply to keep on breathing. Over and over, Ti collapses and I have to wait for her to recover. It soon becomes clear to me that it is not only lack of air bringing her down, but guilt. She rues her role in the passing of Fu Po, who for all his foibles always provided for her, and believes she sees his floating ghost chasing after us. I tell her that any such phantasm is far more likely to be an amalgam of smoke and fire but she remains unconvinced. She tells me that she would never have taken me to the Cinnamon Forest if she had known what her master's reaction would be. She had no desire to hurt anyone, much less see her master die. She tells me everything fell apart because Fu Po was so possessive of me, She tells me that even though I felt ignored, she had never seen him so obsessed with any girl before, least of all herself.

"I know none of this is your fault," she says, even though she doesn't sound entirely convinced.

I want to tell her that if Fu Po was obsessed with me, he did a very good job of hiding it, particularly as our journey together wore on. I want to tell her that I think what happened at the brothel had more to do with his outrage at being defied than it did with his love for me. I want to tell her that Fu Po was selfish and self-centered, that this had been clear to me since the day I met him. Instead, I fuel her view of Fu Po, because I think it is easier for her to bear.

"I encouraged him," I say. "And I felt strongly about him, too. But I am nobody's possession."

Ti nods unhappily. She can't disagree with my point, though that word well describes her position in Fu Po's household and she knows it. We do not speak further about the subject, but she cannot shake her conviction that her master's ghost follows us. She sees him on fiery balconies, gazing down at us with eyes ablaze. She sees him in doorways, his black sword raised at us not in fealty but in fury. She sees his reflection in small canals, and she sees him with my spear piercing his flesh and his hands desperately on the shaft trying to withdraw it from his chest. When she sleeps, she cries his name, and it is during that dreaming time, while I stand guard over her, that I realize how much she loved him and how deeply she must love me to accept, as her friend and guardian, the very person who took his life. This quality of hers impresses me, for she is able to separate resentment and judgment, to dissect away what is right and true from what the heat of passion would have us believe. She has many fine qualities, my companion does, but this may be her finest.

Once we are clear of the city and on the road north, I increase our pace. My body loves to stride, my spear bounces, my satchel rides lightly for I don't need much. Ti, on the other hand, has shorter legs, a rounder torso, ad increasingly pendulous breasts. She has more and more trouble keeping up even as I expect the opposite, expect the road to teach and condition her. During the first week or two, I ascribe this to the fact that we take circuitous treks to avoid the main highway. This latter is easier going but is also filled with garrisons, merchants, beasts of burden, families fleeing the approaching Mongols, supply houses, and checkpoints manned by soldiers in possession of our descriptions.

Through all this, Ti does not issue one word of complaint. Even so, I am concerned not only by how much sleep she requires but also by her appetite, which seems insatiable, particularly for salty fish, stinky tofu, dried sweet plums, and horse jerky. It is a testimonial to my ability to ignore the obvious that I do not realize she is pregnant.

Yes, Ti is with Fu Po's child, which, of course, accounts for her spasms of guilt and regret. Privately, I worry that being a single mother without assets or affiliation will doom her to lowest station. Ti is a person who has an ongoing need to nurture others, and I can only hope she will carry the burden well. She grows rounder as we go and we go more slowly because of it. What should have been a journey of two weeks becomes one of four. In truth, this is a good thing as I relish the extra time we have together, and it spares me idly waiting for Li Quan in my parents' home, listening to arguments about my brother, fictionalizing an account of where I have been and what I have been doing since leaving Yidu Town.

As we near home, I take Ti into the forest and teach her to dig for herbs that will strengthen her body for delivery. Born and bred a city girl, she knows nothing of such things. It is in one of those forests, at a teahouse of my acquaintance, that I hear the innkeeper tell a traveling barber that the lord has perished from wounds sustained in a skirmish with the Jurchens. I keep my face composed and the tears from my tea until we retire to our quarters, a second-floor room at the end of the hall with the smell of stables rising from the floorboards and wafting in through the spaces between the beams. They are poor accommodations, but we are women traveling alone and without much means. Ordinarily, I wouldn't care about such trivialities, but mourning my brother here seems especially bitter.

Mourn him I do. My own tears surprise me, as does the ache in my heart that will not abate all the night through, despite Ti's most tender ministrations. I wail and rock and I will not be consoled. My brother was a hard and arrogant man but he loved me and our parents and he was a wonder with his blade and the kind of leader, despite Li Quan's reservations, who really made a difference in the world. It is during this mourning time that I resolve that I will assume the mantle he has left behind. I will lead the men myself, will strengthen and unite and protect our province. I will keep both the Song Dynasty dogs and the Mongolian wolves at bay. I share this ambition with Ti. I also tell her I will, without fail, avenge An Er's death by slaying his slayers and a hundred more of the Jurchen animals.

I will do so singlehandedly, and with that feat, become a legend.

***

My mother might have been brusque in her inconsolable grief. She might have ignored Ti or, worse, loosed her lashing tongue on her with prognostications of her end, miserable and alone, under a bare tree, shivering with all the other harlots and strumpets, lunatics and thieves. Instead, the loss of my brother has softened her in a way I could never have expected. She takes to Ti like a clucking hen, although the clucks are quiet and punctuated with sighs and, irregularly, with sobs. Father pays her less mind. He has one daughter and she is as a daughter of his should be. By contrast, the way Ti shares every thought and feeling and eats like a water buffalo without pulling a yoke to pay for the food is not very much to his liking. Still, he is a steady and gracious host, and gives Ti my old room in their home while moving me into my brother's quarters.

It is from those quarters, vibrating with An Er's spirit in a way no single doorway in the city ever really burned with Fu Po's, that I set out to meet Li Quan the night of his arrival. I have kept our love a secret from my parents. I want to present him to them in the flesh, not as a tale or apparition that gives soil to the roots of resentment or distrust. The moon that has been waiting for us hangs low and full in greeting, embracing the spring night with a penumbra that makes it seem twice the size it is, and even more welcoming. I measure my steps to my special grove with care. I am always awake and aware when I am in the wild, for the possibility of a tiger is never far from my mind. More, though, I don't want even the smallest misstep to keep me from my man. I am careful not to scratch my legs against a thorn and careful not to twist my ankle in a rut. Even a master hunter can mistake the signature silhouette of trees and become lost in the forest at night. This does not happen to me. In deliberate fashion, I make my way to my love and when I arrive at the grove, he is already there.

Often in life the anticipation is sweeter than the event, the fantasy larger and more perfect than the reality, the intensity of feelings a let-down compared to how one remembers them, the stature, beauty, scent, and touch of a lover less sublime the second time than the first. I grant this truth and I shove it away to the far reaches of the great sea that separates the Middle Kingdom from those of the great turtle who swam to Fu Hsi with the Lo writing on its back. Such sentiments have no place in my grove, no place in my love for Li Quan and his for me. We are complete only when we embrace each other, only when my breath comes through his skin and his through mine. We make love for as long as there is a moon, and once there is none, we play swords and spears with a package of mulberry paper he has brought for the occasion. Big and fast and strong as he is, Li Quan confirms that he is not my match, and because of this, I am his, and perfectly.

It has been some weeks since An Er's passing and Li Quan knows of it. I convince him that a son-in-law is precisely what my parents now need, that a path to grandchildren and heirs will provide them comfort after both secure old age and the perseverance of their blood. When we return home for my man to pay his respects, my mother is with him as I feared she would be with Ti. I don't resent her for this. After all, one can only expect so much. Father, on the other hand, is not only solemn and serious in the way he accepts Li Quan's proposal of marriage, but grateful. Watching the two of them, heads bowed toward each other over the tea table, mounds and furrows of dirt growing between their feet as they conspire and converse, I realize that Li Quan has always been in our lives, that he has long provided balance for Father in his dealings with his own errant son, that nothing could be more natural than that he should be here with us now.

In the time I have been gone, things have changed immensely.

254

Invaders have come and gone, my family has spawned a lord, and that lord has been killed. My transgressions, the deaths of a soldier by dagger and a boy by viper were never positively linked to me. There were only rumors and fears launched by resentment at my solitary beauty and the way I refused to be meat for the butcher. So, despite An Er's fears, when our wedding is announced, the town shows up in force and there is no mention of any of it. My befit one who is a daughter of the town mayor and the sister of the recently-deceased lord.

A surprise guest is Mu, if you can use the word surprise in any connection to that ancient sorcerer. He seems well and truly pleased by the festivities, not the least bit jealous of Li Quan (after all, he had his way with me when I was as good as a virgin and his most apt pupil ever) although at one point he transforms himself into a lynx, enters my bridal carriage, and, restored to his most youthful and appealing form, steals a kiss and a little bit more than a kiss. I can only say I am impressed by how he manages to enchant the four men carrying my palanquin so they don't respond to our dalliance but simply keep walking.

On our wedding night, I share with Li Quan my ambitions for our province. I tell him that we will fight the Mongols. I tell him, too, that we will ally with the Song without selling out our people, our territory, or our souls. He listens to me, but not so patiently, because it is our wedding night after all, and he wants things from me beyond military strategy. Even so, I inform him that it is my ambition that he be governor and I govern with him. I tell him I will train our men not only with spears but with spear

techniques applied to other weapons. With this training, born of tigers and mulberry paper, we will be invincible.

I tell him that we will be betrayed by our allies, I have foreseen this in a dream Hun gave me. I tell him the hordes of Genghis Khan will defeat us but, in the end, accommodate us too. I tell him we will rule the largest piece of land anyone but an emperor ever has. All this talk of conquering inflames him and all he wants is to conquer me.

So I let him.

39

I HID the wasps inside an emptied and opened can of shaving cream and secreted their nectar in a little tin labeled as lip balm. I put these items in my toilet-article kit and the kit into my knapsack. My mission in China accomplished, all I could think of was getting home before the wasps woke up and started buzzing. Feeling as if I had a bomb in my bag kept certain other thoughts and feelings from confusing me, slowing me down, forcing errors that might have gotten me caught. Although Ping's vendetta no longer drove the Yang family's internecine war with the police, my face was surely still on police computers and I was hardly free to move around at will or show up at an airport. After all, I was still married to a wanted criminal and I could be associated with the death of a colonel. That death weighed heavily upon me. Although I had intended no such thing, and it had been Dora who had loosed the gas, it was I who had kicked shut the door that gave the killing bullet its target. As much as I wished I could leave that memory in Tianjin, no such thing was possible.

Nor was simply boarding a cargo ship bound for LA. My wife's life hung by a thread and I gingerly held the spool. I sent my mother a text telling her I was headed home, then swapped my American clothes for typical Chinese ones. Dora bought a hijab at a market and, with only the sea to the east, we boarded a series of bullet trains headed west toward China's center. It was a whirlwind journey too fast to qualify as a tour, although Dora did give me a wonderful travelogue when she was not sleeping, the first real rest, in marvelously comfortable seats, that she'd had since our flight began. What we didn't talk about was that kiss in front of her old nanny, although I caught her looking at me a certain way from time to time and I know I looked at her that way, too.

The first major stop was Xi'an, an early capital of China and the eastern terminus of the famed silk roads from the Middle East and Europe. We had a four-hour wait there and used it to go to the old city and stand atop the ancient walls, looking down at the tourist shops and the bins of spices and brightly-colored goods in the Muslim market. The next stop in the circuitous route we had picked to discourage discovery was Chengdu. We had a bit longer to wait for exactly the train we wanted, and so explored the town for a few hours, visiting a museum dedicated to the period known as the Three Kingdoms and rife with examples of beautiful Chinese landscape painting, sculpture, and calligraphy.

Chengdu has a Tibetan quarter and we cruised it in a taxi so I could photograph the people visiting from the former mountain kingdom to shop for Chinese and international goods at low prices. I snapped images of temple items too: prayer flags and wheels, bells, hanging silk thangkas rendering Tibetan gods meant to represent anger, lust, envy, and other flaws and foibles of the human character, silver jewelry, statues of Buddha and Guanyin. There were also countless bracelets and malas, most plastic and some jade and lapis lazuli, which Dora told me were all fake unless they were mined in Afghanistan and sold with certificates in expensive stores.

When I told Dora how much I liked Chengdu's vibe, she said

she wasn't surprised. "This is where Chinese rebels and artists come. Stubborn people like you."

The next train took us to the major commercial hub at Chongqing, where we found a train to Kunming, capital of Yunnan Province, and the gateway to Vietnam, Burma, and Laos. That was a long train ride and Dora slept the sleep of the dead for almost all of it. The scenery relieved my boredom at watching the dry, brown landscape of northern China. It was dramatic, with peaks and valleys, and increasingly lush the farther south and west we traveled. Color, it seemed to me, made a comeback on that leg.

From Kunming, we transferred to a smaller, slower train to Dali, prehistoric man's entry point into the Middle Kingdom and the capital city of what had been two ancient empires before being razed by the Mongols. The family had people in Dali and Dora's brother, Bik, met us there. We took a several-hour taxi ride to reach the base of a mountain and then had to walk additional hours to meet Bik at a temple to Hun at its summit.

The walk through the mountains was a time of reflection for me. There were scores of deciduous trees I did not recognize along the path, most just beginning to show the earliest signs of fresh, spring foliage, many with beautiful flowers. I thought about my mother's watercolor paintings, about the love of nature that had led me to become a photographer, about the *curanderos* and what they saw beneath the surface of every forest, jungle, desert, and plain. I thought about the black tendrils rendered by the wasp serum and wished I could see them now.

I was glad to see Bik. He seemed calm, relaxed, and aware of every single thing that had transpired since we left Qingdao. He embraced me as a brother would, and his greeting made me realize I had finally gained the Yang family's trust. Almost immediately, I confessed my concerns about having been the agent of Ping's demise, if not her intentional killer. He was quick to reassure me that all this had been going on long before I appeared, and that Ping's death had been an accident. He also told Dora that there had been no casualties from the nerve gas at all, and that Shu Chun had reappeared. Always shy as a turtle, she had simply been waiting for all threats to pass before sticking out her head.

Bik had a very specific plan. Because of his mother's efforts on behalf of endangered species, the family had border officials in its employ. "Our best bet is Laos," he said. "It's less well-organized than Vietnam and more stable than Burma. The friends we have there have been friends for years. They will help you get across and also help you inside the country."

The journey south to the Lao border took a day and was conducted in a family truck, a small one with double tires in the back and a cab attached directly to the cargo compartment. This one smelled much better than the tractor-trailer we had ridden to Tianjin, as it was used by a bakery. We reached the crossing at night, but even in the dark I could see how thick the vegetation was, how dense the cover. We went across in the truck without ever seeing a border guard, although I heard chatter outside as Bik got out and Dora whispered something to me about a payoff. Bik remained behind, ostensibly to assure things went smoothly for us at the border, and we started moving again after he tapped the side of the truck. The moment we were out of China, I felt an easing of tension I had not realized I was holding in my stomach, my shoulders, and particularly in my chest. We stopped to stretch our legs at dawn, already halfway to the capital city of Vientiane. Dora offered a rest when we reached that city but after a shower and change of clothes, I felt we needed to keep going. A family friend met us at the airport and stood at the immigration agent's elbow as he flipped through our passports and ignored the absence of an entry visa tag. We got on an international flight to Los Angeles through Bangkok. I stared out the window in hopes of seeing red birds on the wing, but there were none. Dora fell asleep holding my hand.

***

At the hospital, Lulu was still immobile and unresponsive but looked better. The most significant change was that the bandage over her face was gone. She'd had some reconstructive surgery at the same time her scalp was repaired from the removal of Hector-The-Bullet. Coraline had applied light makeup to her face. The doctors had fitted her with a beautiful glass eye that was a perfect match for the one that had been lost to lead, replete with fine gold lines and brown dots. My father was especially proud of it, as he had been the one to procure it.

"World's best," he told me. "I know about these things. I used my personal connections to arrange it for her. They came and took detailed digital images. You would have been impressed by their gear. Very high tech."

He and my mother were there to greet me, as were Ginger and Nash. They were all a bit taken aback by the presence of Dora.

"Astonishing," my father said, circling her as if she were a department store mannequin and he was a buyer. "Two of the same girl. The wonders of genetics have no end."

My mother was more reserved. Perhaps she saw the way Dora and I looked at each other. If she didn't, my sister certainly did.

"What's up with her," she whispered in my ear. "You two a thing or what? God, that is so weird."

I had no interest in such gossip but was happy for my nephew's hug. Predictably, Dr. Granate was too busy to show up, but the floor resident came in to give me a summary of what had been going on. It was not substantially different from what Coraline had told me on the phone a few days earlier. Coraline herself was there, but very reserved and staying mostly in the corner with her back to us, pretending, I think, to be busy with nurse things so as not to intrude.

The very first thing I did was lay my head on my wife's chest and listen to her heart. Then I placed her arms around me in a hug. I had not expected to cry so loudly or so long, but even my embarrassment couldn't stop the flow of tears. My mother came and touched my shoulder. My father went into the hall to talk to an intern. Dora kept her distance too. She might have shed tears as well, but I couldn't see.

The second thing I did was part Lulu's lips and smear wasp serum on her tongue. Her lips were moist, the nurses had seen to that, but her tongue was limp and did not respond to my finger. Somehow, I had imagined she would lick the stuff like an excited dog, would know on some level the healing it would bring. The healing came, though, and it began almost instantly. The first thing was a rise in heartrate. The monitor showed that right away. It wasn't high enough to cause great concern but it was noticeable. The second thing was an increase in her oxygen saturation, something I'd learned the first day was measured by a sensor on her finger. After that, her breathing deepened.

Then she began to move.

I can't say the movements were purposeful, although, of course, we had no idea what might be going through her mind. To me, it seemed as if her muscles were saying "hey, we've been on vacation for months now, enough of this lying around" and got excited. They contracted, they extended, but everything was leisurely, no panic, no spasms, no pain. It was more like the stretching that happens after a long sleep, the kind that is accompanied by a large yawn and an expulsion of breath. Her mouth even opened as if to say, "Look, I had a bullet in my brain and my cheek and eye were destroyed, but my teeth are still perfect and beautiful".

Coraline went and brought the doctors. They examined her, drew blood, demanded to know what I had given her. They tried to stop me, physically, from putting a second dose of the wasp serum in her mouth my father overrode them and I was grateful. This time, her tongue worked and she made an effort to swallow despite the breathing tube. In fact, she became so agitated at the tube that she began clawing at it and they had to restrain her so she didn't rip it out. They wanted to sedate her, but my father got them to wait a short while. The moment the doctors left the room, I produced the wasps. Even my father balked at those, demanding to know what the hell I thought I was doing, but Coraline put her hand on his and reminded him Lulu had asked for them.

Coraline and I held Lulu's hands while Dora breathed hotly and loudly on the wasps to awaken them. At length they began to stir and then issued their strange, low vibration. At last, they took to the air, assuming the same characteristic spiral flight they had in Tianjin. They made straight for Lulu, first circling her head, which caused my mother to cry out, and then landing on her glass eye and her surgery scars. Nash screamed something about stingers and Ginger had to turn him away. I had the distinct impression Lulu was communicating with them, and they with her. Then, as abruptly as they had landed, they were in the air again.

They flew directly to her arm this time, and then to her hand. Not the hand I was holding, but the fingers interlaced with Coraline's. They formed their wispy cocoon there, beginning at her wrist and then moving up to Coraline's, then to both of their elbows. You might have expected Coraline to be distressed by this, to try and pull away, but her eyes grew dreamy. When the doctors came in again — this time it was my mother who dragged them into the room — Coraline waved them away, saying something that was really helping the patient was going on, whether they understood it or not. I added that I'd seen some amazing things in China and, banking on the way familiar terms can ease the mind, begged them to allow this procedure. All the while, of course, my heart was in my shoes about the way the wasps bound Lulu to Coraline and not to me.

The cocoon grew to the level of Lulu's shoulder, then down to the level of her heart. It followed the same trajectory with Coraline. During this time, Lulu's thrashing stopped and Coraline sat perfectly still, her pale neck straight, her features composed. As shocked as I was by the proceedings, I noticed she looked both peaceful and beautiful. Dora noticed too, because it was she who came to me and took my hand from Lulu's and walked me across the room to sit down on a chair next to my family.

Transfixed, we all watched the cocoon envelop both women. The doctors grew increasingly agitated but my father calmed them down by citing the known analgesic properties of bee venom, the likely still-undiscovered proteins in both plants and animals, and how nature was a repository for healing compounds based upon which doctors of the future would perform new treatment protocols and future pharmaceutical companies would reap untold profits.

After a time — I want to say it was an hour but it might have been longer — we could no longer see Coraline's torso clearly nor Lulu's arms and head. About an hour after that — I remember because Nash began complaining to his mother about how long this bizarre thing was taking and about needing some dinnerwe heard voices from inside the whiteness and Dora somehow knew it was time to tear our way in. We did, and Lulu was awake inside, staring at me. She pointed at the breathing tube. One of the doctors removed it and moments later my wife was breathing on her own, smiling, and gazing mostly at Coraline.

Her voice was raspy from disuse and the effects of the tube, but she answered our questions, mostly silly stuff like asking her if she knew her own name, who was president of the United States, if she recalled what happened.

"I guess I shouldn't have blown my horn," she said. "But the fucker deserved it."

That's when I knew Lulu was back.

40

Ti will serve me faithfully until the end of her days, always soft, gentle, giving, kind, and loyal — everything I am not, save perhaps loyal. She is in my bed whenever my husband is on one of his military campaigns against the Jurchens, who are bent on their own dynasty, against the Mongols, who decimate everything in their path, or against those Song dogs to the South about whom I have nothing good to say and never will. When I need her to be, Ti is my lover, always enthusiastic, always grateful to be with me, always letting me know in what ways I can pleasure her, always knowing without asking in what ways she can pleasure me.

Ti never marries. She says that being with me is enough for her. Li Quan can hardly object, particularly when he too enjoys her luxurious curves, and given that his own path will take him far from both of us for long periods. Ti will have no more children, but her one son is enough. She names him Tam and begs me and Li Quan to adopt him as our own. We do so, and my prognostications about the boy's martial prowess are correct. He is every bit the fighter his father was, and more. Not only that, but no son of ours, no son of the three of us, could possibly be spoiled the way his blood father was. He is raised with the rod but also with kindness and, most of all, with good examples of how to be in the world.

The traitorous Song lure my dear husband into a bog where he kills 37 men before succumbing to his wounds. He dies with the title Governor of Yidu. After I avenge him, I take his rank and wear it until the Song emperor gives me the title Yang Lingren—Lady Yang. With that I rule a larger piece of the Middle Kingdom than any woman, save a dowager empress, ever has. I miss my husband terribly, ache for him day and night, and yet am proud of who he was and what he accomplished for our land and for our family. We brought glory to our family, and before they died, my parents had both reason and opportunity to celebrate that.

There are several reasons for our success. First and foremost is the support and guidance of Lord Hun, without whom I would never have come to understand how to understand events and trends that appear random to untrained eyes but which I know to be anything but. Second is the bond between me and my husband, which leaves me strong in moments of weakness, fearless when I should be terrified, and resolved even in the face of impossible odds. Last but not least is my skill with my special spear, which I came to call *lihua qiang*, the pear-blossom lance. My techniques are always based upon the spirals in nature, those of the stars and rivers and windstorms and leaves.

When it comes time for me to pass away from an illness I can neither forestall nor conquer, I leave our family armies and lands to Tan. I know he will acquit himself to perfection. Ti is with me at my deathbed, and she holds my hand and kisses me as I pass into the care of Lord Hun. On my journey to be with him, I see Mu and Grandmother. I hear the blessed buzzing of the wasps and know that this too shall pass and that I will soon return to the world I love.

I will still be the best. No matter what weapons I encounter, no matter how sharp they may be or how fast they may fly, I will find ways to defeat them. I will conquer everyone and everything, and I will search for Li Quan again, no matter how hard and long and far I have to look, and no matter the body he inhabits. I will find him and I will know him and until I do, I will keep on looking, for if there is anything one can say about love, it is that it is a product of pure randomness and chaos, and thus the ultimate creation of the great, great Lord Hun.

41

LULU DEVOTED herself to her recovery with a demon's energy. At the start, she stayed at a rehabilitation clinic, where she learned to walk again and grow accustomed to her reduced visual field. She fought fiercely to regain the muscles she had lost during her months in a coma, using a treadmill first, then an elliptical machine that worked her arms as well as her legs, and finally weightlifting with a trainer until she regained her strength and tone. All the while, her belly ballooned and she made regular visits to her doctors to make sure our babies were healthy. When they were born, naturally, quickly, easily, and without complication, I can honestly say she looked stronger and oddly more fit than at any time I had known her.

I cannot say the same for her beauty, and that fact pains me. The surgeons had done well and her face was intact, but there had been a subtle shift in her, not exactly a rearrangement but a transformation, and although she was still a very striking woman, her previous glory was no more. Later, my friends would say this was not true, that she was still gorgeous. Perhaps it was just that having learned what I had about her, I could no longer see her the same way.

We named our boy Bik, for her brother, and our girl Ophelia for my mom. The twins were inseparable from the very first moment, even emerging—and the doctors said such a thing was vanishingly rare—in intimate contact. Bik came out first but Ophelia had him by the foot and followed immediately, either because she couldn't accept second place or because she refused to let him go. We kept them in the same crib and Lulu nursed them together, one at each breast, and for the first six months, she was a devoted mother.

My wife and I slept in the same bed, too, but not much happened there. I can't say there weren't moments when I wanted it to, but for some reason I couldn't quite manage it and neither could she. After a while, when I was sure she was stable at night and not exhibiting any after-effects from the coma, I moved to the nursery and slept with the children, changing their diapers when they were soiled and awakening Lulu only when they cried for her milk.

It took a while for me to screw up the courage to ask her about everything, but when I did, she grew enraged. She said her sister had no business telling me such stories. In that state, in her anger, she seemed truly a different person; her reaction itself put the lie to her denials. When I pressed her, when I said it wasn't only Dora who had told me these things (she hated that I used the name Dora and only referred to her sister as Dongmei), but her parents and a certain police colonel, she just grew sullen and said she would not speak with me about things I would never understand.

Such comments wounded me. I wasn't sure she fully appreciated what I had done for her, how difficult it had been for me to go to China and pursue the wasps, to find her family, to learn what I needed to learn to bring her back from her painful limbo. She said thank you, and she seemed to mean it, but it was the kind of thanks you might issue to someone who bought you an ice cream cone or gave you their seat on the bus. None of this was good enough for me, not the silence, not the child-oriented and perfunctory cohabitation, and I suppose it was not good enough for her either.

When she disappeared, I was neither surprised nor mortally wounded, though I was terribly sad and worried for my children. It was in the evening; at a time she customarily went to the gym. I waited for her without success, and when I grew worried, I tried tracking her phone but found she had terminated her service. That was when I realized she was not simply late. I was going to call the police but then I noticed the absence of that little glass statue of Hun. I checked her closet and discovered a few of her favorite outfits gone, along with three pairs of shoes and a small suitcase. If she took any photos of the children, they were on her phone and not printed in frames; all the ones we had about the apartment were still there after she left.

On a hunch, I rang the hospital and discovered that Coraline had not shown up for work either that day or the previous. I identified myself and asked for her cell phone number and, after a lot of convincing, I got it. I called and found that number disconnected as well. I went to my parents' home straight away, as I felt I needed some help with the twins. You can imagine the things my father said, but my mother's venom was beyond imagination. Perhaps that was because of the children. Most women, I think, would have similar judgments to make in that circumstance. I felt so empty, sad, and lonely, that I almost confessed to my parents what I knew of Lulu. Instead, I went to the garage and used my brother's old heavy punching bag until my knuckles bled.

That night, sleeping in the room with my children and listening to their quiet breathing, I wondered whether Lulu had ever really been here, whether she had been just a dream, not a nightmare— nightmares do not leave beautiful children in their wake—but a gale-force wind that blew through my life and turned everything upside down, turned everything into pure chaos.

***

In the year that followed, I spoke with Dora every chance I got. We did video chats every night so she could see the children. She was still afraid to go back to China because of Colonel Ping's passing, so she had settled in the north of Thailand. Her parents had a business there and she ran it for them. Bik came to see her every month or so. These chats of ours gave me a chance to test my feelings for her, to see if they were more than merely the kind of bond that develops between people who have been through things and shared grief. I guess the wasps were right because the feelings were real for both of us, and they only grew stronger. In the end, she moved to LA to help me raise the children. They began calling her Mommy. I expected my parents to raise holy hell, but they had the opposite reaction. It turns out that they had bonded from the very first moment, during that time in Lulu's hospital room. Sometimes, parents can be rigid, judgmental, hasty in their opinions, and just generally difficult. Sometimes, they can be right.

In any case, my relationship with photography changed. I no longer felt that one could see things deeply simply by looking at them. I found myself expecting the impossible all the time and felt disappointed by the merely ordinary. Dora took me to task for all this, reminded me of the wasp serum, told me ordinary things were themselves extraordinary if one saw them correctly. That was the main lesson of Lord Hun, she said, and demanded I stick with my program at UCLA. She was more involved with my daily life, my work, than Lulu had ever been. Even when we argued, I wound up smiling because I knew she had such strong opinions on the subject only because she believed in me.

Even if that was the lesson, and even if things had become stable, I still expected, at any moment, to see a murder of three-legged red crows. The longer I went without seeing them, without seeing anything like them, the more I yearned for answers to things I did not understand. After a while, I did my own research into the woman known as Yang Miao Zhen. I learned she had been a woman of omnivorous and insatiable appetites, as well as an utterly invincible fighter. Her favorite weapon, if one believes the work of a few lesser-known Chinese historians, was the spear. What they called the spear back then was not the sort of thing you see African bushmen throw at pigs, but rather featured a sharp, pointed tip of pattern-welded steel fashioned into a shape resembling a narrow leaf and mounted on the end of a twelve-foot shaft of Chinese white wax wood, a tree known for its strength, flexibility, and resistance to breakage. I found it hard to imagine a woman able to master such an unlikely and unwieldy item, and even more to use it to defeat the Jurchens, Southern Song Dynasty fighters, and even the scariest of all warriors the world has ever known, the soldiers of Genghis Khan.

Defeat them she did, according to records of the day. In the company of her husband, a formidable rebel bandit known as Li Quan, she not only forged alliances across north-central China during one of its most turbulent periods, she returned to the area in which she was born, present-day Shandong Province, shared her genius for spear fighting with an army she and her husband assembled, and with her extraordinary strategy and training established a fiefdom of her own. She became a regional lord, and in that position was just too much trouble for either the Song forces of the south or the nomads of the northwest to bring to heel. She died at the age of fifty-seven — still brazen, self-righteous, and undefeated in battle — and was succeeded by her son, a man she and her husband had adopted. Apparently, she was either unable to conceive or disinterested in having children of her own. Either way, her influence over the area continued

273

after her death and was, by any measure, unique and formidable.

Some of this I learned by reading through documents Lulu left behind on the file-sharing service we both used. But there was more. When I left our apartment for larger quarters, a handwritten journal came loose in the van and dangled by a piece of tape from the bottom of Lulu's desk. Incredulous that her sister could have kept its existence a secret even from her twin, Dora translated it for me. The picture painted it painted was of a peripatetic, itinerant spirit, the spear queen Yang Miao Zhen. The narrative made clear that Miao was a quester driven by a desire for conquest, justice, and revenge, but also a misunderstood woman driven to find the love she craved. The journal brims with such impossibly rich details of Miao's life that it could not have been written by anyone but the woman herself. I have included it here as part of Lulu's story because having access to it surely led my wife to a strong identification with Miao. What role the journal also played in both the reincarnation legend so dear to the Yang family and the uncanny similarities between Lulu and Miao are beyond my ability to explain.

I can't help feeling that Lulu envied this Mistress Miao, which suggests that even before the shooting she didn't feel as if she had found that soulmate in me. This hurts me, even makes me feel a little guilty I guess, because I have found exactly that in Dora. As far as our relationship goes, even though we are very much together, Lulu is still an unspeaking presence in our home. Part of me expects her to just show up unannounced one day.

At one point, I heard she Lulu appeared to give a paper on the Song Dynasty at an academic conference but then promptly disappeared before the event was over. There was also a tantalizing rumor of a pair of women designing feminist clothing combining style and freedom of movement, but when Dora tried to learn more but soon discovered the company had been sold.

Dora's reaction was to sigh and say she hoped her Lulu and Coraline were happy.

"Maybe she's found someone else by now," I said.

"Maybe," Dora answered, fussing over breakfast for the twins. "Wherever she is and whoever she's with, you can be sure she's doing something extraordinary."

I put my arms around my handsome young son and my beautiful green-eyed daughter, then leaned to Dora.

"So are we," I whispered in her ear.

MISTRESS MIAO

ACKNOWLEDGEMENTS

Thanks to Graham Earnshaw for believing in my work and having the vision to shepherd it into the world. Thanks to Alexa Dysch, Jennifer Beimel, and Antoinette Henson for their careful proofing. Thanks always to my Daoist master, Yan Gao Fei, for everything you have done for me, including kindling my fascination with the historical Yang Miao Zhen. Thanks to my wife, Janelle Rosenfeld, and to Connie Holmes for helping get the word out about this work of passion.

About The Author

Yun Rou has been called the "Zen Gabriel Garcia-Marquez" for his works of magical realism, many set in China. Born Arthur Rosenfeld in New York City, he received his academic background at Yale University, Cornell University, and the University of California and was officially ordained a Taoist monk in Guangzhou, PRC. His award-winning non-fiction works on Taoism bridge science, spirituality, and philosophy, while his novels have been optioned for film in both Hollywood and Asia. Yun Rou lives in the American Southwest and travels frequently and extensively in the Far East.